Thank
new. T̶ ̶ ̶ ̶ ̶ ̶ ̶ ̶ ̶ ̶ ̶ ̶ ̶ ̶ ̶ ̶ ̶ ̶a, who helped me tell Nick and Victoria's story the right way. Also, thank you to Christi, who helped so much with my line by line editing. And lastly, thank you to my readers. You rock!

Table of Contents

Chapter One

Chapter Two

Chapter Three

Chapter Four

Chapter Five

Chapter Six

Chapter Seven

Chapter Eight

Chapter Nine

Chapter Ten

Chapter Eleven

Chapter Twelve

Chapter Thirteen

Chapter Fourteen

Chapter Fifteen

Chapter Sixteen

Chapter Seventeen

Chapter Eighteen

Chapter Nineteen

Chapter Twenty

Chapter Twenty-One

Chapter Twenty-Two

Chapter Twenty-Three

Chapter Twenty-Four

Chapter Twenty-Five

Chapter Twenty-Six

Chapter Twenty-Seven

Chapter Twenty-Eight

Chapter Twenty-Nine

Chapter Thirty

Chapter Thirty-One

Chapter Thirty-Two

Chapter Thirty-Three

Chapter Thirty-Four

Chapter Thirty-Five

Chapter Thirty-Six

Chapter Thirty-Seven

About The Author

Other Works

Chapter One

Victoria stretched to ease the stiffness in her back and looked around the combined living room and kitchen area of the condo. The work made her proud. Color and life, furniture and art now filled the previously hollow room.

Rachel would sell this condo in a flash now.

Her cell rang from inside her purse and she dashed to the bar in the kitchen and dug until she found it. She bit back a curse when she saw the display.

Roger. Roger, who was supposed to be picking up Lucia and Helena from school today. Roger, the ex who wanted to "go find himself" and decided a wife and family weren't part of that. He'd only waited two days after the divorce was finalized to date a socialite.

She reminded herself that the divorce was a year old and that bitterness didn't suit her. "Yes?" If she answered the phone with a little bit of bite in her voice, it didn't make her bitter. It showed how tired she was of him bailing on her.

"Hey, babe." Roger still didn't get the fact that he couldn't call her babe. Ever.

A headache started at the base of her skull. "What is it? I'm busy." She needed to meet her dad and the contractor at her new office.

"I can't pick up the girls from school. I'm having dinner with someone and I'll be late if I don't leave now."

"Roger," she sighed and looked at her watch. The girls needed to be picked up in ten minutes. "You promised me you would get them. Plus, I'm on the other side of town. There's no way I can get there in time." Sanctuary Bay wasn't a large town, but tourist season had started, so traffic would be heavy.

"I'm telling you ahead so that you can make arrangements."

Temper ignited at the exaggerated patience in his voice. "You're telling me ten minutes before they're supposed to be picked up. That's not telling me in advance."

"Look, babe. I can't make it. Give my love to the girls."

Victoria glared at her phone when he hung up. She closed her eyes and took three deep breaths. There was a way to solve this situation without maiming her ex. She'd just have to call one of her sisters.

She dialed her youngest sister, Addison, with her fingers crossed. Addie taught at a school not far from the girls. If there were no meetings, Addie should be able to pick them up.

"Who's my favorite sister?" Her voice dripped syrupy sweet when Addie answered.

"God, what? You only act like this when you need something." Addie said.

Victoria heard the smile in her sister's voice and took heart. "Can you pick up the girls?"

"Did Roger back out again?"

"He decided to have dinner in the city." She leaned against the counter and surveyed the condo again to prove to herself that she'd moved on after the divorce. That she was better off. That her girls were better off.

"That douche. I'll leave right now. But you owe me dinner."

"Thanks, Addie."

After she hung up, she changed into a black pencil skirt, a white button up shirt, and red pumps for the meeting. She pulled her black hair into a sleek ponytail, dressed her brown eyes in natural makeup and mascara.

The drive to the ocean front office on the boardwalk took an extra thirty minutes. It didn't bother her, though, because the warm air smelled like the sea, and she enjoyed every minute of it. She pulled her SUV into the shopping center and spotted her father's truck parked close to the office he'd helped her buy. Being a retired contractor, he recommended a friend of his to redo the inside to fit her needs. She had high hopes on the outcome.

"Hey, sweetie." Her father stood outside the door, his salt and pepper hair close cropped. He shared his sloe eyes with his two eldest daughters, and they warmed when he saw his oldest. "How was the staging?" he enveloped her in a tight hug.

"Great, I finished the condo for Rachel and I have consults tomorrow for a few personal interior designs." Victoria looked at the door. Her stomach tightened in excitement. An office of her own. She wouldn't have to work out of her house anymore. "Let's go in. I want to see it again."

Her father gestured toward her oversized purse. "If you can find the key in that suitcase of yours."

Victoria laughed. "Lucia and Helena bought it for me for my birthday. It's a little big, but they were so excited when I opened it. I think they combined both their allowances for a month to buy it."

"Your mother helped them with some." He said as she pulled the key out.

"See? Only took a minute." With a quick smile she unlocked the door and stepped inside.

Wallpaper hung from the walls in tatters, the carpet smelled musty and had black and red stains all over it. A receptionist counter covered in chipped black and white Formica was the only furniture in the room, thank God, Victoria thought.

"Needs a lot of work."

"I know, Dad. Did I make a mistake? Picking this place out?" Worry clouded her excitement.

"Do you know how you want this place to look?" He looked at her and she saw the faith in his eyes.

She regarded the place and imagined what she wanted. Dark hard wood floors, antique furniture, some potted plants. Graphite colored walls with white trim. Elegance and style. "Definitely."

"Then there's no mistake. You're going to build a business here. You're already doing great out of your house. You'll be able to accommodate more clients out of a real office. You can even get an assistant for scheduling and stuff."

Her father was the driving force behind her confidence. Whenever she couldn't imagine herself with her own business, he built her up. Pushed her toward better things. He looked in the direction of the parking lot at the sound of a truck door shutting. "Here comes Nick now."

Victoria turned when she heard the door to the office open and the shock shot straight to her toes. Thank God she'd fixed her hair and makeup. A friend of her father's? No way. This tall and lean guy was nowhere near her dad's age and had muscles that were evident underneath his gray t-shirt. Tattoos peeked out from under the sleeves and twisted down his arms to his wrists. Shaggy black hair framed a face with a square jaw and full lips.

Anatomy that she'd tried to forget about roared to life.

Which was ridiculous because the last thing she had time for was a man, even one as gorgeous as this one. She recognized him from high school, although they'd never been in the same circles since he'd been more of a bad boy.

Catching herself, she held out a hand and said coolly, "Hi, I'm Victoria. Wes's daughter."

His eyebrows rose over ice blue eyes. "I'm Nick."

She ignored the interest on his face as his lips quirked.

"Hey, Nick. Thanks for meeting us. Want to take a look around?" Wes shook his hand.

"Sure." Nick pulled a small notebook from his back pocket and a pencil from behind his ear. "What are you looking to do to the place?"

Victoria tried to bring her thoughts back to the business. Her dad was up to something, she could tell. He would've never hired out the job to someone else, even if he was retired, because he'd want to do it for her.

Wes glanced at her. "Ask her. She's the designer." His phone rang. "It's your mother. I'll take this outside."

Victoria watched him leave with a mutinous glare.

"So, Victoria. What do you want to do with the space?" His voice hinted at his amusement.

"You think this is funny?" She pursed her lips. "They're trying to set us up. It's mortifying." How could Nick not see what was going on? He definitely looked like the type who could get his own dates. If her sisters knew about this she was going to rain hell down on them.

Nick shrugged, the muscles in his torso and shoulders catching her eye. "I think it's funny. Wes told me he had a client for me. Didn't say it was one of his beautiful daughters."

Heat unfurled in her abdomen. She told her brain to tell her newly awakened anatomy to slow its role. "Where do we go from here?"

"I hear there's a new restaurant on the boardwalk we could try out." At her glare, he laughed.

The laugh shot straight to her core.

"I could design you an awesome office space. I am good at what I do. We can ignore the fact that our parents are working against us. Or we can make them happy and go out. I do love my mother very much, and this would make her very happy."

She couldn't help but smile. He was a charmer. "How about you design my awesome office space and we ignore our parents?"

"Sure, we can do that. But you can't blame a man for trying." Nick turned to the room. "So, the space?"

"Well, first of all I want that hideous receptionist counter gone. Demolish it. I need an office of my own in the back, and a small break room with room for counter space, a table, and a fridge. I'm going to design it like a regular kitchen, without the oven. I'll need a unisex bathroom." She continued with details while he took notes.

"This shouldn't be hard to do. I'll have to start the designs and get your approval before going for the permit." He tucked the notebook back in his pocket, the pencil behind his ear.

"How long will the designs take?" She looked out toward the parking lot, past it toward the beach. Anywhere but at him. She couldn't let herself be tempted. A man was a complication she didn't need. Not with her daughters and her expanding business.

"A week, tops. I have a job I'm finishing now but it shouldn't take too much of my time."

The door opened and her dad stepped back inside. "Your mother was having a small dinner crisis. Needs me to pick up some stuff on my way home."

"Does she now?" Victoria narrowed her eyes so that he'd know she knew exactly what he was trying to do. Her dad deftly avoided eye contact. "Anyway, we're done here so I'm going to head home." She handed Nick her business card and tried to ignore the laughter in his eyes as she left.

Chapter Two

Victoria walked into her house and the sound of music from the living room assaulted her ears. Her feet screamed for relief so she slipped off her stilettos and carried them through the small foyer into the living room.

Her daughters and Addie danced across the white carpet with the Wii remotes in their hands, concentration and laughter on their faces. Lucia and Helena's identical features, black hair and hazel eyes, belied their different personalities. Victoria watched them dance, and not for the first time wished she could've chosen better for their father. No other excuse than she was young and stupid.

Her family was supportive, not wanting to tell her Roger wasn't good enough, wanting her only to be happy. All except Addie, who'd protested loud and often that he was nothing but a douche. Victoria watched her sister keep up with the girls and smiled. Her sisters had helped her through the past year and without them, she didn't know what she would have done.

"Hey, Mom." Lucia waved when the game came to a lull. "I'm beating Addie to a pulp."

Addie glanced over, blue eyes from their mother lit with a competitive fire. It didn't matter that the girls were younger. Addie had to win.

Victoria noticed Helena didn't say anything but guessed she was too focused on the game. She continued through the living room and into the kitchen, immediately going for a bottle of wine. She hated that Roger still got to her, even after all these years. His attitude toward marriage--toward her--had been the same for the last twelve years. He wasn't going to change just because they were divorced.

"Pour me a glass." Addie's long black hair fell down her back in a straight waterfall, her make-up light. "Teaching third graders can be stressful. I'll be gray by the time I'm your age."

Victoria lifted a brow, poured the wine into two wine glasses. "Mom always taught us that more wine equaled less gray."

Addie lifted the wine in a toast. "That she did."

The wine warmed her throat and stomach after she sipped. "Thanks for picking up the girls."

"You know you don't have to thank me for that. I love spending time with them."

Victoria moved to the fridge, trying to decide what to make for dinner. "I met with Dad and the contractor today."

"How did it go? Did they say how long it would take for your posh new office to be done?" Addie smiled and slid onto a stool. "What are you cooking?"

She pulled a mix of chicken stir-fry she'd frozen a few weeks ago, held up the bag for Addie. "The contractor is going to draw the designs and blueprints first. Then he'll meet with me and let me know how long it'll take. Did Dad tell you who it was?" She looked at Addie, saw the question on her face, knew Addie didn't know. Addie had the worst poker face. "He's a freakin' hottie." She turned the fan on above the stove, then fanned herself.

"Tell me more." Addie laughed. "You haven't blushed like this since you met dick face."

"Addie." Victoria nodded toward the living room, where the girls argued about who would bowl first on the Wii.

Addie shrugged. "Sorry, but they aren't paying attention to us. Why did you ask if Dad told me?"

"It was embarrassing. He got a phone call from Mom when Nick walked in--"

"Nick is a sexy name."

Victoria tried not to laugh at that. "Shut up. Anyway, we could both tell our parents were setting us up."

"He didn't spook about that?"

Victoria moved the stir-fry around in the wok. "No, he suggested we go out to eat."

"Tell me you agreed. You need some hot sex to loosen you up."

"Stop." Victoria shook her head. "I don't have time for that right now. I need to focus on my girls and my business. Not sexy men in butt hugging jeans and t-shirts. Do you remember him from school? He may have already graduated already when you started high school. He has a younger brother named Luke."

"I think I vaguely remember Luke. They were total cuties, but bad news from what I remember." Addie said.

"He's graduated from cutie to complete hottie."

"I really need to accompany you to your meeting." Addie drained the rest of her wine. "Make sure you two accidentally fall into each other's arms or something."

"You're crazy."

"I volunteer for baby-sitting. Anytime."

Victoria laughed this time. "Quit. I'm not interested in him. I've had enough of men for a while."

"I know a few cute girls who'd be interested in you."

"You really are crazy."

During dinner Addie had the girls laughing about her third graders. Helena pushed the food around on her plate and didn't look at her mom the whole time. Victoria tried to get her attention, but was mainly baffled as to why Helena treated her that way.

After dinner, the girls went upstairs to shower and get ready for bed. Addie went home, promising to watch the girls again. Victoria shooed her out and settled down in her bedroom at her small desk.

Looking at her calendar, she had several appointments this week with real estate agents who wanted her to stage their beach houses, apartments, and homes. She'd always had an eye for dressing up rooms. It was a talent that she was lucky she'd been able to turn into a business. Hopefully it would be a lucrative one. Five years ago she started it, building it slowly, networking, cultivating connections carefully. She did some interior decorating for clients, looking for stuff they wanted at flea markets and antique shops in nearby cities. It was a hobby she adored and fit in whenever she could.

She never did anything rash, other than marrying Roger, and look how that turned out.

"Mom?"

Victoria turned to see Helena standing in the doorway. Ever day she worried about boys because of her daughter's willowy bodies. She dreaded they day they would learn to drive and their first dates. How was she going to deal with it?

"What is it, sweetie?" She coaxed Helena into explaining what bothered her.

Helena sat on the edge of her mom's bed and picked at the white duvet. "Lucia is going to try out for the cheerleading team."

Victoria heard the hurt in her daughter's voice, knew Helena wasn't trying to blame her sister, but something about it obviously bothered her. Victoria moved to sit next to Helena. "And you don't want to?"

Helena shrugged, a small pout on her lips. "No, but this will be the first time we don't do something as sisters."

Victoria's heart ached at the worry in Helena's voice. "It doesn't mean that you two are going to grow apart. You're best friends, and always will be. Like me, Addie, and Halle. We are very different, but very close."

"Lucia said that trying out for the math club at school made me a nerd. But I don't like dancing around, and I love to solve problems. It makes me happy."

There it was. The real reason Helena's feelings were hurt. She was the quiet one, the analytical one, who wanted to be good and please everyone. Especially her twin, Lucia, who on the other hand, was rash, impetuous and loud. Everyone wanted to please her. It didn't surprise Victoria that the girls were branching out, doing stuff on their own.

"Sweetie, your sister is probably sad that you're wanting to do something else. You know how she can be. She knows that you love brainy stuff."

Helena shrugged again, still picking at the duvet. "I'm not a nerd, am I Mom?"

Victoria wished she could explain that being a nerd didn't matter after school, that nerds actually became very successful in life. Halle hadn't listened to it when their dad told her; she knew her daughters wouldn't believe her either. "You're not a nerd. Lucia knows that."

"I didn't mean it that way." Lucia bounded into the room, her radar going off that her sister was in with her mom. She stood at the foot of the bed, glaring at her sister, arms crossed over her chest.

Victoria bemoaned the fact that her baby girls needed bras. Real bras, not the training kind. Next year they'd enter the seventh grade and she thought they were growing up too fast. "Lucia, if Helena wants to be in the math club, it doesn't make her a nerd. And you shouldn't tell your sister things like that."

Lucia glared a moment longer, then sighed. "I know. I just wanted her to be on the cheerleading team with me."

"I don't want to. I don't like the other girls, they're mean. And they kiss stupid boys and worry about their looks."

Victoria's stomach clenched. She remembered what it was like to be a cheerleader. She just didn't think that sixth graders worried about that kind of thing.

Lucia sighed again. "We've never done anything by ourselves before. I don't know how to do it without you."

Jesus, a breakthrough. "You two can't do everything together for the rest of your lives. What if you decide to go to separate colleges? Move to different cities? Which you better not do."

Helena smiled at her mother, then at her sister who shared the joke. "Stop suffocating us."

Victoria laughed at them. "Look, why don't you both try these things by yourselves. You may find that you won't fight as much, and you might actually miss each other."

Both girls rolled their eyes, argument forgotten. They left talking about cheerleading, math, about how their mom was clueless.

These times were especially poignant to Victoria. Not that she missed Roger, she just didn't know what to do with herself now that she had no one to argue with. After the girls settled down, she and Roger would argue about who would clean, what they would watch on TV, or if they would have sex or not.

Now that she had the evenings to herself, even after a year, it was almost decadent to choose what she wanted. Although most of the time she chose work. She changed into boxers and an old t-shirt, switched her contacts for her glasses, and settled into the bed with her laptop. It was time to catch up on emails, update her website and social networking sites. She loved the marketing side almost as much as decorating. Interacting with peers, clients, and potential business partners excited her.

By the time she finished, it was after eleven. She put everything up, plugged her cell into the charger, and got underneath the covers. When she shut her eyes, Nick's face appeared in her mind. His gorgeous face, tanned with a hint of scruff made her skin flush. She remembered how, from just a look, she'd wanted to run her hands along his rigid muscles. The next few months were going to be hard if she couldn't get a handle on her hormones.

Chapter Three

Nick's mouth twisted while he looked over the blueprints. He stood with his hands on either side of the paper, pencil tucked behind his ear and black framed glasses on his face, which he only wore while measuring and working on the blueprints. The smell of sawdust hung in the air and it calmed him. Cold air from the window unit blew over his knees, which were exposed from the holes in his favorite work jeans. He didn't see any point in buying new pairs until the ones he had were completely unwearable.

His mother hated that he never threw them away. She bought him new pairs of jeans anyway, still able to accurately guess his jean size. He had at least fifteen new pairs in his closet at home that he'd yet to wear.

His brother, Luke, banged open the door to his shop, carrying a box. "This is yours. Saw it out by the mailbox."

Nick gestured in the direction of the other boxes. "Ordered some materials."

Luke set it down with the others. "I'm headed to the gym. Have some interviews with a new trainer." Luke was an ex-MMA fighter, like Nick, although he had kept to that line of work. While Nick had gone into contracting, Luke had opened his own gym. "Nice glasses, nerd."

Nick flipped his brother off. "What are you doing here?"

"Checking on my big brother. Heard you got a job redoing something for one of Wes's daughters."

Knowing that his brother had always had a crush on Halle in high school, he put Luke out of his misery. "It's for Victoria."

Luke frowned. "Damn. Thought I could've given you a hand. Would've been nice to set eyes on Halle."

"She's married." Nick decided the plans looked great and rolled them up. "Besides, she's out of your league." He had to tease his brother back, it's what they did.

"She's married to an ass." Luke's jaw clenched. He ran a hand through his dark brown hair.

Nick frowned. "Did you hear something new?"

"Heard from one of the guys that her husband is banging one of the damn chicks at the office."

Nick tampered down the anger that rose at the thought of any man cheating on a woman. He'd never understand the need to lie to a woman, tell her that she was his one and only, then ruin that trust by throwing every other woman they could get their hands on in bed. He feared it was in his blood, since his father had done the same thing to his mother, so he shied away from commitment. He wouldn't cause a woman that same pain. "Maybe it's time to let go of the crush, bro. There have to be other women that interest you."

Luke shrugged. "Maybe. But I haven't been able to get her out of my mind since high school. She never even noticed me, her head always buried in a book, but there was just something about her. Call it fate. I'm going to the gym. Call me if you need me."

Nick waved his brother out, grabbed his blueprints and materials, and walked out to his truck. The door squeaked open, the truck almost the same age as him. But it was reliable and that was all that mattered to him. The sun blared, the beginning of the day surrounding him. It didn't matter where you were in Sanctuary Bay, you could hear the call of the seagulls from the beach. He'd spent some time chasing the MMA circuit all over the country, but home had always stuck with him.

Anticipation coiled in his belly at the thought of seeing Victoria again. Her silky hair, slumbered eyes, and full lips crowded his mind. When they'd met a few days ago, she'd looked like a librarian, but he'd sensed the interest in her eyes. She held herself back, which only made him want to spark a fire between them.

He wondered what she'd be like when she loosened up and enjoyed herself. Laughed, maybe danced, then later...his bed.

No, that thought pattern had to stop. He couldn't get involved with a client and she looked like a woman who wanted more than a one-night stand. From what he'd picked up from conversations around town, she had twin daughters. Definitely not someone who would want to fool around and then go their separate ways.

He parked next to her shiny SUV. Through the window of the office, he saw her. She stood in profile to him, all her curves and legs easily seen, and he took a deep breath. His fingers tightened on the steering wheel. Damn it, he wanted to dig his hands through her silky hair and taste her lips.

"Okay, Nick." He said to himself. "You've worked with sexy women before. You can do this."

Another look, and she stared at him through the window.

"Oh man." He began to understand what Luke meant about the sisters having a certain pull. There was no way he was going to fall though. He was made of stronger stuff than his brother.

§§

Victoria smiled politely when Nick entered the office, carrying the rolled up blueprints and a tool bag. Her heart thumped in her chest, like she was a teenager again. She needed to get control. "Good morning, Nick."

His mouth twitched. "Having a bad day?"

"What gave me away?" Victoria remembered the girls' fight earlier over a curling iron. She'd wanted a glass of wine before she'd even left the house.

"The frown. And the crease on your forehead." Nick grinned and pointed to his own forehead.

Damn if he didn't make her want to smile and forget all about the stress from earlier. "Not that you'd really care, but my girls fought over a freakin' curling iron this morning. Which is crazy, because Helena isn't even interested in the girly hair stuff. But Lucia called her a nerd the other night, so now she's determined to prove her wrong..." Victoria trailed off, aware she rambled like she talked to her sisters. Nick watched her with a grin, brows raised.

"I don't have any sisters so it's hard for me to relate. I can see how it would cause you to have a bad morning, though." Nick set the tool bag down on the counter and Victoria watched him move. He looked so comfortable in his own skin, and that confidence turned her on.

"Yeah, it did." Victoria couldn't believe she'd vented about her girls to him. She didn't want him to think that she couldn't handle her own kids.

"I finished the blueprints yesterday. We can go over them, I'll make notes on what you think should change. The permits will be approved soon, and then I can get started."

"Great." Victoria looked around the space. It definitely had potential.

Nick spread the blueprints out on the old receptionist counter. Victoria moved next to him, focusing on how much she hated the ugly counter and not how good he smelled. She pursed her lips and concentrated on the plans. She pretty much knew enough to get a vague idea since her dad was a contractor, but she pretended to understand it even less, just to hear Nick's smooth baritone. He explained the plans patiently, without even a hint of superiority. When he looked at her, those ice blue eyes warmed her entire body.

"Is there anything you'd like to change?" He nodded toward the plans, breaking the moment.

She swallowed and focused her brain. "Would it be a big deal to add a window in my private office? I love the openness of it."

"No, it'll be easy. I can make the adjustments. Do you need me to show them to you before I get the permits?"

Victoria arched a brow. "My dad trusts you enough to try and set us up, so I think I can trust you to get the permits." Why, why did she bring that up again? It made her seem desperate, like she fished for a date. The smile froze on her face.

Nick's lips quirked up at the corner. "True enough. I'll get the permit and call you so we can go over start times, fees, all that." He pulled out his cell phone, then looked at her. "I need your number to do it."

Her stomach flipped. Relax, she told herself, it's purely professional. After she rattled off her number, determined to act collected, she thanked him.

"No problem." Nick rolled the blueprints back up and walked to the door. "See ya soon."

"Bye," she waved, watching him as he got into his truck. Her heart rampaged in her chest. Roger hadn't even made her feel this way. This...lost. She could still feel his body heat next to her. She was in way over her head right now. She had to keep it under control. This business was important to her, and getting spacy over the man fixing her office was not a good idea.

With one last look at the office space, she grabbed her purse and left. The rest of the day she staged a house for Carmen, a real estate agent she loved to work with. The Texan woman was loud, sweet, and had a sharp mind for business. Carmen welcomed all the questions Victoria asked when she started her own business.

In this house, Victoria worked with an earthy tone to match the walls that were painted by the previous owners. She pulled small yellow pillows out of her duffel bag and arranged them on the couch to brighten the room. The stone wall surrounding the fireplace made an great accent to the room, and Victoria knew this place would attract a lot of buyers.

Her cell went off, and she dug it out of the back pocket of her oldest jeans. She saw Halle's name and answered. "Hey, what's up?"

Halle's breathless voice came over the line. "I'm walking to the deli to get lunch. Had to get out of that office. It gets nuts sometimes."

"I can imagine." Victoria leaned against the back of the couch. Halle worked as a nurse and office manager for her husband's private practice.

"So, Addie told me about your hot contractor."

"She can't keep her mouth shut." Victoria said. "His name is Nick, and Dad hired him."

"Go, Dad," Halle cheered. "It's about time you moved on. You wasted too much time on someone who wasn't worthy."

"I have moved on. And I'm not interested in seeing anyone right now. I have to focus on the girls and the business." She reminded herself again. Something she had to keep in mind when Nick was near.

"Oh bull. You're afraid that it'll end up like it did with Roger. Well, honey, I remember Nick's reputation from high school, but no one can be as self-serving as your ex-husband. It defies the laws of nature."

Victoria forgot that her sisters could see right through her. It didn't mean she was going to give in though. "Halle, I'm serious. I'm not ready." Victoria tapped her nails on the side of the phone.

"Uh huh. I can hear you doing your nervous nail tap thing." Halle sighed. "But, I understand. Anyway, I'm at the deli. Call me later, okay?"

"Okay." Victoria hung up the phone. She wasn't afraid, she was just nervous. He seemed so intense and probably didn't want a ready-made family.

Chapter Four

"Mom! Mom!"

Victoria heard her daughters calling her after they slammed open the front door. Their feet pounded on the hardwood and then they burst into the kitchen where Victoria stood over the stove.

They ran straight up to her, jumping up and down, squealing.

"What is it?" Victoria laughed at the obvious joy on their faces.

"I made the cheerleading team!" Lucia said first, not able to wait.

"And I made the math club!" Helena beamed.

Victoria enveloped them in hugs, held on a little longer than they wanted. She couldn't help it. Those little embraces were few and far between now. What happened to the days when they'd toddle up to her, fighting for a spot in her arms? "That's fantastic! Both of you! We need a treat. I'm going to make cookies for dessert."

The girls squealed again.

"Go take a shower and then do homework. Dinner will be ready in a bit."

"Thanks, Mom! We have paperwork in our folders. We'll get it for you." Helena gave her one last hug before following her sister out of the kitchen.

The girls were a whirlwind she couldn't live without and Helena's happier mood brightened her own.

Victoria reached up into the cabinet and grabbed the ingredients for homemade chocolate chip cookies. Her mouth watered at the thought. She hadn't taken the time to make them in a while.

Her phone's text message whistle rang out. She washed her hands of flour before checking it.

Nick: Hey, got the permit approval. By the way, this is Nick.

Victoria stared at the screen for a minute. Blinked against the rush of butterflies that hit her. God, she really was acting like a teenage girl. Should she text back? Would he see that as a sign that she was desperate? Or would it be rude to ignore it, making him think she was a bitch? When did it become this big of a deal to answer a freakin' *business* text? Before she changed her mind, she answered.

Good. When do you want to start?

Nick: What are we referring to?

Maybe it was because she was at home and not near him, or maybe because she was about to eat the best cookies in the world, but she couldn't resist flirting with him. It was harmless, right?

Contracting, of course. What else would be discussing?

He didn't respond immediately like before. Victoria's insides twisted. Did she say something wrong? Then her phone whistled. She read his text and laughed, surprising herself.

Nick: Our date to the new restaurant on the boardwalk, naturally.

She couldn't believe she found that funny. The attention and flattery stimulated her after so many years of disinterest from Roger.

Whoa, stop it. She didn't want to compare the two of them. It wasn't like she was considering being in a relationship with Nick. She had to stop thinking of him that way. The best thing to do now was end the conversation.

Ha. G2g, cooking for the girls. Meet at the office around 9?

Nick: Sure, see ya then.

Victoria rushed through making the cookies and finishing dinner, eager to get to her desk and drown her thoughts of Nick under book keeping. Once she and the girls ate, discussing all the things they'd have to do for their new extracurricular activities, she tucked them in bed, kissing them good night.

Her laptop beckoned to her. She did the bookkeeping once a month so that it never overwhelmed her. It might be enjoyable now, but wait until there was six months to do. A headache waiting to happen.

Temptation snatched at her and she opened her Facebook profile. Nick may or may not have one, but she could definitely find out. She searched for him, found him. In his profile picture he wore a big smile and stood outside of a gym. Nothing too risqué, or too stuffy. Just that gorgeous, lazy grin. Before she knew it, she started clicking through all of his pictures, which mainly consisted of family, work, and vacation photos. Should she be worried that there weren't pictures of women on there or grateful that he didn't focus on the past?

God knows that the minute the divorce was final, she'd removed all photos related to Roger from her social networking sites. She didn't want any reminders of him popping up when she signed in.

When she saw the time, she frowned. "Oh my God." She shut the laptop and groaned. She'd been looking at pictures of Nick for an hour. An hour! She was officially a Facebook stalker. Her face heated up, even though no one else knew how she'd spent her time. She would be humiliated if he ever found out. She'd meet him tomorrow, and be cool and collected. He'd never know.

§§

"Hey, Nick. Whatcha drinking?" The waitress, a blonde with a curvy body, asked.

Nick scratched his scruff, made a mental note to shave in the morning. "Whatever's on draft is good, Ivy. Bring two, Luke should be here in a minute." He glanced around, waving at some of the guys he knew. He knew mostly everyone here, the bar was older than he was. Although the name and ownership had changed from time to time, most thing stayed the same in the small town of Sanctuary Bay.

Luke walked up to the table at the end of his sentence. "Hey, bro." He sat on the stool across from

Nick. "Thanks for meeting me. Work was insane today, and I needed a cold beer to wind down."

Several conversations hummed throughout the sports bar. A baseball game played on the several flat screen TVs hanging on the walls, volume low. Glass cased sports paraphernalia signed by famous athletes decorated the remainder of the sports bar.

"How did the interview go?" Nick asked.

"Great. He's young, early twenties, but fought on the pro circuit. Quit when his girl got knocked up, wanted to be closer to home." Luke told him. "Has a hell of a resume'."

"When does he start?" Nick glanced around.

"Next week. I'm giving him time to get his stuff moved in and for them to settle in. Told him that any time he needed off for the baby, he's got it."

"That's generous." But Nick knew why.

"Yeah, well. Got to support a guy who takes care of his wife and kid."

Ivy brought their drinks and winked at Nick. "Haven't seen you in a while."

"Been busy. Working." Nick wondered why her smile didn't affect him anymore. Usually he couldn't resist flirting back, maybe ending up in bed. She noticed his inattention, scowled, and walked off.

"You didn't have to piss off our waitress."

"Shut up, Luke."

Luke grinned over his beer. "You have the hots for Victoria. You've been blinded by those incredible genes. I mean, each of the sisters are gorgeous."

"Just because you're in love with one of them, doesn't mean I am. Or that I will be. She's hot, but she also has twin daughters, and a recently ended marriage. That's baggage I don't want to mess with."

"Don't be stupid. Some women are worth it."

§§

"So when can you start?" Victoria gazed at Nick over the edge of the coffee cup he'd brought her. To prove to herself that she didn't care what he thought, she'd worn simple yoga pants, a long yellow tee, and pulled her hair up in the messiest bun possible. She wasn't dressing up for him. "I'm not trying to be impatient. I just can't wait to see it finished, working from home is a big convenience, but I want to have a professional front for clients."

"Understandable." Nick stood about two feet away and she swore she felt the heat from his body on her skin. "I can start Monday. I drew up a budget for the materials and labor. It'll be a small crew, about five men, working with me. After you approve it, I'll get the materials ordered and gut the place on Monday."

Victoria wanted to jump, like her daughters did when they heard good news, but remembered she held a cup of coffee. "That's awesome." She beamed at him. "How long do you think it will take?"

Nick scanned a piece of paper in his hand. "Two months, if all the materials come in on time. I'll email you the budget."

"Great." She didn't even need the cup of coffee anymore. The news had shot a happy burst of adrenaline through her. "Okay, I've got to go. I have a staging in a condo on the beach."

"Cool. As soon as I have your okay, I'll let you know what time we start Monday."

"I'll review it this afternoon." Victoria smiled again. She couldn't keep it off her face, waving at him as she climbed into her SUV. Everything was falling into place, a little at a time. She'd had moments when she was sure the business would fail, that she'd have to move into her parents' house with the girls, but her hard work and determination had paid off.

On the way to the condo she stopped by a Redbox to grab some movies. Tonight Roger was supposed to pick up the girls for the weekend, but she knew it wouldn't happen. So, they could curl up on the couch with popcorn and chocolate, wine for mom, and enjoy some time together. She needed to spend more time with them, work had definitely cut into family time. They needed her more than ever since their deadbeat dad wasn't around.

Maybe she could invite Addie and Halle over, make it a girls' night. The twins loved it when they spent time with their aunts. It made them feel grown up. She'd ask Halle to bring over some spa stuff she used to sell and they'd do makeovers and have fun.

Victoria felt herself relaxing already. It would be amazing. When she pulled into the driveway of the condo, she sent a quick text to both of her sisters. Hopefully they would be down for it.

Chapter Five

As Victoria expected, Roger bailed on the girls. Thankfully, her sisters showed up after work, Addie carrying wine and chocolate, Halle with spa materials and pizza.

"I'm so glad you texted us." Halle's brown hair fell in a short pixie cut that framed her model face. She wore no makeup when she went to work, she thought it unprofessional to be all dolled up in front of the patients. "Work has been extra crazy. Like a full moon every night of the month. Trevor has had double the amount of patients. Too many old men and women with heart problems."

"I needed it, too. I can't wait for summer. Why did I become a teacher?" Addie set the chocolate and wine on the coffee table in the living room. She pulled her hair up in a ponytail and cocked her head to the side. "Where are the girls?"

"Upstairs. Their room was a disaster area. I told them they had to clean it before we watched a movie or played spa."

"Tyrant." Addie grinned. "Tell them to get their butts down here."

"I'll go get them." Halle started for the stairs. "I swear I haven't seen them in months. I miss them. Plus, I want to hear how their tryouts went."

Victoria and Addie watched her go up the stairs, then glanced at each other. "Does it seem a little like something's bothering her?"

Addie nodded. "I wonder what's up. Do you think we can ply her with enough wine so she'll talk about it?"

Victoria smirked. "You know she only has one glass." She grabbed the bags, Addie following her into the kitchen with the pizza. "I know it has something to do with Trevor."

"You two have an uncanny ability to pick complete douches for husbands. That's why I'm staying single forever." She placed slices of pizza on paper plates while Victoria poured three glasses of wine. "Speaking of being down, Helena seems quieter than usual. Do you think she's handling the divorce okay?"

"How does anyone handle a divorce?" Victoria shut her eyes against the pain in her heart. It killed her that she couldn't provide that stability for her daughters. "If our parents had divorced, we'd have been devastated."

"Lucia seems fine." Addie shook her head when Victoria's eyes watered. "Hey, you made the right decision. The girls would've been miserable watching you be miserable. Helena will understand that eventually."

"I hope so. She's been more sensitive to Lucia's comments. Usually she'd give it right back." Victoria took a napkin and wiped her eyes before the girls came down.

"I see this sometimes in my students. Not that it makes me an expert, and I assume it's worse in pre-teens, but she will get used to the idea." Addie placed a wine glass in Victoria's hand. "Forget all of this tonight. Business, divorce. Focus on having a good time with your daughters and sisters. We'll cheer Halle and Helena up, even if it kills us."

Thank God for sisters, Victoria thought. She wouldn't survive without them. They were her rock when the world crumbled, and after the divorce they helped build her back up by taking care of her and the girls.

§§

After eating pizza and watching Helena's sci-fi movie, which Victoria would never admit she liked, they decided it was time for the spa.

Halle beamed, some of the stress falling from her, as she mixed the facial paste and then applied it to Helena and Lucia's faces.

"It's cold!" Lucia laughed, trying not to flinch while Halle spread it around her cheeks. "It smells good."

"Like cucumbers." Helena closed her eyes when her turn came. She shivered when the paste spread over her skin. "Will it get rid of blackheads?"

"Sure. It makes you glow, too. You're supposed to use it once a week for a while." Halle shot Victoria a quick smile. "We'll do the mani and pedi while the paste hardens."

"It's a good thing you only had one glass of wine." Addie giggled. "Because if they let me paint their nails, it'd look like a toddler did it."

Victoria shook her head and laughed. This night had turned out perfectly. Both Halle and Helena smiled freely, and Victoria's own stress melted away with wine and her family's laughter. Earlier, when Helena found out that Roger wasn't picking them up, she'd looked like someone had slapped her in the face. Helena had made excuses for him, swore he would pick them up next weekend.

But he wouldn't come for them. Victoria knew Roger too well. Before the bitterness could swallow her, she watched her girls whispering and giggling to each other, and took another sip of wine. They were going to be okay. Tonight was for fun, so she pushed Roger out of her mind.

"Will you do this for us the night before the first day of school?" Lucia asked Halle. "I'd love to go to school glowing."

"Sure. You'll have to remind me. You're not even finished with this school year."

"I can't wait 'til next year. Cheerleading is going to be so much fun!" Lucia reached a hand out and held Helena's. "So will math club."

They snuggled on the couch once everyone's nails dried, and watched a chick flick. By the end, they were all wiping tears from their cheeks. Nothing like crying over a romantic ending to bring women together.

All in all, Victoria thought the night was a success. Everyone's stress had disappeared. Nails were painted, skin glowing, laughter flowing. It was exactly what everyone needed.

§§

On Monday morning Victoria met Nick at the office. The relaxation from Friday was long gone, Helena's nasty attitude surfacing Saturday when she'd woken up. Nick waited at the front with a crew of men. She self-consciously excused her way to the door and unlocked it. Nick stood behind her, and even in the humid-soaring morning she felt his body heat.

"Morning." His breath tickled the back of her neck and goose bumps popped up on her skin. He followed her in, carrying a clipboard and the blue prints. His crew unloaded stuff from their trucks and carried it inside. She noticed him watching her intently but Victoria kept her focus on the process. "It will take a day or so to rip out cabinets, floors, walls, whatever needs to be done. Demo's the fun part of the job."

Victoria nodded, tried to understand the fun of that, to let loose and demolish something. Had to be a guy thing. She glanced down, wished she'd worn something other than flip flops. A strange urge to demolish something began to unfurl in her, but her choice of footwear held her back.

Nick grinned at the disappointment in her eyes. "I have an extra pair of boots and coveralls in my truck. You can put them on...demolish that counter you hate so much."

"Really?" Victoria tried to hold back her smile but it was nearly impossible. "You would be okay with that?"

"Sure," Nick smiled. "I'll be right back."

Victoria grinned the entire time he went to get the coveralls and boots, even as she changed, and then waited for the crew to finish setting up. The men moved around her, placing tools along a wall and talking about a baseball game that played last night. Two big guys carried a blue tarp by her.

Nick sauntered over, muscles tightening in his arms when he held up a sledgehammer. "Did your dad ever let you handle one of these?"

"No, but I watched him. Besides, all I have to do is hit the counter, right?" What if she messed this up somehow? Would he laugh at her? What if she missed and hit someone?

"It's simple." Nick's crooked smile erased her nervousness. For some reason, he believed she could do this. He wasn't criticizing her for wanting to do something new, and she had a feeling he wouldn't say anything about how she swung the hammer either.

With a deep breath she took the sledgehammer from him, arms dropping from the weight. She hefted it up and Nick moved back a few steps. She closed her eyes and imagined Roger's face, his voice when he callously stood their daughters up. It took nothing to let the hammer fall and it smashed into the surface. Debris scattered through the air and when Victoria opened her eyes she saw that she'd made a softball size hole in the center. The men behind her cheered and it goaded her into hitting the counter again.

Tension eased from her shoulders, which she knew would be sore tomorrow. She hit again and again, releasing the bitterness from every fiber of her body. In all her life it was the most violent thing she'd ever done but it helped. When she finished, most of the middle had caved in. Sweat poured down her back and soaked the front of her shirt. She'd probably have to run home and shower.

Nick winked at her. "Feel better?"

"Definitely. Tomorrow my arms and back won't, but for now I feel great." Victoria set the sledgehammer down, stick up, and sighed. "Thanks,

I'll get out of your way now. I need to do some work so I can finish paying you."

"Yeah, okay." Nick nodded to the back. "Just leave my coveralls and boots in there and I'll get them later."

Victoria listened to him giving his crew directions. He spoke low and calm, and every few words she heard the sound of a smile in his tone. He laughed with his crew when they said something, and her mind stuttered. She could get used to that laugh. She sighed, decided to ignore that crazy thought, and carefully laid his coveralls over a metal chair and set the boots beside it.

She waved to the men and Nick, skillfully darting out the door so that she wouldn't have to talk to him. She'd never been known for a poker face and didn't want him to see the interest she was sure was written all over it.

Chapter Six

Nick couldn't shake the thought of Victoria from his mind all day. No matter what he did, working, eating, glancing at the now-demolished receptionist counter, her face popped into his mind. She was an enigma to him, a new species of woman that he never really dealt with. An independent, confident woman who looked cute as hell in his overalls and work boots. She'd beamed the entire time she'd used the sledgehammer and he'd barely thought straight since.

The guys were beginning to notice his distraction. A few of them shot him knowing looks, like they knew something he didn't. Instead of snapping at them like he wanted, he focused on physical work. He hauled the debris out to the dumpster he'd had delivered to the parking lot, stomped back in, and hauled more out. He wasn't even sure why he wanted to punch something. Nothing had happened between the two of them, it wasn't like she was trying to lock him into a relationship. So why did he feel threatened?

That his crew noticed him reacting this way irritated him more. He grumbled and cussed under his breath and they kept out of his way. When the day was over, Nick headed to Luke's gym. He'd rarely gone in the past month, busy with work, but he really needed to release his frustration. Normally he would've called Ivy over and they'd work it out a different way, but that didn't appeal to him right now.

Luke held a punching bag still for a young teen in sweats. The lanky boy hardly had any muscle, but Nick knew Luke would change that. Luke believed in building up the body and the confidence of his protégés.

"Hey." Luke called out. "What are you doing here?"

Several customers used the weight machines and cardio equipment he had set up off to the right of the ring. In the middle, a large square ring was surrounded punching bags that hung every few feet. They waved or called out a greeting to Nick as he walked toward his brother.

Luke arched a brow at the look on Nick's face. "Bad day? Why don't you call Ivy?"

Nick flipped him off, ignored the curious look from the young boy, and headed to the lockers in the back. He grabbed his gym clothes and changed quickly. The gym reminded him of the one he and

Luke had frequented as kids. It wasn't the same one, but the sweat, the rubber, the testosterone filling the air made it feel like home. They'd made some damn hard decisions during their MMA training as teenagers. Some he regretted, some he didn't.

He taped his hands, watching the people working out, sparring, or cross fit training. Luke had instructed the kid to lift weights with another trainer and crossed the floor to Nick.

"We haven't sparred in a while. Want to get in the ring?" Luke assessed Nick. "You've kept most of your muscle mass in the last month, probably due to your job."

Nick shook his head. "Maybe Friday. I have to work all week."

"Want to impress your new girlfriend? Don't want to look like a wimp on the job, not with the bruises I'd leave on you."

"Right." Nick grinned. "I always kicked your ass."

Luke clapped him on the shoulder. "That's not how I remember it." He pointed toward the now empty punching bag. "That's the only one open for now. After work is one of our busiest times, you know that. Hit that for a little while, see if you can work your sexual frustration off since you won't call Ivy. God, you've got it bad."

Nick clenched his jaw against the string of curse words he wanted to sling at his brother. He claimed the punching bag, starting off with short but strong jabs to burn off the edge of the frustration. He didn't have it bad. He didn't even have it, whatever it was, a little. Victoria had a hot body, but was a mother recently out of a divorce. He didn't want to step into that mess. She wasn't going to just roll around in the bed to satisfy an itch and then wave him out the door. She'd want to make him breakfast, talk about his day, ask him to fix stuff around the house. Things a man would do for the woman his woman.

The jabs got sharper, the bag rocking. The thought made his chest tight. She had pre-teen daughters. He didn't know what to do with kids. Hadn't spent time around any, other than some of the kids at the gym, and he just taught them stuff he already knew. He sure as hell didn't know how to raise a kid.

And why the hell was he thinking about raising kids? The woman confused him, shredded his mind. All at once he wanted the job over so he could forget her, but at the same time he didn't want it to end.

Damn that woman for messing with his mind.

§§

Victoria tapped her fingers on the steering wheel while she waited in the car line at the girls' school. For once she'd finished early enough to pick them up. She eyed the students rushing out of the middle school, glee on their faces because they were finally done with another day of school. She wondered if any of them knew how easy they had it at the moment, how confusing adult life could be. Of course not, she knew that. When she was in high school, all she thought about was moving out of her parents' house. If someone had told her that she'd be divorced with twin daughters, she would've laughed in their faces. Back then she'd thought divorce was for people who didn't want to make it work, who were lazy.

What made it worse was that her parents had a near perfect marriage. They were each other's soul mates. Never once had she heard her parents have anything other than a heated discussion, and after it seemed to solidify them even more. They were a solid unit, even today, best friends and lovers.

Someone tapped on the passenger window and Victoria jumped. She saw Lucia and Helena standing outside the car door.

"Unlock the car door, Mom." Lucia rolled her eyes. "Were you daydreaming again?"

"Sorry. Thinking about a house I have to stage." Victoria hit the unlock button, feeling ridiculous. What had spurred that train of thought anyway?

Lucia slid into the front seat, beaming. "Mom, Jack Browning asked me out today. He wants to take me to the movies Friday night. You have to let me go!"

Victoria hands slipped from the wheel and she turned sharply toward Lucia. "A date? No, I don't think so. You're only in the sixth grade." She glanced in the rearview mirror, saw Helena staring out the window. Helena's arms were folded across her chest and she frowned. "Helena, baby, will you put your seatbelt on?"

Helena made a sour face but complied.

"Mom." Lucia turned in her seat as Victoria drove out of the car line and toward home. "I really want to go. It won't be by myself, a group of friends are going."

"Hmm." Victoria wished she had a partner she could discuss this moment with, someone who could help her figure out how to let Lucia down easily, who could take some of the brunt of the girl's anger at being told no. "Lucia, you're way too young to be going out with a boy, even if it's with friends. I'd need to be there."

"No way." Lucia's eyes widened. "This is so unfair. No one wants their mom there."

"It's the only way you're going, honey." Victoria sighed. Lucia's anger practically swallowed any remnant of a good mood she may have had.

When they went in the house, both girls dumped their bags and ran to their rooms. Victoria watched them run up the stairs, heart aching.

With the way she already handled the attraction with Nick, it only reaffirmed her intentions. She wanted to focus on her girls, not her sex life. The girls were more important than that. She trailed her way upstairs, wanting to talk to the twins, get them to calm down so they could spend the rest of the afternoon happy and together. As she approached their room, she heard their voices escalating.

"Stop it! You don't care what they say about me!" Helena screamed at her sister.

Victoria stopped outside the door. She didn't want to eavesdrop but how else would she find out what was going on with them?

"I do care, Helena. I take up for you, just like Mom asked me to. You know I do."

"No you don't!" Helena screeched. "The only one who cares about me in this family is Dad!"

Victoria's chest clenched. Suddenly she was terrified of facing her girls, Helena especially. What did her daughter think of her? Did she think that Victoria pushed Roger away on purpose? *You're an adult, and their mother, get in there.*

She pushed the door open slowly. Both girls' mouths snapped shut, their eyes widened, and tears ran down Helena's face. On the backdrop of the pink and white stripes on Lucia's walls, the agony in her daughter's stare hit harder.

"Hey, girls." Victoria stepped into the room. "What's going on?"

Neither spoke. Lucia's eyes welled up, but she bit her lip.

"Helena, can you tell me what's going on?" Victoria sank onto the edge of Lucia's bed. Her room, full of pink and white in a Paris theme, suited her perfectly.

"I don't want to talk about it." Helena mumbled and stared down at her favorite, almost worn-out, sneakers.

"You couldn't wait to yell at me." Lucia threw out. She crossed to her desk and took a seat in the chair.

Helena's head snapped up. Before they started a new argument, Victoria held up her hand.

"Stop." Victoria looked from one twin to the other. "We need to have a serious talk, one I should've had long before now. I just thought you were adjusting okay enough to skip it, and that's my fault. Sit down and listen. When I'm done talking, I want each of you to share how you feel."

"God, Mom. When did you become a therapist?"

The venom in Helena's voice hit Victoria like a slap in the face. Where had all this hatred come from? "Helena."

Helena stayed silent, keeping her gaze fixed on her shoes. The defiance in her stance shook Victoria. When had her little girl become this angry pre-teen?

"Your dad left. I know that's a big thing." Victoria watched them both while she spoke. Lucia picked at the nail polish on her fingernails, ruining the manicure her aunt had done. "I understand that it's a lot to deal with and we all have to adjust. I didn't make him leave, and he didn't want to stay."

Both girls shifted. Lucia's breathing was more ragged, but she still held back her tears. Helena looked pissed at the world. Victoria hoped to God this was the right thing to do.

"He wanted to explore things in the city, people and job opportunities that he couldn't get here. I wasn't going to uproot you from the only place you'd ever known, the business I'd built, and we couldn't compromise." She wasn't going to tell them that Roger had basically said they'd held him back in life. "Helena, I heard what you said to Lucia. Please, tell me what's going on." Victoria leaned toward Helena. When Helena took a step back Victoria tried to hide the hurt that crossed her face.

"Nothing." Helena shrugged.

Deciding she'd get nothing from Helena, Victoria turned to Lucia and raised a brow.

Lucia glanced at her sister and sighed. "Kids are teasing her about being in the math club and because she doesn't want to do cheerleading. I told them to stop."

"Are they being really mean?" Hearing all the news stories about kids committing suicide terrified her. She didn't want the same thing to happen to Helena.

"No, Mom, it's cool." Lucia stood from the chair and moved to the bed. "They'll stop."

"I want to know why you think that the only person who cares about you is your dad, Helena. You know your aunts, grandparents, sister, and I all care about you. We would do anything for you. Anytime you need to talk, or just hang out, you know we're here for you."

Helena ignored her, focusing on a strand of hair she kept playing with.

"Sweetie?"

"Sure, whatever."

The venom had disappeared from Helena's voice, but she still sounded numb. It worried Victoria. She'd have to call her sisters and mom and figure this out. Her mom had three teenage girls at the same time, and while her parents never divorced, maybe her mom had some advice for this type of situation. Maybe she could contact the school counselor, about the bullying and the divorce.

"Want to go watch some DVR shows?" Victoria stood and gestured to the door. "I think there's some good episodes of Hell's Kitchen. Maybe some Storage Wars." Reality TV was their guilty obsession.

Lucia nodded reluctantly and when Helena said nothing, she pulled her to the door. "Come on, I know you want to hear Gordon Ramsey yell at people."

Helena shrugged and left the room. Lucia turned to Victoria. "I'll make the kids stop, Mom."

"I know, baby." She pulled Lucia into a hug. "Just don't forget to take care of yourself. You're holding this stuff in because Helena is so upset, but you don't need to. Any time you need to talk, I'm here."

Lucia's breath shuddered but she smiled. "I know. I'm just not ready to talk about it now."

"Okay, but don't hold it in forever." Victoria said. "You go make the popcorn and we'll all try to cheer up."

Chapter Seven

Victoria dropped by the office a few days later, wanting to check on the progress Nick and his crew had made. When she pulled up, she saw her dad's truck parked beside one of the crew member's cars.

"Hey, Dad." Victoria called when she stepped inside. The whirring of drills and thuds of hammering drowned out her voice so she called his name louder. Her eyes swept over the place. The flooring was gone, along with the ugly receptionist counter she'd helped demolish.

"Hey, darling." Her dad straightened from where he removed the old, stained baseboards and walked over to envelop her in a hug. He smelled of sawdust and old paint.

"I thought you were retired." Victoria smiled at him and his eyes twinkled down at her.

"I was driving your mom crazy." He stood with his hands on his hips. "And I couldn't help myself. I want to have a hand in helping you with your dream."

"Dad." Victoria hugged him again. "You helped me buy the place. That's more than I could ask for."

"Yeah, well, I want to have a physical hand in it, too."

Nick walked and Victoria's pulse sped up. He wore jeans with holes in them, a snug t-shirt, and a three day five o'clock shadow. When his gaze met hers, the thrill went straight to her core.

"Checking on our progress already?" Nick's crooked smile did nothing to help her pulse slow down. He removed his thick gray gloves and stuck them in his back pocket.

"I had to make sure you were doing it right." Victoria teased. "But I see my dad is here, so I know you won't screw it up." She sensed her dad watching them, but couldn't help smiling back at Nick.

"We've managed to get most of it gutted, which is the easy part. We need to redo some of the sheetrock, replace the baseboards, and remove all the flooring." Nick looked at her dad. "Wes has been crucial with getting those baseboards. Superman crucial."

Wes laughed. "It's all he would let me do so far. I've only been retired for six months. Not years. I still know how to wield the equipment."

Nick chuckled. "I know, but your wife would kill me if anything happened to you."

Victoria watched the easy camaraderie between the two. This was her father's kingdom, the place he knew like second nature. That Nick appreciated his help, and didn't act like her dad was trying to take over, showed her how much he respected him. Roger had always dismissed her dad's questions and advice and would charm her sisters or her mom instead. Jerk.

"Nothing's going to happen." Wes waved a dismissive hand. "I'm can take care of myself."

"I know you can." Nick clapped him on the back.

Wes pointed a finger in the air suddenly. "Victoria, I know you wanted to go to the antique shops and flea market tomorrow, but my truck is going in for a problem with the water pump. I won't be able to haul all your finds back here."

"Oh, well, that's okay. We can go next week." Her mind whirred with the possibilities of shifting her schedule. She had a lot of high profile consultations next week and a few clients that *hated* being rescheduled.

"I'm sure Nick wouldn't mind taking you out there." Wes shot Nick a look.

Victoria's head snapped up and red stained her cheeks. Why would her dad suggest that? Why was he so determined to get them together? Now he forced Nick to either accept or make it extremely awkward between all of them.

Nick rubbed the back of his neck. Before Victoria could open her mouth to tell him that she'd find someone else, he surprised her. "I'm sure the guys can handle the work here tomorrow."

"You don't have to do that." The thought of being in his truck, next to him, for a full day sent tingles up and down her spine. *Maybe this wouldn't be so bad after all.*

"I don't mind. It'll be nice to get away for a day." He arched a brow and sent her stomach spinning again.

"Thanks, Nick. I appreciate it."

"What time do you want to leave?"

How about now? "Um, how about 8:00am? I'd like to get an early start."

"No problem. I'll meet you here and we'll head out." Nick nodded toward Wes, then made excuses to head to the back.

Victoria glared at her dad. "What the heck, Dad? You put him on the spot. I could've rescheduled."

"Nonsense. It'll be good for you two." He patted her on the back. "Your mother wants you and the girls over for dinner." Wes steered her out the door. "Don't be late!"

She hated it when he steamrolled her, effectively cutting off her protests. How did he get everyone to do just what he wanted? Then again, maybe it was just what she needed.

§§

Victoria walked into her parents' kitchen to see her mom boiling pasta. "Hey, Mom. Need any help?"

Halle sat on a stool at the bar, chopping vegetables for the salad. She waved at Victoria with a smile

"Sure, sweetie. Boil some tea for us. Extra sweet, the way your dad likes." Cecilia's dyed blonde hair, artfully styled in a French twist, had a few hairs that errantly escaped. Her dark blue eyes matched Addie's, and she shared Addie's fiery nature, although she kept hers wrapped up. She ran her hands down the red and white polka dot apron the girls had made her a few years ago and reached to Victoria for a hug. "Where are the girls?"

"They spotted Addie in the living room on the Wii. We won't see them until dinner's ready."

Cecilia's lips quirked. "I don't understand their need for that stuff. Those girls should be in here learning how to cook."

Halle laughed. "Mom, really? Have you seen Addie cook?"

"Honestly." Cecilia huffed and returned to stirring the pasta and starting on her sauce. She always cooked from scratch.

Victoria reached into a cabinet and pulled out a pot and filled it with water. After that, she grabbed two tea bags and set it all to boil. She stood next to the stove, aware that if she walked away she'd forget about the pot and it would boil over. "So, how's work going, Halle?"

"Good. Busy all the time. Trevor's been really busy lately too, not getting home until the sun comes up, if then." Halle sprinkled some of the chopped bell peppers into a bowl. "I swear my blood pressure rises the moment I walk into that place."

Cecilia shot Victoria a look, then said, "That's not good, darling. I think you should take some time for yourself. Stop bending over backward for that job. Try something new. Like yoga, or a gym. Maybe a knitting class."

Halle gave her mom a perplexed look. "You want me to knit? I can barely sew a button, but you want me to knit?"

"Okay, maybe knitting is a bad choice." Cecilia told her. "But you shouldn't let your life revolve around work."

Or your husband, Victoria thought. Especially when his life definitely didn't revolve around Halle. He hardly came to family dinners, always stating some type of work emergency. He'd never been with them on one of the family vacations and seemed to like to do his own thing.

"Honey, I'm home." Her dad strode into the kitchen carrying a bouquet of sunflowers. He kissed Cecilia and waved to his daughters.

"Oh, they're beautiful, Wes. Put them in a vase with water and set them on the dining room table."

"Sure thing." He kissed her again.

Victoria melted at the look of love in her parents' eyes. It made them glow with happiness. It struck her in that moment. She wanted that, so badly, and Roger would never have given it to her. When she glanced at

Halle, she saw the same longing on her face and it pierced her heart. Her sister deserved so much more than Trevor.

She glanced down, cursed when she saw the pot of tea boiling over. She picked it up and carried it to the sink and made the tea.

For dinner they sat in the formal dining room with cell phones placed in a basket on the side table. Cecilia forbade any form of technology at the table, preferring to have actual conversations.

Helena remained quiet, talking to her grandfather only when he pestered her. Addie sat on the other side of Helena and relentlessly tried to make her niece laugh. Lucia sat at the other end of the table with Halle, Victoria, and Cecilia. Victoria listened, but kept an eye on Helena. Lucia had no problems talking, and kept up easy conversation with Halle and Cecilia about boys and school.

By the time dinner was over, the girls were back in the living room with Addie, boxing it out on the Wii. Victoria figured now was the time to broach the subject about Helena to her mom and Halle.

"Mom, I wasn't sure if you noticed Helena's behavior lately. I don't know what to do." Victoria brought the plates to the kitchen and scraped off the leftovers into the garbage can. "She's been so hostile lately, and when she's not argumentative, she's numb. Uncaring on the outside, but I know that's not how she really feels. I can't tell if it's from the divorce, or the kids at school, or maybe both."

Cecilia stopped washing the dishes and turned at the despair in Victoria's voice. She wrapped her daughter in a hug.

Victoria closed her eyes and held on tightly. Her mother always knew that a hug could take the edge off of any kind of pain. When her mom pulled back, she looked Victoria in the eye. "Helena was as close to Roger as anyone could get. She always followed him around, from the time she could walk, even if he ignored her. That was her way of spending time with him. She loves her dad and that stopped her from seeing how miserable you were."

Victoria sighed. "I didn't want them to see how miserable I was."

"In any case, right now all she's thinking about is her dad is gone, and she's probably blaming you."

Victoria opened her mouth to speak, but her mom shook her head. "It's not your fault, we know that. But

Helena is a hormone fueled pre-teen who has to blame someone, and right now, that's you. She'll get over it in a little while. She'll see how her dad really is. Now, as for the kids at school, I can't say. But that can be serious. You need to talk with her teachers. If you need me to go with you, I can."

Halle laughed softly. Victoria had forgotten she was there. "You asked for advice, Victoria. I'd say you got it."

"I did, didn't I?" Victoria smiled at her mom, even though some of it was hard to swallow. "Thanks."

"That's right. Now finish these dishes. I'm going to spend time with my granddaughters. Expect Addie to be coming to help."

Chapter Eight

The next morning, Victoria met Nick outside her office at eight a.m. He waited with two cups of coffee and she wondered if he knew this was the straight line to her heart, the IV that kept her going sometimes. She'd stayed up most of the night, worrying about Helena because of her attitude, and Lucia because of her desire to go on the date Friday night.

"Morning." Nick flashed a smile that made her forget all about her worries, including her lack of sleep. He held the cup out for her.

"Do you ever wear anything other than jeans and a t-shirt?" When she realized how bitchy she'd made it sound, she took the coffee. When his fingers brushed hers, she let out a silent gasp. "Thanks. And you don't have to answer that. I'm just tired."

He leaned against the side of his beat up truck, grinning suddenly like he loved getting up early and going antique shopping.

"Why the heck are you so happy?"

"Why wouldn't I be?" He stood. Flashed that grin again that made her weak in the knees. "I get to chauffeur a beautiful woman around all day, and help her pick out old furniture for clients."

Surprised laughter burst from her. "Old furniture? I'd love to hear what my clients say about that."

He opened the passenger door for her. "Well, let's get to it. I'm sure there's plenty to find at the flea markets."

Victoria slid in, making sure her sundress didn't expose anything, and noticed that the truck smelled like vanilla. Her eyes swept the cab of the truck and knew he cleaned it. The truck was immaculate. Not a fast food wrapper or empty can in sight. "Did you clean just for me?" She asked when he got in and started the truck.

"I may or may not have decided that you might run screaming if you saw the state of my vehicle, so I may or may not have thrown some stuff away."

"Well, maybe I'll thank you or maybe I won't. Since you might or might not have cleaned it."

They both looked at each other and started laughing as he pulled out of the parking lot.

Victoria sipped more of her coffee. "Thanks for taking me. My dad is being ruthless in his efforts, but I really couldn't reschedule some of my clients."

Nick nodded. "It's cool. I figured that by the look of panic on your face when he said he couldn't take you. It was the least I could do," he took his eyes off the road for a quick second and winked. "It's going to be such a hard day."

"Ha." Victoria felt a wave of heat hit her cheeks. Her lips stretched into a wide smile. She hadn't felt this happy in a long time. It was nice to enjoy the attention of a man without there being huge expectations. Without wondering if you said the right things or made him feel flattered enough. With Nick it was easy. Almost too easy.

"So, where to first? I kind of need to know where we're going."

Victoria thought about it. "Let's try the flea markets on the north highway first, and then if I can't find everything there we can go to the outlets in the next town."

He nodded like he did this everyday. "Okay, so what put that frown on your face this morning?"

"What?" She glanced over at him. "What frown? I didn't have a frown."

"Yeah, you even had that wrinkle in your forehead, like the morning you came in after the girls fought."

For a moment she sat, speechless. "You noticed that?"

"Hard not to." He looked at her, then back at the road. "Do you want to talk about it?"

Victoria was shocked. Never had Roger bothered to ask if she wanted to talk about how she felt. What did he want to know? Was he just being nice or looking to strike a conversation? Or did he *really* want to know how the other half lived? What it was like to live with children? "You don't want to hear about the drama in my life." She picked at the sleeve around her coffee cup.

He turned down the radio that was barely audible to begin with. "Sure I do."

Her heart melted. This was too good to be true. Why would he care to hear about her struggles? And did she really want to tell him?

"Were the girls fighting again?"

His question snapped her out of it. "Oh, no. If you really want to know…" He nodded. "…Helena's been having some trouble accepting the divorce. She misses her dad, even though he never really spent time with them, and doesn't now. She's also having some trouble with kids at school." She watched the scenery outside the window go from town proper to fields. They passed a few farmhouses.

"What kind of trouble?"

Victoria twirled her hair around her finger. "I walked in on her and Lucia fighting about it. It seems some kids are making fun of her for being in the math club, which I don't think is a big deal. But kids can be so cruel."

"Have you talked to her about it?"

"I've tried. She's so defensive lately. Right now, I'm her enemy and my advice means nothing."

"What about your sisters? Would they talk with her?"

She immediately turned and looked at him. She was surprised he would come up with that piece of wisdom. With him being a bachelor, she didn't think he'd be able to offer sound suggestions when it came to parenting. "Yeah, they have. Addie spends a lot of time with them, especially if I get caught up at work. Halle does what she can, but she's always working."

Victoria noticed him tense at Halle's name. "What is it?"

"Nothing. Maybe the kids teasing her has triggered the stuff with the divorce or made it worse. My dad ran off when I was seven, and I know it's a tough thing to deal with."

She shifted in her seat. A thin thread of pain laced his voice, but she couldn't see any evidence on his face. "That's awful."

He shrugged and wouldn't look at her. "Yeah. It was hard watching my mom deal with it. But I'm sure you've already heard this from people around town."

"Actually, I haven't. I've only heard about you from my dad and he's always spoken highly of you. How is your mom now?" She was ready to find out more about him and stop talking about her problems.

"She's fine, I guess. We worked hard to make sure she was." He kept his eyes on the road, gripping the steering wheel until the whites of the knuckles pressed through. "Anyway, what about Lucia? Is she handling it well?"

He effectively blocked her from inquiring anything else about his past, about who he was. She could handle that for now. "She seems to be okay, but she holds it in. I know she's hurting, but she puts on a brave face because of Helena. She wants to go to the movies Friday night with some boy named Jack."

"Dating? That's a tough one. How old is she?"

"She's only twelve and in her first year of middle school. That's why I told her no. I want them to wait about ten or fifteen years before they start dating. I'm not ready."

"Hmm. I don't think Mom let us near girls until we were fifteen or so. Or at least she thought we didn't go near them."

"Oh God. Don't give me something else to worry about. Like them sneaking behind my back. Have you lost your mind?"

He laughed. "Sorry. Guess I could've kept that to myself."

By the time they reached the first flea market, Victoria definitely got the sense that while Nick could charm her endlessly but anything serious about his home life was off limits. Any time she mentioned it or asked a question, he deftly changed the subject. He wasn't rude about it, just very unwilling to talk about it.

The air carried a spring morning chill, but she'd anticipated it and brought a gray cardigan to wear over the dress. Her feet were clad only in sandals but the day would warm up before that started to bother her. They crossed the gravel parking lot to the furthermost, tin-roof covered aisle. It wasn't busy yet and only a few people mingled through certain vendors.

Nick followed her patiently through the aisles, making her laugh or just standing with her in companionable silence.

They spotted a perfect 1900's desk and a lamp for one of her clients and loaded it into the truck, then headed to the next flea market. The temperature had risen while they'd been in the truck, so she left her cardigan behind. Victoria began to lightly sweat underneath her dress so she took a rubber band from her purse and pulled her hair up in a pony-tail. Her hair frizzed out in little strands from her pony-tail because of the humidity and she wished that the heat didn't turn her into Cousin It. She snuck a glance at him while they strolled through the aisles. When he reached to pick up something, his muscles flexed underneath the thin cotton material. Her stare followed the sleeve of tattoos, eyeing one of various bright colors. Cherry blossoms surrounded a kneeling samurai. It made him look sexy, especially with the gleam of sweat on his skin. She wondered how he looked shirtless.

He stopped at a table selling water and bought them each a bottle. It didn't seem like that big of a gesture, but it made her feel special. That he cared about her. Just like how he brought her a cup of coffee that morning. None of which he had to do.

"Nick?" A bubbly voice called out.

Both Nick and Victoria stopped, and panic crossed his face. The voice called out again, literally trilling like a bird. Nick winced.

Victoria turned and watched a pin-up blonde come across the aisle, arms outstretched. She launched herself into Nick's arms and planted a raunchy kiss on him, leaving hot pink lipstick behind. Victoria's eyebrows rose.

Nick tried to disengage himself, but the girl clung tighter. "Oh, Nicky. I've missed you. Why don't you come around anymore? I loved playing your nurse, fixin' up all your bumps and bruises." Nick shot her a pleading look. Victoria knew he wanted her help but she was too busy trying to tamp down her irrational hurt at seeing another woman all over him.

"Nicky?" The girl paused when she noticed he wasn't giving her any love back.

"Uh, Sabine, it's been a while." He peeled her arms and legs from his torso and set her down. "I haven't been fighting for the past two years. I quit."

Sabine crossed her arms, pushing her breasts up and out. She even pouted. "But Nicky, that's no excuse. We used to have so much fun."

Victoria wanted to know what he meant by fighting. Was he a violent person? It was weird, she hadn't really thought he was. She turned to give the two of them more privacy, and herself space to breathe, and went further down the row to a seller that had shelves of wood statues. She tried so hard not to listen to the conversation carrying down the aisle but she couldn't *not* hear.

Sabine had that whiny voice that she'd always hated. She remembered a few girls from school who'd talked like that because they thought it made the guys like them. That it made them seem fragile and womanly. Victoria snorted. Ridiculous. She didn't know how men put up with it. She didn't realize that Nick liked that kind of thing.

Victoria snuck a glance over her shoulder while she pretended to sift through lace doilies a stall over. Nick stood with his arms crossed and a frown on his face. Apparently he didn't find Sabine adorable anymore. That little warmth she felt at that could shove it. She didn't care if he had a woman, or several women. It was none of her business.

With a few more words, Nick broke away from Sabine and strode over to Victoria, frown still in place. "Thanks for deserting me."

Victoria scowled. "You looked like you had it handled."

He rubbed the back of his neck. "Is she still standing there?" She peeked over his shoulder, nodded. "Christ."

"Maybe if we walk further down, she'll lose sight of you." Victoria pulled him with her, ignoring the warmth of skin when she placed her hand on his arm. "So, fighting?"

Nick sighed. "I used to do fights when I was younger. With my brother. I quit the national circuit and came home two years ago, opened this business."

"That sounds nice." Victoria said to be polite. She hated fighting, always had. It seemed brutish and primitive. She could understand doing it for self-defense, but for fun? She didn't understand that at all.

Nick searched her face for a moment. "Maybe. But it came at a point in my life where I needed the structure and discipline of it. Me and my brother. If not for MMA, I probably would've ended up a felon."

"A felon? Were you a troublemaker as a kid?" Victoria led them over to a table full of eccentric figurines. Some of them were beachy, and she could use them in some of the condos and beach houses.

"I got into some trouble."

Victoria exhaled slowly. "You're not going to go into it, are you?" She picked up a pink starfish; looked closely and set it back down. "I guess it doesn't really matter."

"Okay." Nick looked at her, confused. "You against fighting?"

"I think it's stupid." She let it slip before she thought about it and heat crept up her neck and into her cheeks. "Oh, God. I'm sorry. I shouldn't have said that."

When Nick laughed it didn't make her feel better. "It's okay. My mother hated it, too. Couldn't stand it when we came home, bruised and beaten. My brother broke a few bones. How about this?" He showed her a picture frame that held real sand dollars in different sizes.

"That's actually cute." She took it from him, checked the price sticker. "Only seven dollars."

"Actually? I have some design sense."

"I bet your apartment, or wherever you live is bare. Only essentials. Nothing hanging on the walls." When he didn't say anything, she laughed. "I thought so. Usually when people leave their homes bare, it's because they don't actually feel like it's home. They haven't quite settled into the house, and don't decorate it because they feel like at any moment they may leave. Or they're afraid of the commitment." She left him staring at her as she went to pay for the frame.

Chapter Nine

Spending an entire day in Victoria's company probably hadn't been his best idea. Nick stared at his empty walls, and his 'bare essentials' and damned if she hadn't been right. He sat back on the couch, propped his feet up on his coffee table, and took a sip from his beer. He didn't like the fact that she made him rethink his bachelor pad. It suited him just fine. And what was that shit about not wanting to commit? How the hell do you commit to a damn apartment? Bare walls didn't mean he had issues and she wasn't going to make him rethink bachelorhood, no matter how much he wanted her in his bed.

When a knock sounded on his door, he swung his feet over and stood. The beer dangled in his fingertips as he opened the door.

"Hi, Nick."

Just his luck. Another of his one-night stands had hunted him down. "Hey, Alyssa." He stood in the doorway, blocking her way in. She wore a short, denim mini skirt and a shimmery halter top that looked like she poured glitter all over her torso. She'd teased up her hair and wore too much make-up. When she stepped closer, she smelled of cheap beer and cigarettes, and it almost choked him. Funny, none of that used to bother him.

"You going to invite me in?" She licked her lips and leaned into him, giving him what she thought was a sexy glare. To him she just looked ridiculous. When had all this changed?

"No, Alyssa. It's late, and I have to work in the morning." He tried to shut the door but she maneuvered her body through the small opening.

"That never stopped you before." She cocked her head to the side. "You look like you could use some fun. You seem tense."

He rubbed his eyebrow, wondering why the hell he'd thought these women were sexy. "I'm fine. I don't need company tonight."

"Oh, come on, Nick."

He could tell he needed to be an asshole to get her off his back. "Alyssa. I used to be interested, but I've grown out of it. Go back to the clubs and hunt someone else down." He pushed her out the door and locked it.

She banged on the door for a good ten minutes, yelling at him. He sank onto the couch and waited for her to go away. He spotted his cell phone, fought the urge to text Victoria and lost.

Hey. Hope you found everything you needed today.

It took her a few minutes to reply.

Victoria: I did, thanks.

He stared at the screen, at a loss. Why did he have this compulsion to talk to her? And what did he want to say? He'd never had a problem talking to a woman. They usually just fell right into his bed, no heavy seduction needed.

Anytime you need a ride, or a truck, you can ask. Let your father enjoy retirement.

Victoria: Yeah, maybe.

Was she deliberately being aloof? Did he do something wrong? He'd never understand females. He thought back over the day, wondering what could have made her give him the cold shoulder. He took another slug of beer, and it hit him. *Sabine.*

The girl practically wrapped herself around him, and it had taken him much longer than he would've liked to get her to leave him alone. Victoria had witnessed that.

She was in a different league than women like Sabine and Alyssa. She had goals and she worked for them. She didn't sleep around. He, who was normally charming when it came to women, was at a loss for words.

He shook his head and drained his beer in one gulp. He really shouldn't care. Shouldn't put too much thought into this situation. Victoria was off-limits and he had to keep it that way.

§ §

The next morning he stood in the office he rebuilt for her. The sounds of tools whirring and his men joking around with each other drifted over him, but he ignored it. They ignored him, noticing his surly mood when he'd walked through the door.

He rubbed a hand down his face and groaned. Victoria's scent had sunk into the bones of his truck. He'd gotten in this morning, breathed, and been hit by a case of desire so hard he thought he'd lose his mind. So naturally, his mood had darkened. Turning down all those women hadn't been a great idea. He was sexually frustrated, but none of them interested him. Only one woman did and her disinterest baffled him. He never had to talk women into his bed, and he always had several texts waiting for him. So why did he care if Victoria wasn't interested?

Why did it feel like she was a challenge he'd love to take on? He had time to win her over, but did he really want to deal with what came after that? Something about Victoria screamed long-time love and he just wasn't that type of man. He was his father's son.

Damn if she didn't make him want to be better than that. That's what terrified him the most.

Nick scanned the office. Wes worked hard for his daughter, helping stain the new receptionist counter. For the first time in Nick's life, he wondered how he would've turned out if he'd had a father like Wes. He'd never focused on it before, preferring not to worry about the bastard who'd abandoned them. He'd only worried about his mother and Luke.

Wes clearly loved his daughters, and from the few times Nick had seen him with his wife, he was clearly devoted to her. If he'd had a father like that, he might be good enough for Victoria.

He really needed to focus on something else.

He focused on the work. He dripped sweat, his muscles ached, and his mind numbed to anything other than measurements and the feel of the tools in his hands. His crew eventually teased him out of his funk, making him laugh over their antics by the end of the day. After they'd rolled up all the extension cords and turned everything off, Nick checked his phone. When he saw the message icon, his heart skipped a beat. He opened it, calling himself an idiot when he saw it was from Luke. Their mom wanted them to come over for dinner.

He rushed home, showered, and headed to his mom's condo on the other side of town. It overlooked the beach, something he and Luke had fought her to accept. She loved the sound of the ocean, looking at the waves and they wanted to give her everything she loved. Even though she was in remission from breast cancer, they both worried that she would get sick again. They wanted her to have everything she wanted, whether she liked it or not.

He headed up the stairs to her second floor condo, knocked, then walked in. The smell of chicken marsala hit him, and his stomach immediately growled. It'd been a while since he'd eaten a good, home cooked meal.

His mother stood in the kitchen wearing a bright pink apron over a navy blue dress, short gray hair pulled away from her face with bobby pins. His gaze raked over her, making sure she showed no signs of sickness. Her eyes sparkled when she caught his scrutiny.

"I'm feeling great, Nick." She raised on her tiptoes and kissed his cheek. Before she turned back to the stove, she patted his cheek. "How's work going?"

"Good." He crossed to the counter and poured himself a glass of sweet tea. "We're making steady progress."

She smiled. "And how is Victoria doing these days?"

"Mom." Nick watched the smile blossom on her face and his heart warmed. For the longest time, he and Luke were terrified she wouldn't make it. Watching her take treatments, vomit for hours on end, and lose her hair was the most petrifying thing he'd ever faced. If talking about Victoria made her this happy, he might just bring Victoria over for dinner. Anything to keep that sparkle in his mom's eyes.

"Is she as pretty as I remember? I haven't seen her since I used to clean her parents house."

"I didn't know you cleaned their house." He commented.

"Is that going to be a problem between you two? She probably doesn't remember it either. It was just after your father left. Anyway, is she as pretty?"

"Even more." Nick thought back to the flea market. "She's feisty, too. You never told me about cleaning for them."

"You didn't need to know. Giving my baby a run for his money, is she?" Charlotte's brown eyes danced. "Good, you need it. Always having women fall over you makes you weak. You need to work for the right one."

Nick arched a brow. "Who says I want to?"

Charlotte tapped the side of his thigh with a wooden spoon. "Sit. You're making me crazy standing about."

He complied, taking his tea and sitting at the table nearby.

"Hey, Mom. Nick." Luke walked into the kitchen just in time, in Nick's opinion.

"You know Luke's still pining after Halle."

Luke stopped just inside the kitchen. Beside the yellow walls, his dirty white shirt stood out. "That's not fair. I just got here. You can't throw me under the bus that quick."

Charlotte laughed. "That's what mom's are for. Besides, I think it's sweet. One day she'll come to her senses and divorce that weasel. Then Luke will sweep her off her feet. Show her what a real man is."

"We're only real men because you taught us how to be." Luke hugged her.

Her eyes misted. "Stop that. We've had enough tears for this lifetime. Now, wash your hands and set the table."

Nick met Luke's gaze, knowing that they both thought the same thing. They were blessed to have her.

§ §

Victoria sat in her comfy chair in her pajamas while the girls watched *Good Luck Charlie* reruns. She wasn't going to lie, sometimes she peeked over the edge of her laptop to watch too. The girls talked quietly about school while she mulled over if she needed a receptionist when the office opened. What was the point in having a *receptionist* counter without someone to man it? Could she afford to pay someone or could she just do it herself?

It would look more professional if she had someone to greet the clients. She knew first impressions were important and she wanted to impress. Her livelihood depended on it.

"Mom, can I go to cheer camp over the summer?" Lucia suddenly asked. She'd finally forgotten her mom's refusal to let her go on the date, and had returned to acting like her normal self.

Victoria looked up from the computer screen and blinked. "Camp? How much is it?"

"I don't know. Some of the girls were talking about it at school today and I want to go. I think it's two weeks long." Lucia rose on her knees and put her hands together. "Please, please, please!"

Victoria laughed at her theatrics. "Get me the information on it, and we'll see."

Lucia squealed and wrapped Helena in a tight hug. "Yes!"

"Get off of me." Helena shoved at Lucia, her mouth turned in a severe frown. "No one cares about your stupid camp."

"Helena!" Victoria snapped.

Helena jumped at the sound of her mom's outburst. Tears filled her eyes. "I hate you! I hate both of you!" She darted out of the living room and stormed upstairs.

Victoria heard Helena slam her door and her stomach rolled. She didn't mean to yell at her, she just didn't appreciate how Helena acted toward Lucia. She refused to cry in front of Lucia, even if the backs of her eyelids were hot with tears.

"What is wrong with her? Why is she being such a bitch?"

"Lucia!" Victoria could feel her world spinning out of control. "Do not say that word again. Especially about your sister. Go to your room, right now!"

Lucia scowled at her, but Victoria didn't back down. She pointed to the stairs and Lucia trudged up them. Her door slammed a second later.

When did everyone start fighting with each other? When did she lose her grip on her daughters? Was it because their dad hadn't spoken or seen them in a while? Well, even if it killed her, if she had to drive the girls to his place, Roger was going to spend time with them.

She wanted to go check on Helena, but lately every time she showed even an ounce of worry or care, it made Helena's attitude nastier. Resigned, she went to bed, hoping that when she woke up tomorrow, everything would miraculously be better.

Chapter Ten

When Nick called and asked her to meet him for a business dinner later in the week, stating a problem at the office, Victoria reluctantly agreed. Even if it was only for business, it made her jumpy. Being with him again, outside of work, tested her resolve to stay away from him socially.

He picked a small seafood restaurant nestled on the boardwalk near her office. She could tell he hadn't gone home by the sawdust on his jeans. He grinned when he saw her look. "I didn't have time to change. I came straight from the office."

She shook her head, trying to resist the urge to let her guard down around him. He could obviously charm women into dropping their walls, becoming addicted to him, and then throwing them away, like the girl at the flea market. She didn't want to end up like that.

He led her to the tables situated on a deck facing the water and pulled out her chair.

Because manners were important in her family, she smiled over at him, let him push the chair in. "Thanks." She glanced over the beach to the water beyond. The sun's setting rays cast pink light over the horizon and only a few clouds floated in the sky.

"What do you want to eat?"

Victoria turned her attention back to the plastic menu in front of her. "I have a craving for fried shrimp."

"Good choice." He grinned at her over his menu. "I'm getting the sampler platter."

Victoria's brows rose. "That's a lot of food. Think you can eat it all?"

"If I don't, I'll take it home." Nick leaned back in his chair. "Since this is a business dinner, does that mean you're paying?"

Victoria couldn't fight her smile at the humor in his eyes. "I guess it could be a write off."

"There's no way you're paying for this dinner. My mother would be disappointed if I was so ungentlemanly."

Watching him move across the table, the cut of his muscles underneath his shirt, the easy way he smiled, awakened more sensations in her body. She wondered what it would feel like to have his weight settle on top of her. She quickly averted her eyes, just in case her thoughts were written on her face.

The waiter took their orders and disappeared into the back. A few people looked over curiously, wondering what the two of them were doing together. She'd have to make a point of letting people know it was just a business dinner. If it got around that they were having dinners, date-like dinners, the gossip would be all over the town in less than an hour.

What was she thinking? It was probably already all over the place.

"What's on your mind?" Nick asked. His head cocked to the side and she felt the intensity of his stare slide over her skin. She resisted a shiver.

"Nothing." She made a mental note to ignore the other people and focus on the business.

He looked like he wanted to say something more but instead asked, "Did your clients like the furniture we picked out?"

"We?" She laughed. "I'll go with that since you helped out. Yeah, so far. The sand dollar frame is going in a beach house I'm redecorating."

"What exactly is it that you do? I've never met an interior decorator." Nick nodded to the waiter that brought his beer and her sweet tea.

"I redecorate for clients and hunt down furniture and accessories they want. Some give me creative control. I also help out the real estate agents around here with stagings, which is basically where I decorate a house they're trying to sell. Decorated houses usually sell easier than bare ones."

"Makes sense." He looked at her over his beer, his stare assessing. She felt naked underneath it, like he was looking for something she didn't know was there. "How long have you been in the business?"

The sincerity in his voice weakened her walls. She was used to Roger's indifference, his questions had always been a roundabout way to talk about himself. "For a little more than five years. Once the girls were older, I could put the time I needed into it. It took a while, but the business grew."

"Because you worked hard." Nick's serious gaze met hers. "My mom worked hard, too. I can appreciate what that takes when you have kids."

A blush crept into her cheeks. "Thanks."

He winked at her. "Anything to see you smile."

Her smile widened and she shook her head. "What did you want to meet me about?"

"Okay, no flirting." He sat back, expression business-like. "We ran into a problem with the old bathroom. We were building your pretty bathroom around the old pipes and fixtures, but they busted when we were taking the sheetrock and wall out."

"Okay. Will that delay things?"

He shrugged. "It wouldn't have if Lowe's had the piping we needed in stock. Apparently there's a lot of construction going on right now. They ordered what we need, but it'll take a few days to come in. Whoever owned the place before you did a horrible job of taking care of it."

"Dad said it was an out-of-towner. They left it when tourism dropped and forgot about it. Apparently they had a lot of money to waste. When they finally put it up for sale, Dad and I decided to buy it."

"Your dad's a great guy." Nick told her. An expression crossed his face that she couldn't read.

"Yeah, he is." She toyed with the straw in her drink, nervous but not sure why. "Him butting in at the office isn't aggravating?"

"No." Nick smiled, all trace of whatever was bothering him gone. "He's a big help. Hell, he could run the place."

"I think he misses working. Mom probably drives him crazy, asking him to do gardening and stuff with her. Thanks for letting him help."

"It's no problem."

The waiter brought their food and set it in front of them. The smell drifted to Victoria and her stomach growled. She couldn't remember if she'd eaten lunch or not. Sometimes she got caught up in work and didn't realize until later that she'd missed it.

"How's Helena doing?" He asked after taking a few bites of his food.

His interest in her daughters only made her attraction more intense. If she wasn't careful, she'd forget all about wanting to focus on her career and fall into bed with him. He made her crave the passion and desire that he could offer her. He'd unknowingly woken an urge in her and she had to fight not to succumb and have him satisfy it.

"She's not acting any better. Lucia hasn't said anything else about the bullies at school, but Helena still feels that I'm enemy number one and that her dad walks on water. Sometimes I wish I could tell her the truth about her dad, but I don't want to be the one that breaks her heart. Not that she would believe me anyway."

"She probably wouldn't. She's focused on her dad, and sees him the way she wants to. Trust me, it won't be long before she realizes it and you'll be there for her. She has a great family that will help her through it."

His bittersweet tone squeezed her heart. He messed with the food on his plate without eating. She wanted to ask again about his childhood, wanted to make him smile and forget it, but he'd made sure she understood that topic was off limits. She steered the conversation back to business. "How long until you start laying the floors and everything?"

His blue eyes warmed as he discussed the work he needed to do. Her heart beat rapidly every time his lips turned up at the corner and his dimple appeared. She glanced at his hands as he ate and suddenly wished for those hands to be on her. Warmth flushed her skin and the air became hotter. She had to get herself under control. Panic set in and she curled her fingers around the napkin in her lap. These new sensations overwhelmed her. How had she lived to be thirty-two and never felt them?

True to his word, he paid for the meal. She ignored more of the curious stares as they left the restaurant. His hand went to her lower back to guide her as they walked down the wooden stairs to the parking lot, and the breath left her body. The hotness of his skin against her shirt soaked through to her back and liquid fire settled between her legs.

"Thanks for meeting me." He rubbed the stubble on his cheek. His eyes roamed over her face.

"You're welcome." She leaned against her driver's side door. He stepped closer, placing his arms on the roof. She held her breath, afraid to breathe in his scent as aroused as she already was. He surrounded her and every nerve ending she had lit up.

His head dipped lower and her lips parted. His right hand came up and brushed right below her lips. Her knees weakened.

Then he leaned back, held out his finger, red cocktail sauce on the tip. "You had something there." The humor in his eyes lit up as he smiled at her, wiped the sauce on his pants. "See you soon." He stepped back.

She drew in air, tried to make it inconspicuous as her body flushed with a different kind of heat. Dear

God, she'd almost melted into him and all he'd done was wipe her face. Had he figured out how he affected her? He'd probably pounce if he did, and she didn't want that.

Did she?

She stared after him for a minute as he walked to his truck, trying to get her bearings. Before he turned around and saw her watching him like a brainless idiot, she got in her car and drove home.

§ §

Helena's attitude got nastier over the next two weeks, so Victoria was happy when Roger showed up at her door to pick them up for the weekend.

"Aren't you going to let me in?" Roger stood on the doorstep in a pair of gray dress pants and a white button up shirt. His reddish brown hair glinted in the waning sunlight and his green eyes too innocent. When he brushed past her after she didn't answer, the smell of his cologne surrounded her. She hated the scent, and he knew it. She followed him into the living room, watched him survey the changes she'd made. She hoped it irritated the hell out of him. He'd never let her have the freedom to decorate the way she liked.

"I wouldn't have chosen these…" Roger waved a hand delicately in the air, "things."

Score one, Victoria thought. He gave her another reason to want her business to thrive. She could prove to him that all of the *things* he disapproved of could make her successful. He continued nosing around, noticing the changes, while she stood silently, arms crossed.

"Where are the girls?" He flashed a grin, one he'd told her could get any girl in his bed--and damned if she hadn't fallen for it--and walked closer to her.

Victoria refused to back down, even though his closeness made her skin crawl. He didn't control her anymore. She stepped around him to the middle of the living room, giving herself space. "They're upstairs packing their bags. They'll be done in a minute."

"Good. I'm taking them to the restaurant to have dinner."

Of course he did. He couldn't wait to show off how he was such a good father to his twin daughters. Victoria pitied him and hated him in the same breath. He had no idea what he missed out on in the girls.

Helena flew down the stairs, beaming at Roger. Score ten to him, she thought. She tried to ignore the pain it caused her to know that she couldn't make Helena smile like that.

"Daddy!" Helena jumped into his arms, her bag forgotten at their feet. "I'm so glad you came."

Roger patted her back absently before stepping away from her. "Yes. Me, too."

Helena didn't see her dad's disinterest and Victoria sighed. When she eventually noticed, it would break her heart.

"Hi, Dad." Lucia offered Roger a smile, nothing more, then hugged Victoria. "See you Sunday, Mom. I love you."

Victoria held Lucia probably longer than necessary, it was so tough to watch them leave. Helena ignored her, not even giving her a smile as they walked out the door. She shut it behind them and leaned against it. This was literally only the third weekend she'd ever spent without them. What was she going to do with herself? Should she call her sisters?

No, Halle had a nursing conference in Long Island and all Addie had talked about this week was her date tonight. Knowing Addie, she'd end up with the guy all weekend, if he didn't bore her to death. At the thought

111

of that kind of freedom, Victoria smiled and shook her head. She hadn't been on a date in years, a decade really. She'd have no idea what to do.

The house creaked in the silence around her. The TV wasn't on, blaring reality shows, and her girls weren't arguing over something or giggling over something else. The quietness settled around her and she sighed. All her life, she'd been surrounded by people. First her family, then her dorm mate, and then Roger and her girls. Being alone like this struck her as unnatural. Maybe she should get a dog.

Her cell phone pinged a message tone from the arm of the couch and she picked it up.

Nick: Hey, you busy?

Victoria laughed at the screen. She was so far from busy and she couldn't deny that maybe, a little, she wished he'd ask her out. After seeing Roger, remembering the years of blandness, of settling, she might just want a hint of the passion Nick had to offer.

No, what's up?

She'd expected him to text, so when her cell rang she jumped. She answered the phone, her belly fluttering. "Is something wrong with the office?"

"No, it's nothing like that." His voice carried over, sending goose bumps over her body. Even though, he sounded nervous.

"Oh? Is everything okay?" She paced, like she always did when she talked on the phone.

"Yeah, yeah." He paused. "Um, I need a big favor. I have this friend, one I used to fight with on the circuit, and he's getting married tomorrow night. With work, I forgot about it."

The butterflies multiplied. "Okay?" She really couldn't think of anything else to say. She sank onto the turquoise, pillow top ottoman.

"I need a date. I know he's invited this girl, one I used to…hang out with…and I really don't want to go by myself."

Victoria pressed her lips together. Those butterflies shriveled up and settled heavy in her stomach. He didn't really want to go with her, he only wanted a buffer. "Why don't you ask one of your many, many one night stands? Maybe find someone who's available?"

Nick's was silent, then he sighed. "That came out wrong."

"I bet it did. Look, I wasted enough time on a man who didn't really want me, who wanted to use me to further his image to get higher in his career. I don't need to be used again. So, good-bye, Nick." Victoria ended the call. She stared at the screen for a minute, then decided she was an idiot. Why did she let herself become even the tiniest bit attracted to him? Was it because she wanted to feel reckless for once? To experience true passion in her life?

She knew she couldn't focus on work now, and pulled up Netflix. Since she wanted to take her mind off of everything, she chose a suspenseful movie that would do so. A little while later, when she heard the knock on the door, she paused the movie. Her sisters had already left for their stuff, and her parents were out on a date night. If Roger was bringing the girls back, she'd punch him in the throat. Unfortunately he was the only one who could make Helena happy right now, so he better step up.

She slung the door open, prepared to go off on Roger. No sound came from her open mouth. Nick stood on the porch, looking delicious in jeans and a dark green t-shirt. She became acutely aware that she wore a pair of cotton shorts and a sleeveless work out shirt. No make-up, glasses on.

"Hey." Nick ran a hand through his hair. "Got your address from your dad."

Victoria blinked. She finally shut her mouth and stepped back from the doorway.

Nick came inside and she shut the door behind him.

"I came to apologize." He sighed. "What I said…it came out wrong."

"I'm not sure that it did." She crossed her arms, aware that earlier she'd been in the same room with Roger. It was surreal. Nick glanced to her chest and heat flushed up her neck.

He snapped his attention back up to her face, his eyes darkening. He stepped closer and she stepped back. "I want you to come because I want to spend time with you."

She arched a brow. "You have a funny way of telling me that." His body heat lit her nerves on fire. Jesus, she wanted him to push her up against the wall and kiss her. "Besides, why don't you take that girl from the flea market?"

"Are you jealous?" His brows rose.

"No." She lied. She glared at him.

"Look, this is new to me." He took a deep breath. She stared at the tattoo that swirled up his left collarbone. "I'm not the dating type." She snorted and he shot her a look. "But I do know that there is something between us. I know you feel it. I want to explore that."

Victoria's breath hitched. It wasn't the sweetest thing anyone had ever said to her, and he didn't state that he wanted to date her, but the desperate look in his eyes, the way he almost pleaded at her to understand, reached her like nothing else. "Oh?"

"I know what you've heard about me. I know that I have the worst reputation. But, it's one night. Come to the wedding with me. If you think that I'm still a lost cause, or that I'm not worth your time, tell me. I'll forget about this craziness in my mind, and finish out the job without bothering you." He observed her expression, waiting on her answer.

She ignored the sinking in her stomach at the thought of him leaving her alone. "Is this wedding formal?"

The grin that spread across his face almost made her rip her clothes off, right there. It softened the edges of his face, made him seem more carefree. "Semi-formal, you got something to wear?"

"I might." She smiled back at him.

"Great. I'll pick you up tomorrow at three. The wedding's at six, and it's a two hour drive. It's supposed to be cool tomorrow night, so have a jacket, or whatever wrap thing you women wear."

"Smooth." Victoria laughed. "Real smooth."

"I try." Nick nodded at her. "Okay. Good. I'll see you tomorrow."

She let him out, then locked the door and leaned against it. Her heart beat rapidly in her chest and her skin flushed. This was bad. Real bad. She wanted him, wanted to tempt that passion in him, have him lose control with her. It surprised her, since she was usually more timid about this kind of thing. She just couldn't help herself.

Chapter Eleven

Victoria hadn't been this nervous in forever. She'd picked out the perfect dress, a navy blue and beige chevron print; with nude heels and a navy, three quarter sleeve fitted blazer. She added a delicate heart necklace the girls gave her for Mother's Day last year and curled her hair, letting it frame her face.

She knew she looked amazing, she just prayed Nick agreed. She'd never wanted to blow a man's mind before, not with this reckless abandon. It was like her hormones had completely taken over. She knew it was crazy to get involved with him. He had a history of moving from one woman to another, never having a girl "over" for more than a few nights. Last night she'd thought about this for a while, and decided that she'd take those few nights.

Passion was missing in her life, in her past, and she didn't want to settle for boring again. If Nick could only give her that for a small amount of time, she'd take it, and be happy.

With one last look in the mirror, she grabbed her clutch and took a deep, steadying breath. It was only one night, like his others. It didn't help to start analyzing everything.

She opened the door right when he knocked and dear God, she almost drooled. He wore a dark gray, three piece suit that molded to his body. His thin black tie was askew and it took everything she had not to pull him inside by it and forget about the wedding.

"Wow." Nick's stare roamed from her feet, up her legs, slowly taking everything in. The heat in his eyes left a caress everywhere he looked. The slow, lazy grin weakened her resolve. "I'm going to have my hands full tonight."

Her heart skipped until she realized he probably meant the way she looked, not that he literally wanted to have his hands full of something. Like, maybe, her. He'd told her the night was going to be cool, but she already wanted to strip off her jacket. Maybe her dress, too.

"Ready?" He held out his hand. "We need to leave before I forget we're supposed to go somewhere."

She placed her hand in his and felt his calloused palm against hers. She wanted to feel those hands on her, trailing over her skin. She let him lead her to the truck because she knew she couldn't form a coherent thought. He opened the door for her, and made sure her feet were inside before shutting it.

He entertained her on the drive with funny stories about his job, some of it from her own remodeling. She laughed in his truck more than she had in the past year, and every time she did his eyes lit up. While he drove, she took the opportunity to watch him. He seemed so comfortable in his own skin. She didn't feel like she had to fake her laughter or smiles. He talked about the happy couple, telling her things about the MMA circuit she'd never wondered about.

Violence was so foreign to her. Her father had never raised a hand against another person. The most violent thing he watched was football. She couldn't wrap her head around someone wanting to hurt someone else, getting paid to do it, or winning trophies. How did that testosterone filled adrenaline not bleed over into their regular lives?

She snuck a glance at Nick. He didn't seem to have a temper, didn't seem to be violent. She couldn't mix the thought of him being a fighter with the genuine way he treated people. His hands held the steering wheel in a sure grip. It didn't seem like he'd lose himself to that violence.

He pulled off the interstate and it only took a minute to reach the church. Once he parked, he opened the door for her. When he grabbed her hand and interlocked their fingers, her breath quickened.

His friends' marriage ceremony was being held in a beautiful, brick church that had a Southern style wrap-around porch with white columns. The dark wooden doors were propped open and an usher stood on each side, passing out programs to guests. Inside, people sat on either side of the aisle in white wooden chairs.

"Hey, Nick!" A redheaded guy clapped Nick on the shoulder as they passed the ushers. "You made it!"

"Colin!" Nick let her hand go and gave the guy a bear hug. "How's Nora?"

"She's great. Ready to pop." Colin turned to the side and pointed to a very pregnant woman sitting down toward the front. "Twins."

"You're in luck then." Nick took Victoria's hand in his again. "Victoria has twin girls, so maybe she can give you and Nora some tips."

Colin glanced at Victoria in surprise and grinned devilishly. "Twins? Nick's actually dating a woman with kids? Never thought hell would freeze over, guess I need my coat." His laughter boomed in the room. "Nora and I could use all the help we can get. We're having girls, too."

They followed the burly redhead to where his wife sat.

"Nick, it's good to see you." Nora had a pixie-like frame, except for the pregnant belly, complete with a platinum blonde pixie cut. She smiled warmly at Victoria. "I'm Nora."

"It's nice to meet you. I'm Victoria." She took the seat next to Nora and crossed her legs. "Twins, huh?"

Nora nodded and rubbed her belly in a way that Victoria empathized with. "Colin mentioned that you have twins too?"

"I do, they're twelve." Nick sat on her other side and Victoria instantly became aware of his every movement, like her body was tuned in to his.

"Is it as hard as everyone says?" Nora asked.

Victoria laughed. "Oh, yes. But it's so rewarding, like with any children. Just double the work."

§§

The way Victoria's eyes lit while she spoke to Nora about her girls planted a seed in the back of Nick's mind. He'd always thought kids were cute, from a distance, and not something he'd ever want to get involved with. Especially as a father figure. That's why he steered away from women with kids. He let his hand trail down Victoria's arm. Distinct satisfaction rose along with the goose bumps on her skin. He knew he affected her, he could tell from how she reacted to his touch.

She was slowly changing something in him and he pushed down the acute panic that rose with the thought. Like he'd told her, it was just one night and didn't mean that they were going to shack up tomorrow and live the rest of their lives together.

The ceremony started and Victoria sent him a sweet smile that knotted his stomach. She was so beautiful. Her ex had to be one stupid bastard to let her go. He couldn't resist interlocking their fingers again and didn't want to examine why he had to touch her tonight, even if it was only holding her hand.

Gerritt's face stretched in a wide smile when he saw Nicola appear at the end of the aisle. Gerritt, who swore he'd never settle down, looked like he'd die if Nicola didn't hurry down that aisle, like he'd found the other half of his soul.

Nick cursed inwardly. When had he become such a girlie bitch? If anyone knew what he'd been thinking, they'd take away his man card.

The short ceremony was sweet with promise. The couple headed back down the aisle, beaming. The families and friends slowly stood and made their way outside for the reception. Golden lights hung from ribbons across trees and surrounding the dance floor. Arrangements of white calla lilies stood on each table, dressed with more lights.

Nick and Victoria walked with Colin and Nora to one of the tables, claiming it as their own.

"I hope you like chicken. I wasn't sure what you'd want." Nick told her.

"Chicken's great." Victoria licked her lips and an electric shock shot to his groin.

He wanted to show her a good time. That didn't include scaring her off. From what he'd heard about her ex, the man was selfish and Nick knew what that translated to in bed. Quick, uncomfortable, and unimaginative. She probably wasn't used to being seduced but she would now. He'd take his time, make her so hot for him she lost her mind. He'd show her how a real man did it.

He cleared his throat and took a swig of his beer. Resisting her was going to be the hardest thing he'd ever done. Especially with her sitting next to him, fresh and beautiful. Every time she smiled, or laughed, it pulled him to her. She'd bewitched him.

"Oh, God. Stella's here." Nora groaned.

Nick's head shot up and he searched for Stella. Victoria watched with curious eyes and he wanted to sink beneath the table before Stella saw him. If she did, it would just strengthen Victoria's resolve to stay away from him.

Stella's auburn hair stood out in the crowd. She wore God-awful heels that made her already 6 foot frame tower over the other women. Her body-hugging green mini dress sparkled in the lights. If a man's eyes weren't on her, she considered it a personal affront.

Unfortunately she saw him looking and wiggled her fingers at him. Her sly smile stretched across her face and Nick knew she was going to head over. They'd had a few whirlwind nights two years ago and ever since he'd refused to continue the liaison, she'd hunted him. She hated that he'd gotten away before she was finished with him.

"Jesus, Nick. Did you have to let her see you?" Colin grimaced. "Now she'll never leave this table."

Victoria raised a brow at him and he knew what she thought. That he'd only proved her right. He had to make sure she understood that Stella was nothing to him.

"Nick." Stella purred as she stopped by his chair. She leaned down, showing her ample cleavage to everyone, and wrapped her arms around his neck. Her thick cloud of perfume stung his nostrils. Before she could slide onto his lap, Nick put his hands on her arms to keep her standing. She pouted at him.

"Stella, I'd like you to meet my date, Victoria." Nick tipped his head toward Victoria, who sat silently next to him.

"Oh. I see." Stella straightened and held out a perfectly manicured hand. "Hello, Victoria. I'm Stella de Noren." Her bold green eyes raked down Victoria. "Such a quaint dress. But, I guess not everyone can buy from Gucci."

Victoria's eyebrow rose again, but this time she assessed Stella. "Hmm. And I guess not everyone can dress like a whore."

Nora choked on her laughter and hit Colin when his turned heads in their direction.

Stella's eyes narrowed and Nick knew that if he didn't get between them, Stella would retaliate. She wasn't above starting a catfight to draw attention to herself.

"Stella, I think you should find someone else to sink your claws into. As you can see," Nick made sure Stella saw the desire in his eyes when he looked at Victoria, "I came with someone else. And even if I hadn't, you'd be the last person I'd be interested in."

Stella flushed, her face matching her hair. She spun on her heels and stalked off. Nora couldn't hold back her laughter.

"Oh my God, Victoria. You handled her so well. I can't believe you called her a whore." Nora snorted. "Stop making me laugh so hard, you'll send me into labor."

"She deserved it. How can you dress like that and not expect people to think it?" Victoria shrugged.

"Yeah, but you didn't just think it. You said it. Out loud." Colin grinned at Victoria. "Nick, you may just have to keep this one. She's something else."

Nick laughed, but on the inside he'd frozen up. What exactly did he want from Victoria? Was it a one night stand or something more? His mind and body were conflicted, and he'd never once felt this way. What was she doing to him?

Chapter Twelve

After the beautiful first dance, where the bride and groom danced under the lights and the stars, Victoria started to get nervous. She'd already had a rise in blood pressure with Stella, but now it really spiked. If Nick asked her to dance, she'd need to get close to him. Could she do that without making a fool out of herself?

Roger had never brought out this want in her before. Addie always went on about how hot her sex life was, how many orgasms she'd had, how she enjoyed sex. Loved it even. Victoria had never understood that. Until Nick.

Then the moment came. Nick stood and reached out his hand. He smiled when she placed her hand in his. Plenty of other couples filled the dance floor, so they had to find a spot on the outer rim. He put his hands on her hips and pulled her to him. "Put your arms around my neck."

His whisper sent tingles through her entire body. She bit her lip and did what he asked, her gaze leveled at the knot on his tie. Her body pressed to his and with each turn, she felt the muscles in his abdomen and chest. His body heat soaked through her dress, making her nipples harden. Slowly his hands slid to her back, resting just above her butt.

What would it be like to kiss him? Instinctively, she tilted her head back and looked at him. Her breath caught at the desire in his eyes. Was she brave enough to let this go further?

He leaned forward, stopping when his lips almost touched hers. She could almost feel the softness of his lips, and her eyes fluttered closed. Want and need entwined in her chest.

Something icy spilled down the back of her dress. She gasped in shock, and Nick glanced over her shoulder and frowned.

"Oh, I didn't see you there." Stella's voice rose above the music.

Victoria spun around and narrowed her eyes. Stella watched her with a satisfied smile, a hand on her hip. The other hand held her now empty wine glass. Stella glanced around the room and saw that most of the other guests watched them.

Nick grabbed Victoria's elbow and pulled her to him. He didn't seem to care that the back of her dress wet the front of his shirt. "Stella, you have serious fucking issues."

Before Stella could snap out a reply, the bride appeared at their side. "Stella, you need to leave. I won't have you starting stuff at my wedding. You won't ruin this night just because you weren't woman enough to satisfy Nick. Now, get your skanky ass out of here. I don't want to see you for the rest of the night. In fact, I don't want to see you ever again."

"Nicola, you don't understand. She bumped into me--"

"Shut up." Stella's mouth snapped shut in surprise. "If you don't leave right now, and I have to beat your ass in my wedding dress, not even the guys will be able to pull me off." Nicola cocked her head to the side.

Victoria saw Nicola's lean and muscled arms. From the way she talked, Gerritt must've met her through the MMA circuit. Stella obviously knew this because she glared for a minute longer before leaving the reception.

"Now, sweetie, come with me. I have a few extra dresses packed for my honeymoon. You can borrow one." Nicola waved her hand to Victoria.

"You don't have to do that." Victoria shook her head. "I don't want to put you through any trouble on your wedding night."

"There's no use in arguing with her. Nicola is one of the most hardheaded women I've ever met." Nick gently pushed Victoria in Nicola's direction.

Without another choice, Victoria followed the bride through the crowd. Nora joined them, waddling inside behind them. They walked into the bride's dressing room. It was small, but beautiful, decorated in whites and deep red. Nicola dug through the suitcase and Nora settled into a chair and sighed.

"I'm sorry about this." Victoria told Nicola.

Nicola held out a lavender sundress. "You have no reason to apologize. I don't know why I invited her. Pity, I guess."

Victoria removed her wet dress and laid it on the back of a chair. She'd been a cheerleader in high school and had two sisters, so she wasn't shy about undressing in front of other women.

"So, I need the juicy details. How did you meet Nick?" Nora asked. "I need to live through someone who's starting a relationship. I've been married for two years. Don't get me wrong, I love it, but sometimes it's nice to hear about the beginning. All the hormones, the adrenaline, the rush of first love."

Victoria let Nicola zip the back of the dress up. "There's no beginning. No relationship." She slipped her shoes back on. "He needed someone to bring as a date. I was available."

Nora smiled. "You don't see the way he looks at you."

"Yeah, I've never seen him look at a woman like that before." Nicola led them back out to the crowd. "And he's never, I mean never, dated a woman with kids. It's like he has a phobia of them."

Victoria thought about what they said while she and Nora walked back to the table to meet the guys. Nick grinned and handed her a mixed drink. "Thought you could use one of these."

"Thanks." She couldn't resist smiling back, even with the worry about him and kids settling in her mind.

"You look great." Nick said sheepishly. "Bet that wasn't what you had in mind for tonight."

"No, but it'll make for a memorable one." She wanted to hint to him that Stella hadn't ruined the night, but would that make her seem easy or too enthusiastic?

He didn't leave her side for the rest of the night. When he fed her a piece of his cake from his fingertips, she wanted to suggest that they leave early. For once in her life she wanted to throw caution to the wind and do something impulsive. Take him home and let him ravish her. But they didn't leave early, waiting instead for Gerritt and Nicola to leave. She swapped numbers with Nora, making her promise to call if she had any questions, or if she just wanted to talk. Victoria had a feeling that she'd hear from Nora soon.

On the way back to Sanctuary Bay, Nick was uncharacteristically silent. He looked deep in thought, tapping a thumb on the steering wheel periodically. She'd had so much fun that she just realized maybe she'd read all his signals wrong. Maybe he didn't have any fun. Maybe Colin joking about Nick dating a woman with kids finally set in. Maybe he really wanted to leave with Stella and thought it would be rude to leave Victoria there.

Her brain started to hurt from all the questions circling. Or maybe it was the alcohol. Addie told her all the time that she over analyzed everything. Was she doing that now? She prayed that the drive would hurry and she could disappear into her house. Maybe if she didn't have him near her she could forget this night even happened.

Even as she thought that, she knew that even if he moved to another country, she'd never forget this night. Never forget how he'd made her feel, the craving he'd woken in her.

He pulled into her driveway, still silent. His grip tightened on the steering wheel.

She waited a second, wondering if he was just going to leave.

"Good night, Victoria." He said it quietly, without looking over at her. He continued to stare out the windshield.

She blinked. He was really going to do this? After all that, chasing her down to be his date, he was going to leave? Not even try for a goodnight kiss? She didn't respond to him as she slid out of his truck, wet dress in hand. He wasted no time in reversing his truck and taking off down the street.

For a minute she stood there. Her stomach clenched. She'd never felt so completely...rejected.

Chapter Thirteen

For the next week Victoria avoided going near her office. She got updates from her dad, dodging his questions about why she wasn't coming by. She put it off to being busy with clients and stagings. Seeing Nick right now would only make the rejection sting worse and she'd had enough of that for a lifetime. She'd been so foolish to believe that Nick would be interested in her for more than one night.

What hurt the most was that he'd acted like he'd wanted her. She could've sworn he also felt the tension and heat between them. But she hadn't been good enough even for a one night stand. That humiliation settled bitterly in her stomach. She could go a while without seeing him and be okay.

Which could be a good thing, considering Helena's attitude had only darkened since her father dropped them off Sunday. She couldn't let what was going on with Nick distract her from her girls. After being married to Roger and buckling every time he thought she did something wrong, Victoria refused to break with whatever Nick had going on. It had been a week, for God's sake; she just had to get the hell over it.

"God, what did that counter do to you?"

Victoria jumped, the sponge flying from her hand. "Jesus, Addie. What the hell?"

Addie's brows rose. "Whoa. Did Roger do something else to piss you off?"

"Not everything is about Roger." Victoria ground out. She picked up the sponge and attacked the stove. It'd been a while since she deep cleaned and she was in the mood now. The next thing she knew, Addie laid a hand on her shoulder and gently turned her around.

"What's the matter?" Addie took the sponge, steered Victoria to the bar, and forced her to sit. "You look like you need a good sister talk and some wine."

"Don't you have a date?" Victoria watched as Addie moved deftly around the kitchen, getting the wine glasses and wine bottle.

"Sure, but he's an idiot. I'd rather figure out why you're being such a bitch." Addie shot her a grin to soften the words. "You haven't been this keyed up in a long time."

Victoria spun the wine glass around on the counter, knowing she stalled. She hadn't told either of her sisters about the date since it had ended so badly. "I went on a sort-of date with Nick."

Addie spit her wine out all over the counter. She coughed. "You can't just throw that bombshell out there. Does Halle know?"

Victoria shook her head.

"Then shut up. I'm calling her right now. Don't say another word." Addie held up a hand. "I mean it."

Halle made it there in record time. She rushed into the kitchen, still in her scrubs, short bob a mess. "Did I miss anything?" She grabbed herself a glass of wine. "If I did, you better start this shit over. When was it?"

"Last Saturday."

"What?" Both of her sisters exclaimed.

"You're just now telling us?" Addie took the glass of wine from Victoria. "You don't deserve this. What kind of bitch keeps this stuff from us?"

Halle spied the lines of tension on Victoria's face. "Give it back. It looks like she needs it."

Addie glanced harder at Victoria, noticed the faint hurt in her eyes. "What did he do? I will kill him. I'll wait until he's done with your office, but after that? His balls are mine."

Addie's words shocked a laugh out of Victoria, although it shouldn't have surprised her. Addie was fiercely protective of her older sisters and had the fire to follow up on the threat. Before Addie could make good, Victoria told them all about the date, from the call Friday night, to Stella, to the unsatisfying end of the night. "He just left."

"That doesn't sound like normal Nick." Addie cocked her head to the side. "He's all about going inside, from what I hear."

Victoria finally gave voice to what gnawed at her. "Is there something wrong with me?"

"Hell, no." Addie shot Halle a worried glance. "Why would you think that?"

"Roger left me to *find himself* and Nick, the renowned womanizer, didn't even want to come inside after the date." Hot tears welled up in her eyes, but she blinked them away. She didn't want to cry over this.

Halle rubbed Victoria's arm. "From what you said, it sounded like he was really into you. Like his friends said, he's never dated a woman with kids. Maybe he's intimidated. You are a very independent woman."

"That's ridiculous. How could I be intimidating? He's a freakin' ex-MMA fighter. He's not scared of anything." Victoria took a long sip of wine. "I'm just not what he's looking for."

"There are ways to be intimidating that have nothing to do with that. You're a woman. You may scare him because he wants more with you than he has with other women. Maybe you're forcing him to reevaluate his life and it makes him uncomfortable?" Addie shrugged. "I think maybe you should wait to hear from him. Text him. Right now. See what he says?"

"I'm not texting him." Victoria shook her head. "I won't. He wants to talk to me, he can text me. He's obviously not interested."

Addie walked out of the kitchen. A second later she returned with Victoria's cell phone.

Victoria tried to jump up from the stool but Halle's arms wrapped around her. Halle may be petite, but the woman had strong arms. She didn't let Victoria move.

Addie's eyes lit up while she typed the message and hit send. "Ha! Whatcha' gonna' do about it?"

Victoria didn't know whether to be supremely pissed that Addie texted him, or relieved that she didn't have to go back and forth with herself about doing it. Halle released her and went back to her wine. "Addie. I didn't want to text him. He rejected me, remember? I'm giving in to him with you texting him!"

Addie set the phone down on the counter in the middle of them and they stared at it. "Honey, sometimes it's not about giving in. You want answers, right? You want to know why he acted like he had a great time? Then ask him. Get him over here for a face to face and find out why he left you standing there. Don't just roll over."

The phone vibrated, sliding across the surface and tapping into Victoria's wine glass. Addie's eyes gleamed with triumph. "See? I bet he was waiting on you to call him."

"That's the point, Addie. It's just a game to him." Victoria's hands shook, but she read the message.

Nick: Hey, I was wondering if you were going to talk to me again.

"See? I'm so right." Addie nodded to the phone. "Don't take everything so literally. Get him over here and make him explain. Text him back."

"What am I supposed to say? I don't know what to say." Victoria tried to stop herself from panicking, but it was useless.

Halle laughed. "Ask him about the office, anything. You're not proposing. Or giving in."

"Shut up." Victoria had to laugh at herself. "I've been out of this game for a long time."

"It doesn't have to be a game." Addie grinned when her sisters both shot her a look. "I know I'm the last person who should say that. But, it doesn't. You can just talk to him like you'd talk to every one else. Stop making it such a big deal and putting all that pressure on yourself."

Victoria blew out a breath. "You're right. I shouldn't be this nervous. He's just a guy."

"So text him." Halle picked up the wine glasses. "Invite him over. I'll pick the girls up from the movies, and you can see where it goes."

That now familiar panic blossomed in her chest. "I can't. The girls need me right now."

"No, they need their aunts right now." Addie smiled at Victoria. "They haven't spent time with us--without you--in forever. You deserve to have a night without work and kids. Just see how it goes."

Victoria knew from experience that when her sisters ganged up on her like this, nothing would change their minds. Besides, she wanted to know what he had to say for himself. "Fine."

"I'm going to pack the girls a bag." Halle winked at her. "They're staying the night."

"I hate when you gang up on me." Victoria muttered. She stared down at the phone and quickly typed him a messaged before she lost her nerve.

Want to come watch a movie?

Her heartbeat sped up as she waited for an answer. It didn't take him long to respond.

Nick: What time do you want me there? Have you eaten yet? I can pick up Chinese.

Victoria: An hour and sure.

"Wear something cute but casual." Addie told her. "Don't worry about cleaning up. Halle and I will do that while you're in the shower. Go." She shooed her out of the kitchen.

When Victoria finished getting ready she glanced around the house and saw that her sisters had lit the candles on her mantle and coffee table. Her face heated. What were they trying to do? She hurried to the first one and blew it out. She went to blow out the second and the doorbell rang. "Crap!" She rushed, blowing the rest out before going to the door.

"Hey." Nick held out a single stargazer lily when she opened the door.

Victoria bit her lip to keep her smile under control. "They're my favorite. How'd you know?" He looked amazing.

"Addie. She took my number from your phone and said that maybe it would soften you up."

"Oh." Somehow that didn't diminish her happiness over the flower. She had to remind herself that he was here for answers. He followed her inside and she put the flower in a vase and set it on the mantle. She prayed he wouldn't notice the smoking candles. "Addie's such a bitch." She laughed at her sister's meddling.

"What happened to the candles?" Nick looked around. "Addie said she was lighting them for ambiance."

"Oh, God." Victoria burst into laughter and the last of her nerves dissipated. "I blew them out. I didn't know she told you about them."

His lazy grin sent heat straight through her. "That's a shame. I thought you were trying to get all romantic on me."

Victoria didn't know what to say to that. She gestured to the Chinese takeout bag he held. "I'm starving." She wasn't really, but she wanted to stall before asking him what last weekend was all about.

They sat at the bar, side by side, eating and talking about the office. Nick filled her in on all the progress they'd made in the last week and he seemed so unaffected by what happened last weekend. Like it hadn't mattered to him that he'd left her at the end of a really great night with nothing more than a good bye.

She pushed her plate away and spit out the question. "Why did you just leave last Saturday?"

His body tensed. He set the food down before turning to look at her. His hooded gaze gave nothing away. "I couldn't come inside."

"Oh? Then why are you here now?" She stood, needing to put some space between them. Hurt and humiliation clouded inside of her. He watched her pace silently before he stood.

"You're not understanding."

"How can I when you don't explain what's going on? I thought we were having a great night. I was, anyway, and then you didn't talk to me on the way home. And then you left." She tried to bury the hurt in her anger but it rose through.

Nick shook his head. He came to her and put his hands on her arms. Victoria stilled. "I couldn't come inside, because if I did, I wouldn't be able to keep my promise."

That baffled her. She looked up at his face, noticed his clenched jaw. She realized that even though his past was seeped in violence, she wasn't afraid of him. He wouldn't hurt her. Not physically, at least. "What promise?"

Nick shoved a hand through his hair, making the ends stand up everywhere, then ran a hand down the stubble on his face. She wanted to feel that stubble on her skin. "It's stupid. Don't worry about it."

"No." He couldn't say something about a promise and then tell her not to worry about it. "What promise, Nick? Did someone make you promise to leave me alone?"

"No, nothing like that." he sighed, shoved his hands into the pockets of his jeans. He looked lost.

Victoria stepped closer and watched his eyes darken. Tension swept into the room. A new kind of power filled her. He wanted her; she knew that with a strong confidence. Something held him back and she was going to figure out what it was. "What is it then?"

"Ah," He swallowed audibly when she stepped even closer. "I promised myself."

"Hmm." She stopped only when there was less than an inch between them. He kept his hands in his pockets. "What did you promise yourself?" She tilted her head back to look in his eyes. Her lips parted.

His eyes zeroed in on her lips. "That I'd take it slowly. Seduce you."

Victoria laughed softly. "I don't want to take it slow."

Nick blinked, then swore. His hands came up to either side of her neck.

Victoria stopped laughing. She may have stopped breathing, she wasn't sure.

He lowered his mouth and brushed his lips gently over hers. His tongue pushed between her lips and she sighed, melting against him.

He meant to keep it soft but she threaded her fingers through his hair and pulled his mouth closer. She slid her tongue across his bottom lip, then nipped it. "Damn it, baby." Nick laid his forehead against hers and breathed hard. "I wanted to seduce you. Give you what you need."

"What is it I need, Nick?" She trailed light kisses down his neck. Her nipples hardened when his hands trailed down her shoulders to her waist. His fingers tightened and he pulled her to them. No space, body to body. The hardness of his erection pressed against her stomach.

"Christ." Nick said. "I'm trying here. To be good."

She lifted up on the tips of her toes, her breasts rubbing against his upper body. The sensation made her core clench. She bit his earlobe. "I don't want you to."

Her words crumbled the last of his resistance. "You asked for it."

When he kissed her hard, she moaned into his mouth and pressed closer. his hands shifted and he lifted her on the counter, stepping between her legs. His hard-on pushed right into her center and she gasped.

Chapter Fourteen

Nick pulled back and looked at her. Took her in. Fuck, she was gorgeous. Her hair tumbled around her face and chest, a hot mess in his hands. Her slumberous eyes dark with desire, and her lips swollen from his mouth. He'd never been so hard in his life, his cock strained painfully against his jeans. Something primitive rose in him. He wanted to leave his mark on her so that no other man thought she was available. He wanted to make her his, but he also wanted to show her how beautiful she was to him. He wanted her to feel it.

She looked up at him questioningly when he scooped her up and carried her out of the kitchen.

"Room?" His brain couldn't make complete sentences right now. Somehow she understood and pointed him in the right direction. He kicked the bedroom door shut behind him. Two long strides and he was at the bed. He set her down, trailing his fingers down her arms, still loving the goose bumps that popped up. Using his body, he pushed her down onto the mattress and settled over her. He didn't understand the gentle urges that rose in him, but he followed them anyway.

    His lip trailed down her jaw and along her neck. Her chest rose and fell underneath the kisses, and he pushed her tank top up and off. She laughed softly when he threw it, but the laugh caught in her throat when his stare lowered to her chest. Good, he wanted to demolish her thought process. Wanted her thinking of nothing but what he was doing to her.

    He pulled her shorts down, tossing them too. His thoughts stuttered when he saw the matching red lace panties and bra covering her tanned skin. It took him a minute to remember what he was doing. He moved lower and dipped his head to lick right outside where her bra covered. "You are so fucking beautiful, Tori." He didn't know why he gave her the nickname, he just wanted this to be an entirely new experience for her.

    Her moan urged him on. He unclasped the front of her bra and pushed it aside. His breath caught when her breasts spilled out. "Perfect." He pressed a kiss to her mouth before turning his attention back to her chest. She bit her lip when he took one nipple in his mouth, swirling his tongue around it.

He smiled against her breast when her fingers tightened in his hair and her body arched against him. After a minute he moved to the other, using the pad of his thumb to tease the one he left. The noises she made spurred him on. He'd never been so hard, not just from giving his partner pleasure. It was usually something he did to get to the end result, but with Victoria...he wanted to make her feel amazing.

Slow down. Be patient. He kept repeating in his mind. If he rushed this, he could mess it up. He glanced up as he moved lower, saw her lids drop, hiding what she felt from him. His hands brushed the waist of her panties and she stilled. Like this was completely new to her.

"Tori." He paused, waited on her to look at him. After a tense moment, she did. "Did Roger ever do this for you?"

She blushed, shook her head.

"That bastard." Nick rubbed his fingertips over her hip bones. "Lie back." He hooked his fingers in the edges of her panties and pulled them down slowly, pressing soft kisses here and there when skin was exposed. He crawled back up her legs and pushed them apart. His muscles tensed and he shut his eyes, counting to ten. She was wet and his mouth watered. He couldn't wait to taste her.

Slow down. Patience.

"Nick." She sounded on the verge of panic.

"Shh, baby. Relax, and enjoy this." He ran his tongue up the middle of her, loving it when she gasped. "Damn it. You taste amazing." His voice turned husky with need.

Victoria tightened her fingers in his hair, pulling his head closer. Holy shit, how had she missed out on this her whole freaking life? No wonder Addie talked about sex all the time. His fingers tightened on her thighs and fire pooled in her belly. She felt amazing, beautiful. Drunk on her power as a woman. She didn't want this to ever stop.

As he used his tongue, his teeth, and then pushed two fingers into her, sensation built in her lower abdomen. Her every sense focused on that one area and her body tensed. The feeling coiled, tighter and tighter, then he sucked on her clit.

She couldn't stop the way she moaned, or whispered his name as she splintered. He didn't stop, just kept going, pulling another orgasm out of her until she was left shaking and out of breath.

He slid a condom on, then crawled back up her body, leaning over her on his elbows. His grin widened when she smiled breathlessly up at him. The tip of his cock brushed her already sensitive clit and she gripped his arms. He kissed her and without breaking it, pushed his cock into her slowly.

The sensation of fullness was new to her, her body stretching to accommodate him.

"Are you okay? Am I hurting you?"

"Hell, no. If you stop I will cut your balls off."

Nick's laugh choked off. "That would ruin your fun."

She ran her hands up and down his chest, loving the feel of the tight muscles bunching underneath her hands. And if she was being honest with herself, his tattoos were hot as hell. He started to move and she leaned up and traced one of them with her tongue.

"Christ, baby." Nick groaned. "You are so fucking wet. I'm trying not to hurt you."

"This isn't my first time, although so far it's definitely been the best. But if you don't stop asking me if I'm okay or stop worrying about hurting me, I'm going to kill you."

"You asked for it." He kissed her lazily, then pulled out to the tip and pushed back in.

"That's...much better." Her breathless words made him smile. Every time he moved, harder and harder, she quit trying to think. A flush started on her chest, moving up her neck.

He rolled his hips and she cried out. She nipped at his shoulder, urging him to go faster, harder. He complied, in and out, until her body tensed again. She tried to bite her lip, to hold back her cry but it was useless. A second later he thrust hard, whole body tensing, before he said her name on a whisper. She loved the nickname, Tori, and hoped he'd keep calling her that. She loved the reverent way he said it, like this was a new experience for him, too.

"Baby, that was amazing." Nick brushed back a strand of hair that had fallen in her face. "You are amazing."

Victoria smiled sleepily up at him, spent in a way she'd never been before. "That was phenomenal. I've never...." She frowned, embarrassed.

"Never...what?" Nick kissed her forehead and something in her softened. She ignored it and muttered the answer. "I didn't catch that."

"I've never had an orgasm before."

Nick's brows rose.

She sighed, completely humiliated now. She turned her head and stared at the lamp on her bedside table.

"Hey, that's nothing to be ashamed of. That's on him, not you." He slid out of the bed, not hiding his nakedness, and held out his hand to her. After a second she took it and allowed him to take her into the bathroom. "That just means the men you were with had no idea what they were doing. You deserve to feel that."

She watched him gather two towels and start the shower. If she wasn't careful, she could want too much from this and she knew that wasn't possible. Nick wasn't that type so she had to be okay with what they had now. She'd already seen the funny, charming side. She'd seen the hardworking one. But this--this was entirely seductive. The tenderness in how he made love to her, of how he took care of her now. If she didn't watch it, she'd slip.

§§

After the shower, they'd both realized they were starving. Victoria warmed up the Chinese while he picked out a movie. He kept giving her gentle kisses or brushing a hand over her waist, or her ass, or softly down her hair, like he was afraid she'd run off.

It was hell on her heart and her body. His touch turned her on again, so soon after they'd had sex but she knew if they were going to go again, she'd have to eat something. She settled onto the couch with him and laughed when she saw his movie preference. "I love this movie."

"You've seen it?" Nick's brows rose again. "Not many women I know have."

"Snatch is amazing. And hilarious. Maybe you just hang out with stupid women." Victoria leaned back and enjoyed the shock in his eyes.

"You keep surprising me."

"That's a good thing, right?" She wondered if he preferred women who let the men lead.

"Oh, yes." He nodded. "Keeps me on my toes."

Maybe that was why he went through so many women. Maybe they bored him.

By the end of the night, well--the early morning hours--after he'd made love to her until she couldn't move, Victoria realized that she'd given him a piece of herself. He'd been so tender, then rough in an entirely exciting way. He'd awakened a side of her she didn't know existed. She craved things she'd never thought about before. With Roger, she'd always been timid, letting him lead, letting him finish and not caring whether or not he enjoyed it. But with Nick, her dominance had escaped, and she'd used it to drive him crazy.

    He didn't stay the night, which was almost okay with her since she wasn't sure what time her sisters would bring the girls home. She didn't want the girls to know about this yet, not at least until she could define what it was between them. Her daughters did not need to know that she was having a friends-with-benefits thing with the man renovating her office.

Chapter Fifteen

Still sleepy and glowing from the night before, Victoria stumbled into the kitchen and headed for the coffee pot. Caffeine needed to be in her bloodstream so she could function today. She grabbed the pot and stepped over to the sink--right into cold water. She let out a squeal and set the coffee carafe on the counter. Looking down, she saw that water pooled around the cabinet underneath her kitchen sink. She sighed, bent down, and opened the wooden cabinets. Her morning glow evaporated in the face of her kitchen sink leaking, or whatever it was. When she looked inside the damp area, a steady trickle fell from the pipes that came from the sink. Knowing she probably shouldn't, she reached out and tried to tighten whatever might be loose.

Something creaked, then snapped, and water flooded up and sprayed out of a pipe that led through the wall. It hit her full in the face, soaking her boxers and cami, and left her hair plastered to her face.

She shoved her hair back, knowing that she at least had to turn the water off to the sink, and reached back under and twisted the knob on the side as fast as she could. It screeched and then finally the water stopped. She sat and stared bleakly at the mess. How the heck was she supposed to fix this? Her dad was at church with her mom and the girls--she'd skipped today to bask in her sexual glow--and he was the only one she knew who could fix it. Now she'd have to wait on him to get home.

The only thing to do right now would be to clean up the water on the floor and in the cabinet, then figure out what to do next. Her phone rang from the living room and she went to answer it. Her wet feet left prints on the carpet and she groaned. Another mess.

Nick's name flashed on the screen and she answered, trying not to let the irritation of her morning seep through her voice. "Hey."

"Whoa, what's going on?" Nick's smile brightened his tone. She liked that, but it did little to cheer her up right now.

"Nothing." She didn't want to pull him into this.

"Really? You sound irritated." He said. "You can tell me."

She exhaled. "The pipes underneath my sink busted. Water's everywhere. Dad's at church, so I have to wait on him to get out, and he usually goes to lunch after with Mom and the girls."

"I could fix it."

She paused, stared at the phone. "You want to help me?"

He laughed. "Of course. I'll be there in thirty."

"Oh. Okay. If you're sure. I can wait for Dad..."

"You don't have to do that. I'll be there soon."

She hung up and glanced around. She didn't expect him to start fixing stuff around the house just because they'd slept together, but if he was willing to help her with this, she could use it. Waiting on her dad would be a while and she just wanted it done. While she waited on Nick to get there, she changed and then cleaned out the stuff from under the sink and wiped up as much water as she could. The towels she used for that she put in the washing machine and started them immediately. She hated the smell of mildewed towels.

When Nick arrived, she let him in and led him to the kitchen. He kissed her softly, placing both hands on the sides of her neck, drawing it out until she was breathless. Until she thought about forgetting the pipes and taking him to her room. He pulled back, though, and smiled. "I'm going to check under the sink."

He laid down and stuck his head in the cabinet. He reached his arms in and his shirt rode up, showing his abs and the V that led into his jeans.

She looked away, determined to not jump his bones right now. "Thanks for coming over, Nick."

"No problem." He sat up. "I brought some piping with me. From what you said, I figured you'd need a new pipe here. It shouldn't take me long to do it."

"Okay." She gestured a hand in the air. "Do you need help or anything?"

He shot her a lazy grin. "I've got this. Do whatever you were doing before I got here."

She laughed. "I was making coffee. But, for now I'll clean around the house. If you need me, just yell." She would've preferred to watch him work, but felt that made her a little obsessed, so she focused on cleaning the living room.

§§

The piping was a cinch and only took him half an hour to install, but every second he was under the sink, the more the walls closed in on him. He'd never been claustrophobic, but damn it, his breath got more and more ragged with each turn of the wrench.

He finished quickly and sat up, throwing his tools back in their box. His skin crawled and he clenched his jaw. Something didn't feel right here. Pressure hit him from all sides and he felt like he was in the ring again, battling some unknown enemy.

He grabbed his stuff, hoping to escape her house with little confrontation. Maybe he could call her later, tell her he had to run.

Victoria appeared from the entrance to the living room just as his hand touched the door knob, and he winced. "Thanks for helping me. Do you want anything? Tea or lunch, since you helped out?" She stepped closer, smiling up at him.

For some reason that pissed him off. He didn't need payment. He was being nice, fixing it for her because her dad was unavailable. Just because they were sleeping together didn't mean she needed to get ideas. They weren't a couple. "No."

Her eyes widened and she blinked the hurt away at his sharp tone. "Okay. If you're sure."

"I am sure." His temper snapped. "Just because we slept together last night doesn't mean that I'm going to run over here every time you need help with something."

Her eyes narrowed as she stepped closer, her body tense. "You offered to help me. I didn't call you. You called me."

He did, and he couldn't figure out why the hell he'd done that. "It doesn't matter. We're not a couple, we had sex. It doesn't mean anything."

She froze and he saw the wall come over her. She wiped all expression off of her face. "It's good to know you feel that way. Thank you for helping me." Her voice was flat as she slung the door open. "Next time I'll make sure to say no when you offer to help."

"Fine." He stepped outside and flinched when she slammed the door behind him. "Fine." He repeated to himself, even though he didn't feel fine. He wasn't even sure why he'd freaked out. It didn't matter right now, he needed to get away from here.

The sun shone bright in the sky, but the world was dark around him. His panic and anger faded away as he drove, and he realized he'd just royally screwed up. She'd even made sure he was okay with helping her and he'd thrown it back in her face. He wasn't sure what to do now. Did he turn around and apologize? Let her calm down, then call her?

He knew he was clueless. This whole thing with her? Entirely new to him. This was all new territory to him. He hadn't outlined this as a one night stand with her, and what the hell did that mean?

§§

Victoria didn't know which emotion dominated the rest. She was angry, hurt, confused, frustrated. Nick had *offered* to come and fix the pipes. After she'd made sure he was okay with it. When she'd left him under the sink and went to clean, everything had been fine. Normal. Then when he left, he'd blindsided her. Went off about coming to fix her stuff and then threw in that they weren't in a real relationship.

She knew that and still his words had sliced into her. The sting had settled into her chest and stayed ever since. As she moved through the house, deep cleaning everything now to work off her emotion, she went over the fight again and again. Nothing jumped out at her, no red flags that she knew of. All she did was offer him something to eat, maybe some tea. Was that code for marry me in men's eyes?

Hell if she knew.

Her shoulders and arms ached from dusting high and low, from wiping down nooks and crannies. By the time her parents dropped the girls off, she looked a hot mess.

"What happened to you? We were only gone a few hours." Cecelia gave her a once over as she stepped inside.

"The pipes under the sink broke. Nick fixed them for me, then I tackled some deep cleaning I hadn't done in a while." Victoria avoided eye contact with her parents so they wouldn't see the pain in her eyes. So they wouldn't ask questions.

"That was nice of him." Wes said.

"Yes." Victoria nodded. "Thanks for taking the girls."

Her mom pulled her into a hug. "It's no problem, sweetie."

Her parents left after that, and Victoria hated that she was glad for it. She just didn't want to put on a front for them. The girls were oblivious, wrapped up in shows and games, and for once that was okay with her. She didn't want them looking too closely either.

While she cleaned earlier, she'd finally sorted through her emotions and decided that something else was going on with Nick. Something deeper, that made him react like that. She knew from rumors around town that Nick had a heartbreaking past and while she didn't know all the specifics, she imagined it might mess with his relationships today. It didn't excuse his behavior, but it helped her understand the reason behind it.

§§

Nick couldn't concentrate on his work, he'd even put his shoes on the wrong feet this morning. It wasn't the best way to start off a Monday, but what could he do? Victoria had soaked into his bones and everything he did reminded him that he'd hurt her yesterday. That didn't sit well with him.

It also annoyed him. No woman had ever monopolized his thoughts like this. He grabbed the blue prints and laid them out on the receptionist counter, looking twice to make sure his measurements were correct. His crew was getting ready to lay the hardwood in her back office. The job would only take about a month or more and for some reason that irked him. Would he still be in Victoria's mind when he wasn't working on her office every day? Would she still be in his?

He needed to stop being a girl and focus on work. He had plenty of jobs lined up after Victoria's office and he needed to make sure he finished this one on time. He had an excellent reputation, one he'd worked hard for. Not everyone had wanted to hire him in the beginning. Wes had helped him out back then, giving him a chance when no one else would, giving him jobs that he himself couldn't get to because he was so busy.

The man was a saint, and Nick prayed to God that when Wes found out he'd slept with his daughter, he wouldn't think differently of him. That wouldn't be good for business or for his relationship with the man.

"Boss, the floors are being delivered in half an hour." Steven, his right-hand man, held out the paperwork. He was a short, stocky man with a hilarious personality. He'd been with Nick since the beginning. "Just need you to sign these."

Nick scribbled out his signature. "Are the bathroom fixtures still arriving next week?"

Steven was a hell of a foreman, and an even better friend. Nick relied on him, trusted him. "Yeah, Joel and Paul will finish with the piping this week. All in all it's been a smooth job."

"Good, I'd hate to mess up Wes' daughter's office."

Steven gave him a side-long glance. "Is Wes's daughter the reason you've been pissed and scatterbrained this morning?"

Nick shook his head, but when Steven continued to look at him, he sighed. "Yes, okay? I acted like an idiot yesterday, said some stuff I didn't mean, then left her angry."

"Smooth." Steven pretended to look at his clipboard, but said, "And does that make you feel relieved or worried that it's over?"

"What are you, my shrink?" Nick snapped, then sighed again. "Worried. Damn it."

Steven slapped him on the back. "Then maybe you should apologize. I've never seen you act like this over a woman. It just might mean something. And don't let her stew in it for long, it'll be harder for her to forgive you."

"Yes, Yoda." Nick shot out.

Steven laughed and walked back to the crew.

Nick grabbed his phone and walked outside the office. He'd be damned if the guys heard him groveling to Victoria. He dialed her number and waited on her to pick up.

"Hello?" She answered.

He listened to the impersonal tone in her voice. His pride stung that she could sound like that after the amazing night they had together, but he had no one else to blame but himself. "Hey." He hesitated, then, "I was calling to see if you would come by the office tonight, after the crew is gone, so I can show you around. Show you how the progress is going."

"I don't think that would be a good idea, Nick. You made your stance perfectly clear to me yesterday."

The coldness in her voice chilled him. He started to pace the office fronts. "Yes, I know. And I'm an idiot. Will you please come by? You deserve for me to apologize to your face."

A silent moment, then, "Fine. I'll be there at five-thirty."

After he hung up, Nick went to the flower store. It couldn't hurt to get her something pretty, right?

§§

Victoria approached the door to her office, running her palms down her pants. She hoped she wasn't walking into another argument, or more disappointment. She hoped he was sincere about his apology.

He looked up when she entered. He looked delicious, dirty from work, and that stirred up her desire. She knew she wouldn't let that happen though. She had more respect for herself than to just jump into bed with him because he apologized. "Hey."

"Hey." She stopped right inside the door, let it close softly behind her. She wasn't sure she should step closer to him.

He straightened, set down the blueprints he looked over. His lips quirked. "You can come closer."

"You wanted to say something to me?"

His smile vanished and he shoved his hands in his pockets. He seemed to respect her need for distance and stayed where he was. "I handled yesterday all wrong. In fact," he shoved a hand through his hair, "I was all wrong."

She watched him steadily, saying nothing.

"I panicked over nothing, over helping you. I have this rule that I don't fix stuff for women I'm sleeping with, because it's too close to what a man does for a woman when he's in a relationship."

She arched a brow at him. Would it be so bad to be in a relationship with her?

"I know you've never said anything about a relationship, and that I was the one to offer to help you." His gaze settled on her. An emotion she couldn't name shone there. "I was under the sink, and suddenly the walls closed in. I panicked, and I took it out on you. What I said was cruel and not true. Can you forgive me?"

Could she? That was the question that rattled on in her mind. He was doing something entirely new with her, spending more than one night, right? She could give him some growing room for a while. Besides, his apology was sincere. "I will."

The smile that stretched his lips was breathtaking. Her stomach fluttered. "Great. Now, do you want me to give you the tour?" He reached out his hand.

Because she wanted that contact with him, she took the steps, and placed her hand in his. "Yes."

Chapter Sixteen

Luke walked into Nick's shop a few days later, a scowl on his face.

"What's your problem?" Nick looked up from his worktable. He was starting more blueprints for his new client. The meeting had gone well, and he was now signed up to remodel the woman's kitchen.

"Don't be a dick." Luke grabbed a beer from Nick's mini-fridge and ignored when his eyebrow rose. "Shut up. I need this. I'll buy you another damn pack."

"Seriously. What the hell happened?" Nick set his pencil down, took his glasses off, and focused on his brother. Luke was a normally easy going guy.

"I should punch the guy in his face. Break some bones." Luke took a long swig of the beer.

Nick swallowed a groan. He understood now. Luke rarely got mad, yes, but if it involved Halle and her cheating husband, his brother lost his mind.

"Look, I'm done here. It's dinner time anyway, so let's go to the bar and get something to eat. You can tell me all about it."

"I'll buy." Luke walked out, not waiting on Nick's answer.

Nick stretched his taunt muscles and geared himself up to give his brother advice.

People filled the bar almost to capacity. Conversations rose and fell, and the brothers were lucky to find a table. Several different games were on the TV's, on low volume, and an MMA fight caught Nick's attention. Sometimes he missed the adrenaline rush of defeating an opponent, of being in the ring, fighting to win. A different waitress came up. Ivy glared at him from across the room, so Nick assumed she wouldn't be taking their orders any time soon. After they ordered, Nick sat back and waited on Luke to start talking.

"Damn it, Nick. I don't know what to do. Trevor is banging a chick named Jenna, a nurse at the office. Right underneath Halle's nose." Luke clenched his jaw. "I want to break his face."

"Luke, I realize that you care a lot for Halle, but what happens in her life is none of your business. You've only talked to her a few times. You crushed on her in high school, and she doesn't even remember you from then. You won't even walk up and talk to her, much less tell her what's going on with her husband. I don't understand where this protectiveness is coming from."

    Luke stared down at his beer. "In school, she once stood up for me when a group of kids were bullying me. Before we got into the MMA stuff. She didn't know me, didn't know anything about me. She wore glasses, carried a bunch of books in her arms, and she was the prettiest thing I'd ever seen. Those guys backed off and she helped me up. I know it's crazy, but since then, I've felt a connection with her."

    "When did you become such a romantic?"

    "Fuck you, Nick." Luke flipped him off. "I need to kick that guy's ass."

    "It wouldn't be a fair fight." Nick reminded him. "The guy is a yuppie. He's probably never thrown a punch in his life."

    The fight drained out of Luke. "Yeah, I know. It just makes me so damn mad. She deserves so much more than that."

    "I agree, but you can't do anything about it until she wakes up and realizes she doesn't want to be married to that piece of shit. If you tell her what he's doing it will seem like you're trying to break up her marriage. Not a good way to start a relationship."

"It's hard to sit back and watch her get treated like that. Back then, she'd been so brave to stand up to those kids. Now, she lets that man walk all over her."

"Maybe you should move on."

"Hell, no." Luke looked at him across the table. "Now that you've had a taste of Victoria, do you think you will?"

Nick shrugged, uncomfortable with his confusion over the answer. Normally he could've said he'd move on instantly. With any other woman he would've already let her go and focused on someone else.

Luke tipped his beer in a salute. "Welcome to my hell."

§§

Victoria slipped on her tennis shoes as Nick pulled into her driveway. Nora had given birth to the twins earlier than day, and since Roger was actually keeping to the every other weekend schedule, she and Nick were going to visit them. She was a little nervous about spending time with him again. While she kind of understood what made him panic the other day, she didn't want a repeat.

She climbed into his truck and gave him a hesitant smile. "How are they?"

"Everyone's good. Colin said that they did a C-section and that the kids have jaundice, so they have to be under a lamp for a while."

"Lucia and Helena had to spend time under the lamp, too." She told him as they pulled out of the driveway. "Colin and Nora are in for an exhausting but extremely rewarding time."

Nick was silent, then asked, "Did Roger help out with the girls when they were little?" Nick glanced over. "I'm sorry if that was too personal. You don't have to answer it."

"No, it's okay." Victoria glanced out the window. "He was always too busy with his restaurant, first as a chef, then as an owner. I always got up with them, not that I minded."

"I bet it would've been great to have some help." Nick hated men that couldn't take part in the responsibility of raising kids. It was one of his greatest pet-peeves.

"Oh sure. My parents and sisters helped out. Addie especially, because she was still in high school." She remembered how much they'd helped her and was immensely grateful. There were plenty of single mothers that did it all on their own. "With twins it's very important to have them on a schedule so that they get up at the same time at night to eat. If not, you'd never get any sleep."

"Make sure you tell Colin and Nora." Nick smiled at her, looked back at the road. "I'm sure they'd appreciate all the things you could tell them."

"I didn't know anyone with twins, much less children. All my friends were still single. They weren't even thinking of having kids yet. Learning by experience made it so much harder."

"Do you regret having kids?"

It was such an off the wall, intensely personal question, but Victoria could tell by the true curiosity in his voice that he didn't mean it to be insulting. "No, I don't. Yes, it was hard because I was so young and I didn't finish college. And Roger had other stuff on his mind, but if I was at the end of my rope, no sleep, no personal time--I couldn't even go to the bathroom by myself--all it would take was a single look at them, or a hug, or to hear them laugh. I would fall in love all over and over again."

Nick waited a moment to speak, seeming to know she was lost to those memories. He acted more restrained with her tonight, like he didn't want to say or do something wrong. She hated it. Before she could say that, he asked, "Is Helena still having trouble adjusting to the divorce?"

Victoria frowned. "Yes. And Roger isn't helping. Apparently he's telling Helena he left because I didn't love him enough."

"That's bullshit. How can he tell her that? Does Lucia believe it?"

"She said she's never heard him say anything like that."

"He's such a coward that he can't tell her the truth?"

"Guess so. He's a shallow person, and image is everything to him. It would tarnish his reputation if it got out that he left because he couldn't handle being married and having children."

"You sure you don't want me to kick his ass for you?"

Victoria laughed and let him lead the conversation for the rest of the hour drive. She wanted him to get comfortable with her again, she just wasn't sure how to get him there.

They pulled into the hospital parking lot while the sun set behind the nine story building. A slight wind brushed past them, chilling the air a little. They stopped at the gift shop, picking up balloons, flowers, and two matching polka dot onesies. While they rode the elevator, Victoria glanced at him. He kept looking down at the onesies in his hand, like they would bite him.

Nick knocked on the door to Nora's hospital room and Colin called for them to come in.

Colin sat in a rocking chair, a small bundle in a pink blanket in his arms. Nick leaned over and kissed Nora on the cheek and set the gifts on the counter. Nora smiled sleepily while she fed the other twin.

"What did you name them?" Victoria asked. She leaned over the hospital bed and peeked and the baby's face. Both girls had a shading of downy hair. "Oh, they are just precious."

Nora beamed. "Thank you. This here is Lola, and daddy is holding Grace."

"Such beautiful names." Victoria smiled at Nick. "What do you think?"

What did he think? Victoria looked absolutely gorgeous when she softened over babies. "They're so tiny. Aren't they breakable?"

Colin laughed. "At first I was nervous, but they're surprisingly resilient and sturdy."

"Thanks for the gifts." Nora set the empty bottle on the table beside her hospital bed, eyes a little glassy.

"May I?" Victoria reached out her hands. It had been so long since she'd held a small baby. "It's been so long since I've burped a baby."

"You have to burp them?"

Victoria bit her lip to contain her laughter. "Of course you do." She settled Lola's tiny body over her shoulder and gently patted her back. "If you don't, it turns into gas, and that can be extremely painful for a baby."

"Oh." Something shifted inside of him at the sight of her cuddling the baby. She looked so natural, like she was born to be a mother.

"Do you want to try?" Victoria asked.

He quickly shook his head, took a step back. "I might drop her. Then Colin would take me outside and kick my ass."

Colin chuckled and Nora said, "I'd beat him to it."

Victoria took a seat in a chair and hummed to Lola, continually patting her back. A few minutes later

Lola let out a manly burp. "There we go, sweetheart. Nick, come here and sit down. You need to try. She's practically your niece."

His throat constricted but he did what she said. He couldn't tell her no, no matter how terrifying holding Lola would be. After he settled into the chair, Victoria showed him how to arrange his body, then set Lola gently into his arms.

"There, that's not so hard. Relax, you won't hurt her." Victoria placed a hand on his shoulder. When Lola's eyes fluttered closed, Victoria smiled. "See? She feels warm and protected."

A deep sense of wonder overcame him as he stared down into her tiny face. When Lola wrapped her tiny fingers around his thumb, his heart warmed. It suddenly became amazing to him that two of his friends could create such a sweet, tiny baby. He heard the others talking, but couldn't stop staring at Lola.

"Nick, you look good with a baby in your arms." Nora winked at him. "Maybe you should change your rule about never having kids."

His gaze shot to Victoria, who looked away from him. He wasn't sure what was going on between them, if she'd fully forgiven him for acting like an ass the other day, but he hated that he'd ever made that stupid rule. He needed to explain to her why he'd said it in the first place, make her understand that he wasn't so sure that's what he wanted anymore.

They stayed for a while longer, then left when Nora couldn't keep her eyes open. Victoria didn't speak on the way down to the truck, even when he tried to talk to her. He tried to give her some space on the ride back, but it ate at him. When he couldn't keep it in any longer, he asked, "What's going on?"

Victoria sighed. "I just don't understand what we're doing. I'm not trying to force you to make us official, or even offer a relationship. I'm just confused. You obviously don't like kids, and I have twins. You don't like relationships, and I'm not so sure I can keep sleeping with you without one. I'm not like those other women." Her eyes shimmered, wise and confused.

He hated seeing the emotions, knowing that he was the one who put them there. He wanted to give her his full attentions so he pulled off the side of the road and put the truck in park.

"I'm not making you choose or giving you an ultimatum, Nick." Victoria implored him to understand. "I just keep hearing from all you friends how surprised they are that you're with me. It makes me feel like a challenge, something you want to cross of your list."

    He wanted to be insulted by that but he could understand where she was coming from. He had a reputation and it wasn't a great one. "The fact that you're not like the others is why I'm with you. You're definitely a challenge, but not because I want to cross you off my list. You're a challenge because you speak your mind. you're independent and know what you want. I know that if I fuck up, you'll kick me to the curb, not lower your standards to keep me around."

    Her eyes widened. In a second his seat belt was off and he leaned toward her. "The thing about kids…" He shoved a hand through his hair, his stomach knotting. "I've told only a few people about this." Her fingers intertwined with his, giving him the strength to keep talking.

    "My father knocked my mother up, twice. He stayed a few months after Luke was born, and split on her when she needed him the most. When he was around, he was a drunk who liked to use her as a punching bag."

"Oh, Nick." Victoria wrapped her arms around him, laying her head on his chest. His heart beat rapidly against her ear, his body tense. She could hear the pain in his voice and her heart ached for him.

"I swore to myself that I would never have kids because I didn't want to treat them like he did us. I didn't want to risk his blood turning me into something I didn't want to be. I couldn't hurt my own kids like that."

"That's ridiculous."

He frowned when she sat back.

"You are nothing like him. I have never seen you so much as raise your voice at someone. You are thoughtful, and you held and looked at that baby with kindness. Even though you were terrified, you held her. That isn't something someone would do who had the attitude of your father." Victoria placed her hands on the side of his face, forcing him to see her. She looked him in the eyes, trying to make him see what she saw in him. "You always ask me about the girls, and I know that you are genuinely interested in hearing the answer. I've heard about the little boys you and your brother foster at the gym, kids who grew up like you, with no father."

The earnestness on her face and in her voice reached inside him. "You really have that much faith in me?"

"Absolutely." She pressed her lips to the corner of his mouth. "I've never seen you be anything but gentle."

He kissed her again. "Am I staying the night?"

Victoria allowed him to change the subject, not wanting him to feel too pressured. "Yes."

Chapter Seventeen

Victoria woke up to the smell of bacon and pancakes. She snuggled deep in her covers, smiling wide, remembering the way he'd made love to her last night. The way he'd lingered over her body felt different, more emotional. It scared her and made her blissfully happy at the same time.

She needed to get up, but she felt so amazing. She couldn't believe she'd stuck around with Roger for ten years and missed out on being this well taken care of. The smell of the food made her stomach growl, so she stretched, got up and pulled on some clothes.

Nick stood in front of her stove in a pair of jeans. No shirt, so the muscles in his back were there for her to drool over. When he heard her come in, he looked over his shoulder. "Good morning, babe. Want to start the coffee?"

She hugged him from behind, loving the feel of him here with her. She kissed his shoulder. "Definitely."

He grinned. "I need it. Someone wouldn't stop attacking me. I couldn't get to sleep."

"Oh, that's how it was?" She laughed. "I seem to remember it differently." She stepped to the coffee maker, brewed some.

"What time are your sisters coming?" Nick carried their plates to the table.

"Around noon. We haven't been shopping in a while. Addie's having withdrawals." Victoria bit into her pancakes and moaned. "These are amazing!"

"I made them for me and Luke a lot when we were kids. Mom had to work crazy hours and we usually let her sleep as long as she needed. Luke was better at dinner foods."

"Well, you're amazing at pancakes. What else can you make?"

"Omelets, French toast, home made cinnamon buns." He grinned at her look. "I can tell you like cinnamon buns."

"They're my favorite. I've never had homemade ones before."

"I'll make them next time."

She smiled so wide it felt like her face would split in half. He was thinking of *next time*.

"So do your sisters mind that I'm with you?" Nick asked.

"No, what kind of question is that?" She wondered why he would think they minded.

He shrugged. "We didn't run in the same circles in school. I wasn't exactly the best behaved. I'm not exactly the upper cream of society."

"I'm going to pretend that you didn't just imply that me and my sisters were shallow snobs." Victoria pointed her fork at him. "They encouraged me to talk to you after the wedding date."

"Then I need to buy them some flowers for making you change your mind."

"They'd love that." She laughed. "Well, Halle would. Addie hates flowers. She'd rather get chocolate. That girl is a chocolate fiend."

"She seems a little wilder than you and Halle." He got up and made them cups of coffee, then sat back down.

"Oh, she is. I don't know if it's because she's the baby, or just her personality, but she has this take no prisoners attitude that skipped me and Halle." Victoria wished she had Addie's strength. The girl knew what she wanted, and she went after it.

"Are you shopping for your mom?" Nick finished his breakfast and started to clean up.

"Yes, and stop cleaning. You made breakfast, I clean. That's the rules." Victoria grabbed the plates from him and set them in the sink.

"If that's what you say." He kissed her. "I'm going to hop in the shower. Luke wants me to meet him at the gym soon for mentoring. You don't mind if I use your shower, right?"

"No." She wondered where all this indecision of his came from. "Go, take a long one, relax. It's going to take me a minute to clean."

He left the kitchen and for a minute she stood there, staring after him. After a year, it felt weird to have a man in her house again. Not a bad weird, just something she'd have to get used to if he hung around.

§§

"What about this?" Addie held up a gorgeous white sweater. "Do you think she'd like this? It'd be perfect with the grey slacks she has."

Victoria appraised the sweater. "It would be perfect. I just don't know what I'm going to get her. You're getting the sweater, Halle's getting the cute mixing bowl. I have no idea what to get."

Addie cocked her head to the side. "You never have a hard time picking out something for Mom.

Usually you have this amazing piece of furniture or pottery to give her."

"I know! This is ridiculous." Victoria glanced around the clothing store. Saturday's were always busy, but it seemed like everyone and their grandmother were here. This weekend seemed to be *the* weekend for Mother's Day shopping.

"You're distracted." Halle laughed at her sister's expression. "Let's stop shopping, get lunch, and you can tell us all about how it's been going with Nick. Maybe if you talk about it, you can focus on other things."

"Good idea. I'm starving." Addie held the sweater up. "I'll pay for this and then we can go."

They decided on a sushi place in the food court that Halle loved. After getting their food, they made for one of the tables.

"So, how has it been going between you two." Addie asked.

"We had a sort of fight, you know. When he panicked." Victoria shook her head. "He freaked out about fixing my sink."

Addie wrinkled her nose. "Why did he freak out about that?"

Victoria told them about that day.

"Sounds like he's got to work through some of his misgivings about being in more than a one night stand." Halle told her.

"That's why when he apologized, and it was sincere, I decided to let it slide. And last night was amazing." Victoria knew she smiled like an idiot but she couldn't make herself care. "He's sweet, sexy as hell, and the way he treats me...it's crazy that I ever thought Roger cared about me. Even if Nick doesn't care, he treats me respectfully."

"Oh, he cares." Addie nodded. "Definitely cares. He was so worried he'd fucked up on the wedding date. He asked me how he could make it up to you. That's the worry of a man that cares."

"Maybe." Victoria said. "But I don't want to focus on that yet. I just want to enjoy how it is right now. If I start thinking about wanting a relationship, it could scare him off. He already panicked over fixing my sink, what do you think could happen if I pressured him. I could be setting myself up for disappointment."

"I think it's a great." Halle told her. "You deserve to be swept off your feet. Roger was a dumb ass that only cared about himself and how to climb the social ladder."

"It kills me that I had children with him. Why didn't I see how selfish he was and know that there was no way he could be a good father? Lucia and Helena deserve better." Victoria wanted to beat herself up forever for that. "That's another reason I don't want to focus on a relationship with Nick. Several people have already talked about his aversion to children."

"He doesn't have an aversion to children. Didn't you say he mentors boys at his brother's gym?" Addie said. "That doesn't sound like a person who hates children."

Victoria thought about what he'd said about his father. She couldn't share that with her sisters, it was too personal. "Yeah, I know. I just don't want to get too attached to him. I feel like I'm already too attached, so it scares me. But I'll choose my girls over a man any day."

"Hopefully that won't be an issue." Halle smiled. "I really don't think it will be. I think he adores you. You may just change his mind about everything."

Victoria didn't think that would happen. She didn't have a great track record with changing men's minds. Roger was proof of that.

They searched through some more stores, and Victoria was able to focus on finding the perfect gift for her mom--a mirror that would look great over the table in the foyer. Her mom had talked about replacing her old one for a few months now.

She tried not to let thoughts of Nick enter her mind, but they kept sneaking in. It was hard for her to imagine a man treating his sons like that, her own father had been nothing but the best to her and her sisters. How would it have changed her if either of her parents had abandoned her, had abused the other? Could she really blame Nick for the way he felt? Her sisters had talked about changing his mind, but if the wounds were that deep, was it even possible?

§§

The gym was closed two Saturday's a month for mentoring the troubled boys. The brothers were able to fully focus on helping them when there wasn't a lot of men around. Nick watched the ten boys warm up and glanced at Luke. "I see some new faces."

"Yeah, two boys were signed up by their mothers yesterday." Luke crossed his arms, also watching. They both wore gym shorts, tennis shoes, and white t-shirts with the gym logo on it.

The boys that came for the mentoring usually belonged to single mother households. The mothers were at their wits end with the boys' behavior and decided they needed to enroll them in the mentorship program. Nick understood, because he remembered how wild he and his brother had been.

When the boys finished warming up, Luke had them line up. "Okay boys. You're moms have put you in this program because you've either been acting up at home, or getting yourselves in trouble with the law or at school." Luke walked the line, looking each boy in the eye. Most of the boys knew this already, but he liked to reiterate it so that they didn't get any ideas about ruining the progress they'd made so far. "During this mentorship, Nick and I will be teaching you self-discipline, respect, and self-esteem. If you have high self-esteem, you'll be less likely to be swayed into making bad choices."

The two new boys stood with their bodies tense, staring at the floor, unlike the others who stood tall and paid attention. It was normal for the new kids to be insolent, to reject what they taught. Every kid was different, so they learned at different speeds, but they never left the program until Nick and Luke were satisfied. They understood the mothers' frustration. They'd caused their own mother plenty.

After the speech, Luke split them up into two groups, putting the two new boys in different groups. Nick took his boys to the weights and Luke took his to the cardio center.

"hey, Mr. Nick. I aced my reading exams. The tips you gave me helped!" Noah, a thirteen year old with shaggy blonde hair and big brown eyes, high-fived Nick. When Noah first came to the gym, he'd had problems respecting his teachers and his mother.

"Awesome. I knew you could do it." Nick had worked hard, even helping Noah with his homework. When Noah's father had still been around, he'd told Noah he was stupid, beating it in to him, so Noah had thought he was and that he couldn't do anything. His father had committed suicide two years ago. It had taken three months in the program before Noah had begun to turn around. "Ok, guys. Start small on the weights. Jude, I'll show you what we're doing before you start."

Jude shrugged, shoulders hunched. "Whatever."

It took a lot of patience when starting out with them, Nick reminded himself. Their attitudes were part of the reason the kids were here. He steered Jude over to the dumbbells. "Have you ever worked out before?" When Jude shook his head, Nick handed him two of the three-pound dumbbells. "That's okay. Most of the others hadn't either."

Jude glanced at the other kids before he stared at the floor. "'Kay."

"Look at me." Nick said gently. It took a minute, but Jude's gaze rose to his. "You don't have to worry about the other kids. They've been where you are now, started out the same way. We don't tolerate bullying here."

"Whatever." Jude rolled his eyes.

"First thing. 'Whatever' is not considered an answer here. I've let it go so far, but the next time you say it, you'll give me thirty push-ups." Nick spoke firmly but without anger. He wanted Jude to know he was serious, but not mad. Anger was the quickest way to raise a kid's walls. "The other kids had to learn the same lesson. You answer with a sir, look us in the eyes, and speak clearly."

Jude's eyes narrowed. "What. Ev. Er." He enunciated each syllable, daring Nick to lose his temper.

The other kids in his group paused.

Nick nodded at Jude, making sure his demeanor stayed calm. "There is a mat right there on your left. Give me thirty push-ups." The new kids liked to see how far they could push the brothers until they lost their tempers. Sadly, it's what most of the boys were used to.

Jude lowered himself to the mat. Nick knelt down to help him into the correct positioning.

"We're here to teach you respect for yourself and for others. We're not here to boss you around, to make you do stuff just so we can laugh. I want to help you believe in yourself." Nick moved Jude's arms out a little so that they weren't right beside each other.

He kept an eye on Jude, silently counting the push-ups, and also watching the other boys work on lifting weights. He and Luke helped the kids build their immune system and used the hard work to tire the kids out. That usually kept them out of trouble for a while. The brothers also gave the boys their cell numbers and told them to call whenever they needed to talk, or needed their help.

For the next four hours Nick worked extra hard on talking to Jude, showing him what's going on, and pairing him up with Noah. Noah was a sweet kid, just a little misguided, and he thought the boys' personalities would mix well. Maybe Jude would respond better to the program if he had a friend. One who had been through the same stuff he had. Nick knew he'd never have survived if he hadn't had his brother.

After all the boys were picked up, the brothers showered then headed to their mom's for dinner. An idea had been rolling around in Nick's mind and he wanted to talk to her about it.

Charlotte smiled when the boys entered the kitchen. "How did the mentoring go?" She kissed each of them on the cheek. "I'm so proud of you two."

"Mom, you say that every time." Luke smiled down at her. "You're going to make us egomaniacs."

"Don't be silly. What you do for those boys, it warms my heart." She pointed to the bathroom. "Wash your hands and get ready for dinner. I made meatloaf, mashed potatoes, and green beans."

"You're not only going to make us egomaniacs, you're going to make us gluttons." Nick's stomach growled at the smell of home cooked food.

He waited until they'd all sat down to give voice to his idea. "Mom, I'd like to pick something out for Victoria for Mother's Day. Will you go with me tomorrow?"

Charlotte's eyes misted. "Oh, of course, baby. You want to get her a gift? Am I going to meet her soon?"

"Mom, don't cry. It's just a gift." Nick frowned. "I'm not marrying her."

"You're getting her a gift. For you, that's pretty much proposing." Luke leaned back in his chair. "I think you've got it bad. More than you think you do."

Nick shook his head, that familiar panic rising. He forced it down. "It's not a big deal. We've just been hanging out."

Charlotte paused. "She has daughters, right? If you get that girl's hopes up, or her daughters, and then leave them in the dust, I will make you regret it."

Nick gave her a solemn look. He knew why his mom would get angry over that. "I won't." The thought of hurting Victoria like that made his chest ache.

"Besides, she hadn't introduced me to her girls yet."

"Smart woman." Charlotte nodded her approval. "I want to meet her soon."

"Yes, ma'am." Nick ignored Luke's grin. "I'll talk to her about it."

Chapter Eighteen

Victoria bit her lip nervously. Nick had just walked in the door and she was worried about what he would say when she told him what she wanted. Would he think it was a horrible idea?

"Hey, babe. What's wrong?" Nick asked when he saw her expression.

"Will you take me to get a tattoo?" She said it really fast, afraid if she slowed it down she wouldn't finish the sentence.

Nick grinned. "Yeah, you want one?"

Victoria nodded shyly. "I want to get the girls' birth date in roman numerals with their birth times on my left ribs."

"Are you sure? You know tattoos are permanent?"

She elbowed him in the side. "Of course."

"Let's go. I know the perfect person to do it, he'll fit you in for me." Nick twirled his keys on his finger. "Put your yoga pants and a sports bra on. He'll have to remove your shirt."

"Okay." Victoria beamed. "I'll be right back."

She couldn't believe she was doing this. Ever since the girls were born, she'd wanted to get this tattoo, but Roger always forbid it. He thought tattoos were trashy and pointless. He'd always through the biggest fit when she talked about it. Now that she could do it, she wanted Nick to take her.

When they entered the tattoo shop, Nick asked for a guy named Logan. While they waited, Victoria surveyed the lobby. Pictures of tattoos and tattooed men and women hung on posters around the lobby. A set of three chairs sat against the left wall. No one waited at the moment, so it seemed they'd come at a good time.

The receptionist had her bright blue hair pulled up in a pin-up do'. She had face piercings that looked cute on her, although it was something Victoria knew she'd never be able to pull off. The girl smiled at Victoria before she went to find Logan.

"You nervous?" Nick ran a hand up her arm.

"Definitely." Victoria smiled to show she wasn't backing out. "But I've wanted this tattoo ever since the girls were born."

"Let me guess. Roger didn't approve." Nick frowned. "That guy needs an ass kicking."

Victoria laughed. "I still agree and if it ever happens, you'll have to beat Addie to the punch."

"Not sure I want to get in her way." Nick smiled down at Victoria. "Do you want me in the room?"

"Hell yes. You're going to hold my hand."

A tall, lanky man covered in tattoos walked out from the back. He shook hands with Nick, then smiled at Victoria. "Shelby tells me you're looking to get a tattoo."

"Yes." Victoria shook his hand, liking him instantly. "My girls are twelve, so it's been a long time coming."

Logan clapped his hands together. "Let's get to a room and you can tell me what you want. I'll draw it out, then you tell me if you like it. If you do, we'll get started."

"Okay." Victoria took Nick's hand and followed Logan into the small room. An exam table stood in the middle. Posters of various rock stars and their tattoos hung on the walls.

"Have a seat on the table and tell me what you want." Logan sat on a swivel stool and pulled out a sketch pad. He drew as Victoria described what she wanted. It didn't take him long to sketch out the tattoo since it wasn't very detailed. "Are you wanting it in color or black?"

"Black. I want it on my left ribs, not big." Victoria's fingers tightened around Nick's. "Nick says you're great at what you do."

"He should." Logan chuckled. "I've done all of his."

"Then I'll be happy with what you do." Victoria tried not to blush as she thought about how she'd seen all of Nick's tattoos.

"Is this what you're looking for?" Logan turned the sketch pad around.

Victoria's grin widened. "That's perfect!"

"I'll need you to remove your shirt and lay on your right side, facing me. Nick can stand at the head of the table and talk to you." Logan pulled on rubber gloves and started getting everything ready.

Victoria laid down, like he told her, after she removed her shirt. Nick's stare heated and she swallowed. Her own desire rose in response and she swallowed.

"Okay, I'm going to clean the area with antiseptic. After, I'll draw the tattoo out on your body with a surgical marker. You approve the placement and we're ready to go."

"Okay." Victoria took a breath. She prayed she wasn't shaking. She was nervous, but determined to do this. When he asked her to stand and look in the mirror, she realized that she really did want this. "I love it." If Nick's stare in the mirror was any indication, he loved it, too.

"You should probably take a bathroom break while I set up the machine. You don't want to have to hold it." Logan pointed down the hall. "It's the last door on the left."

Victoria hurried and used the restroom, ready to see the finished product. She returned to the room and laid back down the way he'd told her to.

"It's going to look great." Nick leaned and kissed her forehead. "You're going to love it."

Once Logan started Victoria forced herself to be still, the burning sensation spreading under her ribs. She shut her eyes and thought back to when she'd given birth to the twins. That pain was much worse than this. Nick distracted her with talk about the renovations he was doing. Soon her endorphins kicked in and she was able to focus on more than his voice.

When Logan finished, he cleaned the area with soapy water. "Go to the mirror, have a look."

Victoria slid off the table, moving gingerly at first, and crossed to the mirror. Her smile widened as she looked at the small tattoo that ran along her left ribs, up high and close to the bottom of her sports bra. "I absolutely love it." She glanced at Nick over her shoulder. The heat in his eyes blazed now. "What do you think?"

"I think it's amazing." He cleared his throat. "Logan always does a great job."

Logan placed the bandage on and gave her a paper packet on tattoo care. "If you have any questions you can ask me, or ask Nick. He knows what to do."

"Okay. How much is it?" Victoria reached for her purse.

"Nothing." Logan grinned. "I don't charge beautiful girls who are dating my friends."

"Are you sure? I don't want to be a free-loader." Victoria slipped her loose work out shirt back on.

"it was a pleasure to work on you. Besides, tattoos are addicting, so just promise you'll come back to me for your next one." Logan winked at her.

"Okay. If you're sure." Victoria nodded.

"I'm sure." Logan clapped a hand on Nick's shoulder. "Now, take that lady out to get something to eat."

"That was nice of him." Victoria said. They headed to pick up burgers for dinner.

"He's a close friend and doesn't charge us." Nick smiled over at her. "We've fostered his nephew, so he feels like he owes us or something. It really looks sexy on you. I thought I was going to lose my mind watching you get it. I don't know why it was so fucking hot, but damn."

"You're crazy." Victoria tried to laugh, but his hand rubbed up her thigh. Her breathing hitched. "Nick."

"Hmm?" He kept his eyes on the road, but continued up between her legs.

"Oh God." Victoria leaned her head back. Even through her pants, his fingers made her boil.

"When we get home, I want you to ride me. We have to be careful of your tattoo, and rubbing it on the bed would be bad for it." Nick moved his hand, took hers and kissed her fingers. "I want you so bad."

"I want you, too." Victoria took in his profile. "I've wanted you since you left this morning."

"I'll have to fix that." Nick pressed the gas pedal down.

Chapter Nineteen

Nick dropped the burger bag on the counter and walked Victoria to the room. He took his time with her shirt and bra, making sure they didn't brush her bandage. He pressed a kiss to her collarbone and she tilted her head back, hands undoing the button on his jeans and unzipping them.

He slipped his tongue inside her mouth and reached his hands up to her hair. He pulled the ponytail down, tossing the rubber band. His fingers ran through her hair, the curls wrapping around the tattoos on his wrists. She fit so perfectly against him.

"Nick." Victoria bit down on his lip, then laved it with her tongue to soften the sting. "I want you now. Hurry."

Nick chuckled, deep and husky. They both tossed their pants and underwear at the same time, which made her giggle. His abdomen tightened at the sound. She was so beautiful. He sat down on the edge of the bed, slipping the condom over his stiff cock.

She straddled him without hesitation, sank down. He breathed through clenched teeth as her wetness surrounded his cock. When she started to move, his hands tightened on her hips. He didn't want to accidentally brush her tattoo and hurt her. Her hair fell over her shoulders and breasts, teasing him with the sight of her nipples every time she moved.

"Tori." He breathed her name, getting her to look him in the eyes. He wanted to see her reaction. "I'm addicted to you."

Her lips curved and her hands drifted up his chest. She moved faster, rocking her hips, her head falling back. Her skin flushed and when he reached a hand between them, she gasped.

"Tori, I need you." Nick nibbled her neck, keeping his fingers moving between them. Her body tensed, her toes curled against his thighs. She was close, he could feel her tighten around him.

When she came, she bit his shoulder. It pushed him over the edge and he came too, thrusting into her a few more times.

Her head dropped to his shoulder and she tried to catch her breath. "Just...once...I'd like to eat first." She laughed breathlessly.

"That wouldn't be any fun." Nick ran a hand down her hair. The feel of her cuddled on his lap snuck into his heart. He didn't want her to move yet.

"Hmm, probably not. But I'm starving now. The last thing I ate was sushi with my sisters." Victoria's stomach rumbled.

Nick laughed. "Okay, I get it." He let her slide off his lap. "Let's clean up and we'll eat."

After scarfing down the burgers, they settled onto the couch.

"You pick." Victoria pulled up Netflix. "I can't think straight."

Nick took the remote. "I know just the thing." He searched and found it.

"City of Angels?" Victoria looked over at him. "Isn't that a little girlie for you?"

He poked her side, far below the tattoo. "This is an awesome movie. I happen to be a huge Nicholas Cage fan."

She smiled, shook her head. "Are you picking this movie because I got a tattoo tonight and you want to show me how awesome you think that is?" She raised a brow, humor in her eyes.

"Yes, sweet thing. I know how much you wanted that tattoo, so I'm rewarding you with a movie, that I happen to like."

"Shut up and start the movie." She moved closer and laid her head on his shoulder.

He might have pushed play, but he couldn't have said how much of the movie he watched. It had been since high school that he'd been with a woman this long, that he'd been on dates or just watched movies. Hung out, like he'd told his mom. He knew he walked the slippery edge of the cliff here, but he was beginning to realize he didn't care.

§§

Victoria approached her office, heard all the tools and conversations coming out into the parking lot. Through the window she saw Nick, standing with his feet planted, keeping a ladder steady. Her heart skipped a beat when she saw her dad standing at the top, attaching wires to the chandelier light she'd picked out. She swung the door open. "Dad! What are you doing up there?"

Wes glanced down at her as the crew and Nick stopped working at the sound of her voice. "Hey, sweetheart. I didn't know you were coming by."

She stopped at the bottom of the ladder and glared up at him. "Dad!"

"Relax, Victoria." Her dad went back to work. "I've done this a million times."

"I know that." Victoria sighed. "Sorry, it just freaked me out to see you up there." She glared at Nick. "Why didn't you go up there?"

"Whoa, hang on. He was up here when I got back from picking up materials." Nick looked up at her dad. "I tried to talk him down, but he firmly refused."

"I'm almost finished, then I'll screw in the chandelier and you'll have your pretty light fixture." Wes told her. "By the way, we're having the Mother's Day barbeque this weekend. I'd like for you and the girls to be there."

"Of course, Dad. Just focus on what you're doing." Victoria sent Nick a look. He winked at her.

"I want Nick to come too. Bring your mom and brother." Wes gestured to one of the crew members. He climbed the ladder and held the chandelier on place while Wes operated the drill.

Nick looked swiftly at Victoria before he answered. "Sure thing, Wes. We'll be there."

Victoria didn't relax until her dad's feet were firmly planted on the ground. "Do we need to bring anything?"

"Nothing but yourselves. You can get there early to help your mom cook and set up." Wes assessed the chandelier. "Frivolous, but it's going to look great when the room is finished. You always know how to fix up a room." He put an arm around Victoria's shoulders and pulled her into a side-hug.

"Thanks, Dad." No more ladders. Mom would freak if she knew."

"Then don't tell her." Wes squeezed her shoulder before letting go. "The barbeque will start at two o'clock, so be at the house around eleven."

"Okay, Dad." She kissed his cheek. "Do I need to call Halle and Addie or have you already?"

"I called them this morning before they went to work." Wes sighed. "I extended the invitation to Trevor, which he'll probably refuse."

Victoria watched her dad's expression. She could never tell if her dad liked Trevor for real, or if he just put on an act for Halle. Her dad's cell phone rang from his pocket.

"It's your mother. I'll be right back."

The crew went back to work. Nick gestured for Victoria to follow him into her back office. He left the door open, so the crew wouldn't get suspicious. "I didn't realize he was going to ask me to the barbeque. Do you mind?"

"Do you?" Victoria wondered if he did. If it put them more toward a couple instead of friends-with-benefits. She glanced at the crew steadily working, and out through the window where her dad faced the parking lot.

He shook his head. "Any time I get to spend with you, I'm cool with it."

"Helena and Lucia are going to be there." Victoria's excitement faded. "I don't know think I'm ready for you to meet them."

"Oh." Nick shoved his hands in his pockets and frowned. "I can give an excuse."

"No." Victoria sighed. "Dad will get his feelings hurt. He really likes you."

"I can pretend we aren't sleeping together."

"I..." Victoria's mind and heart were conflicted. "that's not how I want it to be. I'm just worried how Helena and Lucia will take this because of their father. Plus, I don't even know how long you're going to be around, and I don't want them getting attached."

Nick nodded slowly. Her lack of faith in him stung, but he couldn't really blame her. "I get it. I do. We can wait to come out to your family."

"Okay. Thanks. I'm going to get back out there before Dad gets back in."

Nick watched her go, the frown still on his face.

§§

"Wes invited us to his barbeque this Saturday, for Mother's Day. With Mom." Nick told Luke. He dodged Luke's half-assed punch. "Am I distracting you?"

Luke chuckled, brought his hands back up. "The thought of seeing Halle distracted me." He circled the mat. "Have you told Mom?"

Nick shook his head, threw his own punch, connected with Luke's headgear. Both wore it, since neither wanted to sport bruises on their face. They tried to look professional most of the time. Looking like they had bar fights constantly could scare off clientele. "I'll call her when we're done."

They sparred for another thirty minutes; throwing punches, kicks, and using moves to maneuver each other to the ground. The competiveness stayed at a healthy level, unlike when they were kids. They'd worked that aggression out long ago. When they finished, Luke passed Nick a water bottle.

The gym was starting to fill up, since most of the clients were getting off of work. Nick was proud of what his brother had accomplished here. It just proved that neither of them had to be like their dad. They could overcome his laziness, but what of the other more toxic part of his genes? The abuse and alcohol addiction?

"What did Victoria say about us going?" Luke interrupted his thoughts. "With her family and daughters being there?"

Nick scowled. "She's making me pretend we're not sleeping together."

"Ouch." Luke tipped his water bottle at him. Both of their shirts were soaked with sweat. "That's cold."

They walked toward the lockers to shower, giving up the mat to some of the gym goers.

"I know why she's saying it. She's nervous about the girls and how they'll react because of their father. So I do get it."

"You just didn't think it would bother you so much." Luke opened the door and crossed to the lockers to get fresh clothes.

Nick shrugged. He wasn't trying to analyze why he felt shitty about it. "it's no big deal."

Luke whistled at the hardness in Nick's eyes. "Sure it isn't."

"Fuck off," Nick resisted the urge to push his brother into the lockers.

"Luke, I've got a session at seven. They called to book it a lunch today." A tall, blond guy with tattoos and brown eyes, came around the corner of the lockers. He wore gym shorts, the uniform gym t-shirts, and boxing gloves. "It's a doctor from the hospital. Wants to impress his wife."

"Nick, meet Matt. The new trainer I hired a few weeks ago." Luke introduced the two. "He's been great."

Matt looked to be in his early twenties. "Hey, Matt." Nick shook his hand. He had a confident grip. "Heard you're going to be a dad."

Matt's grin was wide. "Yeah. We're excited. I'm going to have a son."

Something tightened in Nick's chest. "Congrats. That's cool." He turned to his brother. "I'll let y'all talk business. I've got to shower so I can tell Mom about the barbeque."

Luke waved him off and Nick headed to the showers. He stripped off his sweaty clothes and stepped under the hot spray. The water loosed some of the tight muscles in his shoulders and back. It had been a while since he'd sparred and the adrenaline still ran through his blood, putting his body in defensive mode. He breathed slowly, trying to ease the stiffness out.

He was confused about the stab of envy he'd felt at Matt's happiness about a son. He couldn't feel envious about that, it was ridiculous. There was no way he wanted kids.

In his heart, he knew that statement wasn't as strong as it used to be.

Chapter Twenty

When Victoria and the girls arrived at her parents, Halle and Addie's cars were already in the driveway. Lucia practically bounced in the car, excited to see her aunts and grandparents. Helena actually had a small smile on her face. Victoria wasn't sure what had caused the change in her demeanor, but it made her happy. It lightened her own mood, even though she was nervous as hell to see Nick today.

Her mom called her into the kitchen when she heard them come in. "Don't you look pretty!"

Victoria glanced down at her coral summer dress. "You like it? I bought it last winter, so this is my first time wearing it."

"I'm jealous." Addie gestured for Victoria to take a seat at the bar. "You can help me peel potatoes for the potato salad."

"I love potato salad!" Lucia hugged her grandmother tight. Both of her girls wore chevron dresses and looked so grown up that it put an ache in Victoria's chest. She knew it was impossible to stop them from growing, but it seemed to fast for her.

"Good. Because I'm making a ton of it. Helena, come give me a kiss, sweetie." Cecelia waved Helena over, who had a real smile on her face. She pressed a kiss to Cecelia's cheek. "Now, I heard Grandpa saying something about decorating outside and blowing up balloons. You girls head out there and see if he needs any help." She waited until the girls were outside before saying, "Helena's smiling."

"I know." Victoria started peeling potatoes. "It's amazing. She just woke up like that."

"Maybe she's starting to realize that it's over between you and Roger, and that you're happier without him." Halle said from where she iced one of the cooled cakes on the end of the bar.

"Yeah, maybe. Is Trevor here?" Victoria wanted to know if he actually showed up for one of the family gatherings.

Halle nodded but didn't take her eyes of the cake. "He's out back with Dad."

"It's good he got off work." Cecilia said. "We're expecting about fifty people. Your father will grill the chicken and burgers around the time people start arriving."

"Just like last year and the year before." Addie teased. "It's tradition, Mom. It never changes."

"Addie, I swear." Cecelia laughed at her. "just peel those potatoes. And when you're done with that, chop the celery."

"Yes, ma'am."

By the time people started arriving, Victoria's stomach fluttered insanely. How was she supposed to pretend that she didn't want to be close to Nick? Would she even be able to hide it? Her sister knew, and she was pretty sure Nick's mom and brother knew. Would they say something to her family or in front of her daughters? Had Nick talked to them about it? She wanted to relax and enjoy the barbeque the way she always had, but wasn't sure that was possible today.

She greeted the guests as they walked in through the gate. People brought desserts and drinks and she told them where to set them.

"Mom, can I help Halle with pouring the drinks?" Lucia wrapped an arm around Victoria's waist and leaned in for a hug.

"Sure, baby. She'd love the help." Victoria scanned the ever growing crowd and saw Helena manning the grill while Wes looked on. The green lawn stretched for an acre or so, and her mom had placed flower trellises near the picnic tables. Lucia grinned up at her and skipped over to the table that Halle stood behind. Trevor stood next to Halle, but his eyes were on a busty blonde who stood nearby with her husband.

"Hey, Victoria. It's so good to see you." Blanche, one of her mother's best friends, leaned in for a hug, holding her cupcake pan to the side. "You look amazing."

Victoria smiled warmly. "So do you. I swear you look younger every time I see you. What's your secret?"

Blanche leaned in to whisper, "Great sex, dear."

Victoria laughed even as she blushed, although she should've guess what Blanche's answer would be. Blanche was known for her free mouth. "I'll have to keep that in mind."

"You should." Blanche winked. "Is your mother still inside?"

"Yeah, go right in. She's probably waiting on you so you can gossip without anyone hearing."

Blanche laughed and headed inside.

Victoria could see Addie acting that way when she was Blanche's age. Free, not caring what anyone thought. Her students would definitely get a kick out of her then, if they didn't already. She turned back around and her mind stuttered. Nick stood in the gateway, his eyes locked on her.

"Hey." The corner of his mouth quirked up. "Victoria, I'd like you to meet my mom, Charlotte, and brother, Luke."

A short, petite woman with a pixie cut of gray stood in between the brothers. She smiled warmly at Victoria and reached out her hands. "It's very nice to meet you."

Victoria saw the strength in the woman. It practically exuded from her in quiet confidence. "It's nice to meet you, too." Her attention swung to Nick's brother. They looked a lot alike, except Luke's eyes were green. Luke even had the bit of stubble on his face and tattoos on his arms.

"Where should I put these?" Charlotte held up a plate of cookies.

"My mom is inside, she keeps all the desserts in there until after everyone eats. I can walk you in if you need me to."

"Oh, that's okay. I can manage." She smiled wider. "You stay here."

Victoria watched the woman walk away, afraid to turn her attention back to Nick. This was going to be harder than she thought.

"So, I'm going to go grab something to drink." Luke glanced over to where Halle served drinks to the guests. Victoria thought she saw an expression cross his face, but a second later it was gone.

"Do I need to talk to you in public, or should I steer clear? Maybe talk to your dad?" Nick moved to the side of the gate so that people could pass through.

"It might look weird if we don't talk. You are working on my office." Victoria greeted a few people. She'd heard the bite of sarcasm in his voice and wondered if this was bothering him as much as it was her.

"It's going great, by the way. We should be finished in two weeks. Are you ready?"

"Lord, no. I still have to hire an assistant. Create a new website, put out ads. People need to know I'm there. I've got pretty much all the furniture picked out, the technical stuff. It's such a big step. I hope I'm not making a mistake."

"You're not." Nick looked down at her. She barely reached his shoulder and even in the day time heat, she could feel how hot his body was. Something about the look in his eyes sped her heart up. "I have faith in you. You'll not only succeed, you'll flourish. I've heard a lot about your style and people love it."

"It's good during the off season. A lot of summer vacationers like to redo their beach houses almost every year. Like it's a competition. It's ridiculous how much money they spend doing it, but it works for me." Victoria glanced over when her mom called. "Looks like we're done with gate duty. Time to mingle."

"Fine, but damn it. It's going to be torture being near you and not able to touch you." Nick gave her a single heated look before walking to his brother.

Victoria understood that. In the few minutes that he'd been here, women were checking him out, staring unabashedly. Jealousy twisted ugly in her stomach. She wanted to march over to him and mark her territory. Instead, she went to stand with Addie.

"You and Nick are pretending not to be sleeping together. I can literally see both of you holding back." Addie said when she noticed where Victoria's attention was.

Victoria nodded. "Yes, for the girls. I wasn't ready to introduce them. Not in that way, not yet."

"I understand why. This most be so hard then." Addie squeezed her hand. "If any bitches try to hit on him, I'll get them to stop."

"Oh God. Don't start a fight. Mom and Dad would be pissed."

"True. Look at Trevor." Addie told her.

Victoria watched her sister's husband flirt with a twenty-something blonde. The way he stared down at the girl made her uneasy. "You don't think he'd cheat on her, do you?"

Addie took a sip of her drink. "Men are stupid and disloyal and that's why you don't hitch yourself to them. It's messy."

"What about Dad?"

They both looked over to where he showed Helena how to flip burgers.

"He's from a better generation. They don't make them like that anymore."

Victoria saluted her with her plastic cup. "Truth."

"And look at Halle. Isn't that Nick's brother?" Addie told Victoria. "He's totally eyeballing her."

Victoria thought back to the expression she thought she saw on his face. Now he talked to Halle, making her smile in a way that Victoria hadn't seen in a while. "Wow. She's glowing."

"He showing her attention her own husband doesn't." Addie watched them. "She's so beautiful and deserves so much better than Trevor. A man that completes here. You sure there's not a way to get rid of him and make it look like an accident?"

Victoria laughed. "No."

"Damn. I'd commit murder for you two. Just so you know."

"I have no doubt." Victoria continued to watch Luke and Halle for a moment. Halle seemed to open up, flourish, under Luke's attention. What did that say about her home life with Trevor? Did he ignore her as much at home as he did here?

§§

Nick tried to keep his stare off of Victoria, but it was damn hard. She wore a dress that stopped above her knees and showed of her long, tan legs. He kept thinking of them wrapped around his waist, and it made ignoring her impossible. His mother had already repeated herself to him several times, and finally she sighed.

"Nick. Why don't you just go talk to her?" Charlotte nudged him softly.

"Because she wants to wait to tell her daughters about us until she's more sure about how long we'll last." He tried to keep the hurt from his voice, but his mother knew him.

"Baby, can you blame her? Even I know your reputation." Charlotte looked over at the girl that had captured her son's attention.

"No." Nick breathed out. "I can't. I just want to be near her."

Charlotte mulled over that. "Do you know how long you want this to last?" She smiled when her son glanced down at her, perplexed. It seemed he hadn't really thought of it. "Are those girls hers?"

Nick glanced to where the twins stood next to Wes. He couldn't tell them apart. "Yeah. They look a lot like Victoria."

"They do." Charlotte nodded. "They're so beautiful and polite. She's raised them well, a fine job without her ex husband, I hear."

"How exactly do you and Victoria's parents know each other? You've never really told me." Nick asked.

"Oh, well, they helped me out some before you boys came home from the MMA circuit." Charlotte shook her head at Nick's look. "Now, I wasn't calling you home yet. You boys had a life to live, I wanted you to do so as long as possible. Wes and Cecelia found out about my diagnosis and helped me out."

"How did they help you out?" Nick wondered how he and Luke had never found out about this. "Why didn't Wes say something?"

"I made them promise not to. I didn't want you thinking they did it for charity reasons. Wes and Cecelia are nothing but kind and loving people. They have such big hearts. They didn't want it to be a spectacle, just wanted to help me get through a tough time."

Nick's admiration for Wes and his family grew in leaps and bounds in that moment. That man had done so much for his family. "I don't know how we can ever repay them."

"That's not what they're about, baby. They see someone in need and they step in to help. It's not about payback." Charlotte explained.

"Yeah, I guess." Nick watched Victoria's smile slip when she looked over at the gate. He turned his head and saw a red-headed man walk through.

"I think that's her ex-husband." Charlotte laid a restraining hand on Nick's arm. "I don't think he was invited."

On his arm stood a young brunette Nick bet was barely in her twenties. She had on a white dress that could've qualified for lingerie and too much make up.

"Don't go over there unless Victoria wants you to. Don't jeopardize her trust." Charlotte got Luke's attention and gestured him over. It might take the both of them to keep Nick from punching the guy in the face.

Nick watched as Victoria's sisters flanked her, giving her solid emotional support.

"Dad!" Helena ran to the man and hugged him. The brunette eyed the girl with disdain. The man let Helena hug him for a second before disengaging himself.

If his mother hadn't been there, he would've given in and beat Roger to a bloody pulp. He hated men that didn't take care of their kids, who didn't take the time to spend with them. How did Helena not see how much of an ass her father was? He noticed that Lucia hung back with Wes, glancing between her parents. Her hands were clasped in front of her and her eyes round. He could understand why Victoria worried about her daughters knowing about them. The girls had a lot to deal with as it was.

Chapter Twenty-One

Victoria stared across the lawn in shock. She couldn't believe that Roger showed up uninvited. With a date, no less. Guests surreptitiously peeked over their shoulders or plates of food to watch the drama. Roger stood there in khaki shorts and a polo like he belonged, the girl on his arm not that much older than their daughters. Her sisters stood beside her, and she was grateful, because his obvious affront to their marriage made her want to strangle him. She couldn't deny that it hurt that he couldn't find himself with her, but he thought he could with someone younger. Someone who looked like they didn't know how to dress herself.

    She didn't know how to handle this diplomatically, without hurting her daughters in the process. How could he show up, knowing that her parents hadn't invited him? People had stopped talking now, stopped pretending they weren't watching. She had to handle this the right way. Somehow.

"Victoria." Roger made his way to her, smirking in satisfaction. "You forgot to tell me the date of the barbeque."

Victoria's mouth nearly dropped at his nerve.

"That's because we didn't invite you." Addie stepped forward. "Or your whore."

"Addie." Victoria's hissed. Schoolteachers did not use that type of language and a few of her students and their parents stood nearby.

"I don't believe you own this house." Roger looked down on Addie. "And I did receive an invitation from Helena."

So that's why she'd been so happy today. She'd invited her dad and didn't tell anyone. Victoria sighed. If she kicked him out, she'd only look worse to Helena, who shot her mom a pleading look. Victoria bit her tongue, stopping the slew of angry words she wanted to spit out at Roger, and asked, "Would you like something to drink?"

"Very much." Now Roger's eyes gleamed with satisfaction. "So would Candace."

"I'll get it." Halle saved Victoria from the humiliation of serving him and his girl-toy drinks.

Halle led the two away, and Helena trailed dutifully behind her dad.

Victoria let out a long breath. People turned back to their meals and companions. "Is it too early in the day for wine?"

"Hell no. I'll go get us a glass. We'll put them in plastic cups, so no one will be the wiser." Addie rubbed Victoria's arm. "Want to come with me?"

"No, it'll just make it worse if I look like I'm hiding." And she hated that. Now she'd have to face this humiliation until the barbeque was over. She raised her head, smiled at the crowd, and crossed to Luca. She needed to make sure Lucia was okay.

Lucia smiled weakly up at her. "I didn't know he was coming."

"It's okay, baby. Do you want to talk to him?" Victoria hugged her close. "I don't mind. You don't have to choose between us. He's here, and I know it's not your fault." She stepped back, trying not to pressure Lucia. "I promise I'm okay with it."

Lucia glanced over to her sister and dad. "I don't want to. I don't like Candace. She hates us. She hates when dad pays attention to us instead of her. I'd rather stay here with you."

Suddenly Victoria understood violence because she wanted to punch that woman in the throat. Roger had a lot to answer to after this, and he damn well would explain why he hung around a woman who wasn't nice to the girls.

Her dad shot her a questioning look and she shook her head. He couldn't tell Roger to leave without making Helena upset, and if her little girl was happy, she could deal with Roger for a few hours. She glanced over at Nick and saw the frown on his face. This wasn't how she wanted him to see Roger, but it wasn't like she could help it.

Nick smiled at her, encouraging and solid. She wanted to go to him so bad but knew that would only cause more gossip. The girls didn't need that on them right now. She smiled back, hoping he knew why she couldn't go to him.

The next few hours dragged by painfully slow. Victoria was aware of where Nick and Roger were at all times, although for different reasons. Helena followed her dad around everywhere, refusing to let him out of her sight. Victoria watched Candace, saw that Lucia was right. After the third dirty look Candace gave them, Victoria's hands curled into fists. Yes, she could definitely understand the violence now.

When the barbeque was finally--mercifully--over, Victoria helped with the clean up. She was picking up plastic cups and putting them in a garbage bag when Nick walked over.

"Let me hold the bag." His fingers brushed hers when he grabbed the bag and his eyes raked over her. "You look beautiful."

"Thanks." She smiled at him. "I thought you'd like the dress."

"I want to take it off of you." He whispered as he leaned past her to grab a few cups.

Victoria checked to make sure no one was paying attention to their corner of the yard. Roger, Candace, and the girls stood next to Trevor and her Dad. She didn't think they were paying attention to her, so she ran a hand down Nick's chest. "I want that, too." She appreciated the fact that Nick didn't bring Roger up, that he wanted to distract her.

They moved around the backyard slowly, neither wanting to finish the task too soon. The warm spring day had given way to a cooler evening and Victoria wished she'd thought to bring a jacket. The irony of the moment hit her. If she and Nick were "public" they wouldn't have this need to sneak around. She just wasn't sure she was ready for that yet.

Too soon their night came to an end.

"It was so nice to meet you." Charlotte pulled Victoria in for a hug, squeezed her. "Thank you for making my boy think." She whispered.

Victoria smiled at Charlotte, even though she wasn't sure what the woman thanked her for.

"Your daughters are beautiful." Charlotte hugged both of the girls, too. "You and your mom will have to come visit me soon."

"Mom." Nick rubbed the back of his neck. "Don't freak the kids out."

Lucia smiled up at him. "You're mom is very sweet."

"Thanks." Luke laughed. "We think so, too."

Victoria watched her parents say good-bye to Charlotte and her sons. She was so glad that Roger had already left with his side piece. The moment was awkward enough already.

Luke stood silent, glancing at Halle every few moments. Victoria wanted to shove Halle into his arms and tell him to kidnap her away from Trevor.

Trevor watched the two, eyes narrowed. If Halle ever decided to leave him, it looked like he was going to have trouble letting go.

§§

The next morning Victoria woke up to someone ringing the doorbell repeatedly. She sat up in the bed, shoving her hair from her face. It was Sunday, her favorite day to sleep in, and when she glared at the clock she saw it was only eight in the morning. She threw the covers off and rushed to see who it was.

"Open up, Victoria!" Roger's voice filtered through even as he pounded his fist on the wood.

"Jesus Christ, Roger!" Victoria hissed at him and slung the door open. "What the hell is wrong with you?"

He brushed past her, impeccably dressed in slacks and a button up. "Is he here? Is he in your bed right now."

"What?" Victoria shut the door behind him. "Will you be quiet? The girls are still asleep."

"Is he?" Roger ignored her and walked straight to her room. He stopped when he saw the bed empty.

"Who are you talking about?" Victoria stood in the hallway, hands on her hips. "Are you drunk?" She hadn't smelled alcohol.

"The guy, Nick. Helena said that you were flirting with him yesterday. I know he's renovating your office." Roger turned back around and sneered at her.

How had she ever thought this man was handsome? He was always so demeaning. "Are you freaking kidding me?" Victoria's temper finally snapped. She'd held it in yesterday for her parents, for the girls, for the barbeque, but there were no witnesses now. "It is none of your damn business if I'm flirting with somebody else. In case you haven't noticed, we're divorced. Which means that you do not get a say in my life, in who I date. And you sure as hell can't show up at my house, charging in to see if I've got a man in my bed!"

"Stop yelling. You always had a poor temper." Roger pretended to fix his shirt cuffs.

Victoria closed her eyes, focused on breathing in and out, to keep from punching him. She'd never felt the need to hit anyone but her life but was about remedy that real quick like. "Roger, if you don't get out of this house right now I will show you how poor my temper can get.

"You have no right to talk to me this way." Roger's calm demeanor infuriated her. "You can't let anyone around our girls unless I approve of them."

Victoria took a step closer. Roger's eyes widened a fraction at the venom in her voice. "I can do that, because I am a *much* better judge of people's character, even if I was married to you for ten years. That bitch, Candace? She's mean to *my* girls. I don't approve of her. I will date who the hell want, because you don't get a say in the matter. Now get the fuck out of my house."

"Victoria--"

"No." Victoria cut off his reprimand. She pointed toward the door, seething. "Now."

She didn't move until she heard the door shut behind her. Her heart raced and she shook from how much anger she released. Although it had felt good to finally say what she'd held in for years, her stomach rolled. She wanted--needed--to talk to Nick. She went into her room, picked up her cell phone, and sent him a text.

Hey, are you awake?

He replied instantly.

Nick: Only for you at this ungodly hour. Is everything ok?

Tears stung her eyes and started to trail down her cheeks. She hated that she cried when she got angry. It made no sense to her.

No. Roger just showed up at my house.

Nick: Did he hurt you? Do I need to call the police?

No, it's nothing like that. I just really need to see you.

Nick: What about the girls?

Victoria sighed. Maybe it was time for them to meet. Helena wasn't going to change the way she felt about the divorce whether or not Victoria dated someone. She thought it was funny that Roger, in trying to keep her and Nick apart, had actually pushed them together. A surety grew in her. Nick was amazing with little Lola, and from what she heard he was great with the boys he mentored. He would be great with them. He just had to believe it.

I'll explain it to them after you leave.

Nick: I'll be there in fifteen minutes. I'll pick up breakfast.

Chapter Twenty-Two

Victoria opened the front door as soon as she heard Nick's truck pull up. The girls were still asleep, usually sleeping until late morning, so she'd have a little time to spend with him alone. She saw him and immediately her anger evaporated. He came up the sidewalk, easy smile on his face, his five o'clock shadow still there. He hadn't even taken the time to shave before coming to make sure she was okay.

"You okay?" He pulled her close, right there on the porch where any of her neighbors could see. She laid her head in the crook of his shoulder, breathed in his scent, and nodded. He rubbed her back in slow circles and Victoria's shaking finally subsided. "Let's get inside. I brought doughnuts and coffee."

"Yum." The heavenly scent of coffee reached her nose. She needed a cup like she needed her next breath.

He made her sit at the bar and gave her the coffee, a doughnut, and a napkin. "Want to talk about it?"

She nodded and took a sip. Her eyes closed as the warm liquid slid down her throat. "It was about you."

"Me?" Nick crossed his arms and leaned against the counter. His body wasn't tense, but there was unease in his look. "If I caused you trouble, I'm sorry. I'm not sorry if it pissed him off, though."

That startled a laugh out of her. "He's my problem, not you. He showed up a little while ago, banging on the door and ringing the doorbell. He actually came right inside the house and went straight to my room, asking if you were here."

Nick's eyes narrowed. "Uninvited? Did you feel threatened, because I can take care of it."

"No. I'm pretty sure he was the one feeling threatened. If he hadn't left when he did, I would've broken my violence cherry."

Nick grinned. "That's my girl."

"He said that he had to approve of who I dated because of the girls."

"That's ironic, considering the slut he brought with him."

Victoria tipped her mug toward him. "That's exactly what I said. I also told him what Lucia said about Candace being mean to them."

"That bitch is being mean to them?" He didn't seem aware of the heat in his voice.

Maybe he cared already, before he hadn't really spent time with them. "That's what Lucia told me. She said that Candace gets angry when Roger spends time with them." Victoria shook her head. "He's too selfish to see it. It's all about what he wants. I'm not sure I can do anything about it. I'd love to say they couldn't go over there, but that would only hurt the girls."

"I'm sorry I don't have advice to give you." Nick's lips turned down. "I've never been in this situation before."

Victoria smiled. "I know, but it helps just to talk about it. He had the nerve to tell me that I had a poor temper when I got mad at what he said."

"He's not worth it." Nick glanced at the clock. "I can leave before the girls get up, if that's what you want. I don't want to rush you or meet them before you want me to."

Victoria cocked her head to the side, watched his expression. "Do you want to meet them? Think about it for a minute. I want you to be completely honest."

He stared down into his coffee cup, brooded for a minute. When he looked back up at her, his serious expression tugged at her heart. "I'm not sure how great I'll be around little girls, I'm used to the boys I mentor. I'm not sure I'm even cut out to be the guy their mom is dating. But I do know this. I care about you, Victoria, which translates to your daughters. I would never do anything to hurt you or them."

Dear God. She might just have tipped a little further toward love right then. His words touched her because she knew he meant them. That he wouldn't have said anything he didn't mean. "Wow."

His lips twitched. "I don't want you to worry. If this...thing...between us doesn't work out, I promise not to turn on your daughters, to ignore them like their father does."

"Keep talking like that and I'll melt to the floor." She walked around the bar and wrapped her arms around his waist. He was solid, powerfully built, but so tender when it came to her. She wasn't worried. "I'm not sure what's between us either."

"We don't have to rush, we have plenty of time to figure it out. The thing we have to remember is that neither of us wants to them to get hurt."

"If only their father thought that way." Victoria kissed the stubble on his chin.

He pulled back from her a little. "I need to get something out of my truck."

"Okay." Victoria turned back to the bar, getting the coffee cups up. His lips brushed the back of her neck and she shivered. A second later he was gone. This was dangerous, she knew that. She wasn't the type to love 'em and leave 'em, but she liked to think that he felt the connection between them as strongly as she did.

When he returned, she was in the living room, settling on the couch. He carried a rectangular present that was almost as long as he was, wrapped in bright blue and white paper tied with a pretty bow and ribbon. She sat forward, her heart fluttering.

He set it down on the floor in front of her. "I...uh...Happy Mother's Day."

She looked from the present to his sheepish face. "You got me a present?" She couldn't keep the shock from coloring her words.

"Yeah." He didn't say more, gestured for her to open it.

"Okay." She beamed at him, reached for the wrapping paper. Her hand hesitated before touching it. The wrapping paper was so beautiful, and she was nervous about what it was. Not because she wouldn't like it, but because he picked it out, and somehow the gift would tell her how he felt. If he *knew* her.

"It's not going to bite you." Nick laughed at her.

She smiled again, tore the wrapping paper open, saw stained wood. She pulled the paper all the way off. Gasped. Couldn't stop the tears that misted. "Oh."

Nick shoved his hands in his pockets again, something she knew he did when he was uncomfortable. If she was making him that way, she couldn't help that. His gift was so incredibly perfect.

"You got me a sign for my office." She sighed, tried to talk again. "It's...amazing."

"You like it?" He crouched down to look in her eyes.

"I love it." She threw her arms around his neck. It was such a thoughtful gift. "I love it," she repeated. His arms came around her, steady and warm. Yeah, she was definitely in dangerous territory now. He knew her like she'd always wanted to be known and he'd taken the time and consideration to pick out the perfect gift.

"I'll hang it up outside the office tomorrow, if you want." He said into her hair. His hands shook from where they rested on her back.

She leaned back and stared into his face. "Yes, please." She smiled even wider so that he knew she loved it.

He nodded, gave her a quick kiss. "I'll go put it back in the truck so I don't forget it."

She took the few minutes he was out of the house to catch her breath. She didn't think it mattered if she was in dangerous territory or not, she was already gone.

When the girls stumbled downstairs at noon, they both stopped short in the kitchen doorway when they saw their mom and Nick sitting at the table. Lucia's face split into a huge grin. "I knew it!"

"Maybe we weren't as good at hiding it as we thought." Nick grinned over at Victoria.

"I'm beginning to see that." Victoria patted the table. "We made BLT's for lunch. I know you're hungry."

Lucia plopped down in the chair next to Nick. "So, are you and my mom dating now?"

Helena trudged to the table, scowling, and plopped into a chair.

"We're working toward that. Do you mind if I am?" He passed out the paper plates, setting a sandwich down on each one.

"No." Lucia bit into her food, then talked with her mouth open. Victoria let it pass this time. "Mom needs a good guy."

"Dad is a good guy." Helena snapped.

Victoria also let this slide by only giving her a warning look. Helena dropped her gaze to the table. She knew that Helena wasn't going to accept Nick right away, but she could at least be polite. "Let's eat."

After lunch, Victoria found herself back on the couch. The girls brought her present, a white bag with pretty pink tissue paper. Nick sat down, far enough away on the couch that Helena wouldn't freak out.

"You're going to love it!" Lucia bounced up and down, smile wide. "Open it."

"I am." Victoria laughed. She pulled the tissue paper out, reached inside.

"Do you like it?" Lucia asked. Helena stood at her side, quiet.

They'd gotten her the matching wallet to the giant purse they'd bought her for her birthday. "I do. It'll go perfect with my purse."

"Yay. Great. Grammy helped us pick it out." Lucia twirled. "Can we play Wii now? Nick can bowl with us." She looked at him. "It's our favorite game. We always beat Mom."

"Thanks for throwing me under the bus." Victoria took her remote and moved to the edge of the couch. She was the only one she knew who loved to bowl on the Wii sitting down.

"She usually is the one with the lowest points." Lucia grinned at her mom. "Here, Helena. Are you going to play?"

"No. I'm going upstairs to read." Helena crossed her arms over her chest.

"Why don't you want to play, sweetie?" Victoria stood and placed her hands on Helena's shoulders. Helena stepped back from her, letting Victoria's arms fall to her sides.

"I don't want to play with him." Helena glared over at Nick. "He's not my dad."

That was it. Victoria was tired of Helena's attitude. "You're right, he's not and he's not trying to be. But he is an adult and you'll treat him with respect."

"I won't." Helena sneered, and Victoria hated to see that she looked just like her dad when she did that. Her daughter stormed off, running up the stairs. A second later, the door to her room slammed.

Victoria went to go upstairs, but Nick placed a hand on her shoulder, stopping her. "Let her calm down. I know it's a big adjustment, and I don't want to force me being here on her. If you want, I can leave."

"No, it's okay." Victoria told him. "Stay, play with me and Lucia. Helena's going to have to learn that she can't throw a fit just because I'm dating someone. Hell, she throws a fit over everything these days. It's gotten out of hand."

"If you're sure." Nick said. "I don't want to come in between the two of you."

"You won't." Lucia started the bowling game. "She's just being rude because she wants to live with dad, and he won't let her."

Victoria knew that comment shouldn't have knocked the breath from her lungs, but it did anyway. Lucia was oblivious to the hurt it caused, already leaning in to bowl. She forced herself to let it go.

Even though Helena stayed in her room, Nick and Lucia both coaxed laughter out of Victoria. She even enjoyed losing to them, and watched as they entered their "tournament round". Nick picked up his game when he realized Lucia was an ace at it.

Victoria ended up in tears laughing at the both of them. Lucia fairly glowed under the attention Nick showed her and it warmed Victoria's heart.

"I'm going to go upstairs with Helena. Try to get her out of her bad mood." Lucia waved at them.

Nick sank onto the couch beside Victoria. "That girl is really good at that game."

"She plays all the time." Victoria intertwined their fingers. She liked having him here, with the girls, next to her on the couch. His body heat scorched her right side and she started to think about dragging him to her room. "You held back until you figured that out."

"I was going to be nice until I realized she was going to annihilate me." Nick turned his head to look at her. "I'm sorry about Roger and Helena."

"It's not your fault. I've tried to be easy with Helena but she's going overboard. I understand why she doesn't want me to date, but she's going to have to face the fact that Roger left me, because he wanted to go find himself. I didn't make him go." Victoria let go of the pain of that horrible moment. "Don't get me wrong, I'm much happier now. But Helena still sees me as the bad guy."

Nick tucked a strand of hair behind her ear. "I can understand that and I can understand why Helena is upset. I'm sure she'll see it eventually."

"I think she's getting bullied at school. Emotionally. I'm not sure exactly what I do with that. She hasn't told me anything about it, I've only overheard the stuff when she and Lucia were fighting."

"I could always teach her some moves. She could put an end to that real quick."

"No." Victoria shook her head firmly. "I don't want her resorting to physical violence unless it's self-defense."

"I got that. but, like mentoring with the boys, we're not teaching them how to hurt someone. We're teaching them self-discipline and respect. Boosting their self-esteem. Maybe one day I can help with that." Nick brought her hand to his lips and kissed it.

The fact that he wanted to help her daughter, even when she'd been so rude to him, only strengthened Victoria's faith in him.

Chapter Twenty-Three

Victoria met Rachel at a quaint beach house Thursday morning. Rachel was putting it on the market next week and she wanted Victoria to look it over, figure out if she had what Rachel needed.

"Thank you so much for coming on such short notice." Rachel pulled Victoria into the house. "The owners put it on the market and want it sold as soon as possible. It's a big family drama, and I'd like to get it off my hands. The quicker the better."

The house was small, but cute. Victoria walked through the small living room and kitchen, into the back to the master bedroom, single bath, and bunk room. It would be a great rental, enough room for a family to have a week of fun on the beach. In the living room French doors opened onto a small deck that faced the beach. People sitting in the living room would be able to see the ocean at night, and that would be a huge inspiration for her design.

"I've got a lot of stuff that I could use. It's all in the shed at my dad's." Victoria took a last glance around the living room. "The coral walls are a great backdrop for the beach, so that will help us out a lot."

Rachel hugged Victoria. "Thank you! I wasn't sure you'd have time to do it. I know you've been busy."

"I need an assistant." Victoria said. Her office would be opening soon and she didn't want to spend every waking moment on the things she could source out. "I was going to wait until Nick finished the office, but I'm about to lose my mind. I think an assistant would help me stay organized."

"I can find someone else to do this." Rachel said.

"Oh no, the girls are going to their dad's for the weekend. I can come up here this weekend and set it up."

"Then let me help, at least." Rachel held up a hand when Victoria started to protest. "You are going out of your way to get this done for me. It'll go faster if you let me help."

"Okay." Victoria gave in. "Meet me here at ten a.m. Saturday and we'll start."

"I'll bring my niece. She's looking for a job, just graduated from college and can't find anything. Maybe you'll like her."

Victoria smiled. "I probably will, if she's anything like you."

"Thanks so much, Victoria. I don't know what I'd do without you." Rachel led the way outside. "I'll see you Saturday."

Victoria started her SUV and headed just out of town to meet with a long-time client who wanted to re-do her living room. Mae did this about every two years to help deal with the grief of losing her husband of fifty five years. Victoria couldn't even imagine being married to someone that long. Sharing those life changing moments, the happy and the sad, and missing them so much when they passed. Her parents seemed to be heading that way, and she wished so much that she'd have that in her life one day.

The six bedroom estate sat in the middle of twenty acres of land. Mae's husband had been a acclaimed director years ago, and she'd been a playwright. It was how they met, and Victoria listened to the story every time she came. She didn't have the heart to tell Mae she'd heard it a thousand times before. She also didn't mind the forty-minute drive, Addie was picking up the girls, and Victoria knew Mae wouldn't get out of the house easily.

The girls last day was next Tuesday, with those two days that week being exams. After that, Victoria wondered what she'd do with them for the summer. Maybe they'd like to go to work with her, see what she did. She'd already decided to let Lucia go to the cheer camp in June, it would make her so happy. She'd also found a math and science camp that Helena would enjoy. She didn't want to think she was bribing her, but she just wanted Helena to be happy, too.

Mae answered the door with a flourish, wrapping Victoria in a flowery scented hug. "Thank goodness you're here. I was going crazy thinking of what to do in there."

Victoria held on, letting Mae draw the hug out. The poor women was all alone now, her two children living overseas. "Well, let's see what we can do." They crossed the marble foyer and went to the left of the grand staircase.

The "living room" was as big as Victoria's house. Three steps down and she entered the sunken room. Blue marble floors and pale walls, all the furniture decorated in floral patterns. She remembered how long it had taken her to match all the pieces she found to the exact colors Mae had wanted.

"What do you have in mind?" Victoria shook her head when Mae offered her a drink. The woman was

258

fond of whiskey and drank it constantly, although Victoria had never seen her the least bit tipsy.

"Darling," Mae sank down onto one of the pale blue couches, drink in hand. "I want to do more of a modern looking area. Sharp edges, bright red and white, maybe some black to darken it up a bit. Lots of glass and chrome."

"When do you want it finished?" Victoria started to imagine what Mae wanted in her mind. She didn't have anything on hand, but she could take a trip out of town. Antique shops wouldn't work for this. There was a modern-y furniture and accessories store two towns over. She'd have to look online to make sure.

"I know you're probably busy, so two months? You can do it around all the stuff going on with your new office." Mae pulled out a long cigarette and lit it. She took a drag, then released the smoke in a puff. "How is your new office going?"

"Great. My dad's gotten a hand in it."

Mae's raspy cackle warmed with humor. "Did you doubt he would?"

"No." Victoria laughed with her.

"I heard about the handsome young man that's working on your office has his eye on you."

"How did you hear that?" Victoria asked. She willed herself not to blush, and failed.

"Aha. It seems you've got your eye on him." Mae tapped her cigarette against a crystal ashtray. "Is he good to you?"

"Yes. And to my girls. But he's afraid of relationships and children because of his dad." Victoria sat in the white chair near the couch. "I'm trying to prove him wrong about it."

Mae nodded, eyes bright. "I remember his rascal of a father. Such a shame. His mother was such a pretty young thing, and sweet as anything. She helped around here, did some cleaning for me after the man left her with two kids. I always paid her generously. How is she doing?"

"She came to our Mother's Day barbeque and she looked great. Very healthy." Victoria told her.

"Good. That woman deserves some happiness." Mae nodded. She put the cigarette out. "Now show yourself out dear. I'm going to go lay down." Mae stood slowly, bones creaking. "I'm just not sleeping like I used to."

Victoria left after telling Mae that she'd get a concept folder ready for her to approve. Her heart felt heavy for a number of reasons. She hated that Mae was lonely and desperately wanted a love like that in her life. When she was younger, Victoria had just known that she'd have a love like her parents. Her children would grow up in a house with both parents still around, surrounded by love and laughter. It had taken her a long time to realize that wasn't how her life was going to be, and that when Roger had left, it had actually been a good thing.

Her errand out to Mae's hadn't taken as long as she thought it would, so she called Addie to let her know that she could pick the girls up.

The girls hopped into the car, Lucia brimming with excitement. "Mom, I found out when cheer practice starts next year. And, I got to try on my cheer uniform so they knew what size to order for the new ones." Lucia's black ponytail bounced as she did.

"Buckle up." Victoria laughed at her. Her happiness was infectious. "That's amazing. I can't wait to see them. Helena, how was your day?"

"It was okay." Helena glanced up at her mom, then back to her lap.

Victoria sighed. "Have you found out when your mathelete club starts? Are any of your friends in it?"

"One. Julie." Helena gave up grudgingly.

"That's great." Victoria made a mental note to find out who Julie's mom was and see about Julie going to the math camp too. Maybe Helena would enjoy it more. "Can you get her mom's number for me?"

"Why?" Helena snapped.

Victoria raised an eyebrow and looked in the rearview mirror so she could see Helena. "I want to put you in a math and science camp this summer, but if you want to act like this, you obviously don't want to go."

Helena's head jerked up and she glared at her mom.

Victoria shrugged. "Well, I'll forget about talking to Julia's mom about it too." When Helena remained silent, Victoria wondered if it was a small victory on her side or her daughter's.

She helped them with some of their homework, what they needed help with, and worked on her business plan. Her office would be finished within two weeks and she needed to make sure everything was ready. All furniture was ordered or in her parent's garage. It was all coming together.

Chapter Twenty-Four

"What do you want for dinner?" Nick asked Victoria. She moved around the living room, cleaning up after Roger picked the girls up. He wished he'd been here when the bastard was. It would've certainly been entertaining.

"I don't know." Victoria threw the small square pillows back on the couch. "How do they make such a mess in a few hours?"

Nick watched her. "Me and Luke used to tear the house up."

"God, I can imagine. It's been all girls for me, and my parents, so usually the bathroom and bedrooms were the rooms that suffered the most." She stopped cleaning, walked over to him, and put her arms around his neck.

His hands automatically went to her hips to pull her closer. She only came up to his shoulder, and he loved that she had to crane her head back to look up at him. Her body was made for his and he loved the way it felt pressed up against him.

"What do you want?"

"Hmm." He nuzzled her neck. "I can think of something."

She laughed and pushed him away. "Well, I'm starving. For food." She clarified when he grinned.

"Fine." Nick pressed a quick kiss to her forehead. "Let's get groceries and I'll make us an actual home cooked meal."

"Well, well. Mr. Domestic, all of a sudden?" Victoria grabbed her purse.

"No, I'll buy them. I'll cook, too." Nick watched her struggle with letting him pay for the groceries. "Tori, it's not a big deal. It's how my mom raised me, and it's hard to go against the grain."

"Let me at least buy the wine?"

He could see that it really mattered to her that he not pay for it all. "Deal."

"You do know that people will see us together." Victoria told him as they drove toward the store. "Are you ready for that?"

"Sure. Are you?" Nick asked. "I mean, you're the one dating the trouble kid who came back home. The one moms hate because he's slept with all their daughters."

Victoria's face fell and he grit his teeth. Way to go, dumbass. Just rub it in her face that he'd been with more than a few women. "Ah, Tori, that's not what I meant."

She refused to look at him. "Sure."

He'd really fucked that up. "What I meant is that you're a smart, independent woman. They're just going to be surprised that you're with me."

"Why?" Victoria turned that temper on him, eyes shining. "Why is it so hard to believe that I would be with you?"

Nick focused on the road. His stomach knotted and he suddenly felt ashamed of his past. "You know why."

"No, Nick, I don't. That's why I'm asking." She looked at him. "You are a successful man who owns his own business. You have your own apartment, a shop, and you take care of your mother. On top of that you mentor lost little boys, changing their lives forever." Her voice firmed. "That doesn't sound like someone that I'd be ashamed to be with." She crossed her arms and stared out the window.

Wow. She was insanely hot when she was pissed. He wanted to turn his truck around and drive straight back to her house, forget the food, but he wouldn't. He didn't think that was the point of everything she said. "Okay."

"That's all I get? Okay?" She glared at him.

"I'm agreeing with you." Nick took her hand, kissed her palm while keeping her eyes on the road. "You are damn lucky to be with me." He smiled when she laughed at him.

"You're insane."

He picked up groceries for steak, salad, and baked potatoes. When they got back to the house, she sat and the bar and watched him cook. He moved with the grace of a fighter, expertly sautéing the steak. Neither spoke, but Victoria felt the bond between them strengthening.

The food smelled delicious and when he made their plates and joined her at the bar, she told him. "Why didn't you become a cook?"

"Not enough physical labor, I guess." He handed her a glass of wine. "I wanted to do something that didn't involve being indoors constantly, and while I do like to cook, I love construction more."

"God, this is good." She bit into her medium cooked steak and closed her eyes as flavor burst on her tongue. "Don't tell dad, but I think your steaks are better than his."

"I'll keep that secret between us." Nick tipped his wine glass to hers.

By the end of the meal, Victoria felt pleasantly full. She put her plate in the sink. "I've never had steak like that before."

"That's right, boost my ego like a good wench." He pinched her butt. "Now, leave the dishes for after."

"After?" She squealed when he threw her over his shoulder. A thrill ran through her at how feminine she felt at being carried by him.

"I need a shower and I want company." He smacked her butt.

She gasped, not sure if she wanted to admit that she liked it. He went straight to her bathroom and started stripping off her clothes in efficient maneuvers. She thought she might have a heart attack right there in the bathroom, her heart was beating so fast. He took off his shirt and her eyes instantly traced the tattoos on his toned muscles. When he lowered his jeans and boxers, her heart stuttered. She'd never thought the male body was attractive, but right now she wanted to eat him up.

He opened the glass door and turned the water on. When the spray was hot enough, he stepped in, turning around so that she could get in too. His blue gaze lit a fire in her abdomen. He looked as desperate as she felt. Her eyes traveled over the muscles of his chest, lower to his abs, then even lower. She wanted to do something for him, show him the pleasure that he'd given her. His eyes narrowed as she went down on her knees, letting the spray rain down her back. She bit her lip, eyeing his cock, ready to do something for him she'd never done to anyone else.

When she ran her tongue up the bottom side, his hands went to her hair. It spike a quiver of delight to run through her when his fingers tightened, and she could tell he fought with himself to keep from taking control. She swirled her tongue around the head and heard his sharp intake of breath. Never before had she wanted to do this, but she wanted to give him as much pleasure as he gave her. She wanted to drive him wild, make him lose control.

She took him in her mouth, slowly pulling his entire length inside. It took a minute to adjust and she relaxed her throat.

"Fuck, Tori." His thighs tensed underneath her hands.

Taking her time, she pulled her head back to the tip, then took him back inside her mouth. Her nipples tightened to buds, sensitive to the shower spray. When she picked up the pace, he groaned. His hips started to move, pushing shallowly into her mouth, but she didn't allow him to do more than that. She was in control. Her hands brushed his skin and she grabbed his ass, pushing him deeper.

"Tori." Nick pulled her hair back, forcing her to look up at him. His pupils were wide, he took in every inch of her. "If you keep this up, I'm not going to last."

In answer, she sped up, using one of her hands at the base of his cock, twisting it along the shaft. His abdomen clenched and he raised up on his toes. When he growled, heat roared through her.

Desperately he pulled her head back and off his cock. "I want inside you . Now."

He lifted her up and bent her over. Her hands rested on the shower wall. he ran a hand down her back, over her butt, then smacked it. Holy shit, she didn't even have the energy to deny that she liked it. The sting only aroused her more, made her wetter.

"Do you know what you do to me, Tori?" He slipped a condom on from the pocket of his jeans.

She shook her head. Her thoughts tripped through her brain. She had no hope them forming. The hot tip of his cock pushed against her wetness.

"I think about you like this, about you, all the time." He filled her. Pure sensation rushed through her, lighting a fire underneath her skin. She moaned his name and it woke something in him. She felt the moment his control broke. His fingers tightened on her hips and he thrust into her, harder and harder. Her fingers curled on the shower wall, searching for something to hold on to. A cyclone of emotion and sensation overtook her. It terrified her, because she felt like she was losing herself to him. It was almost too much.

His hands gripped her waist, pulling her back as he pushed forward. Her body tightened, every thought narrowed to between her legs, to the sensations he awakened in her. He shifted positions, brushing against just the right spot, and her eyes slammed shut. It pushed her right over the edge, and she climaxed around him.

"Squeeze me tight, baby. Just like that." Nick's voice roughened. "Yes, baby." Two more hard thrusts and he came inside her. When his body relaxed, he laid his forehead on her shoulder. "Shit, baby."

"Keep talking like that and you'll romance me right into bed." She laughed softly. Her legs shook beneath her.

He spun her around, brushed his fingertips over her cheek, his expression serious. "You are so beautiful, you take my breath away. No matter what I do during the day, you are on my mind. When I wake up, I think about texting you just to make sure you're thinking of me too."

"Oh." She stared into his eyes, seeing an emotion there she was afraid to name.

His lips twitched. "Who's being romantic now?"

She pushed on his shoulder, smiling. "Shut up. how can you even think right now?"

"I am a man." He puffed his chest up, playfully beat on it. "Hear me roar."

"Women roar." She laughed. "I need to sit."

"Let me get you a towel, dry you off." Nick stepped out of the shower, dried off fast, then held out a hand. He helped her step out, then set to work, slowly toweling her off. Every time he dried a section, he kissed her skin gently.

There went another piece of her heart.

Chapter Twenty-Five

"Are you sure you don't have anything else to do today?" Victoria asked Nick as he backed up his truck to her dad's shop.

"I'm sure." He put the truck in park. "I want to spend time with you."

"I'm sure you had something else in mind. Not helping me take a bunch of furniture to a beach house and helping set it up." Victoria got out, saw her dad waiting outside. "Hey, Dad."

Wes hugged her, then shook Nick's hand. "She rope you into helping out?"

"No, sir. I volunteered." Nick grinned.

"I see." Wes looked between the two of them, then his face split into a grin. "So, Rachel need anymore help?"

"No. She's bringing her niece with her. It's a small place, so it should only take today to get it done."

"Okay." Wes opened the shop door. "Point out what you need and Nick and I will put it in the back."

She pointed out the furniture, and by the end they realized they'd need her dad's truck to help haul the stuff out there.

"Looks like I'm helping anyway." Wes winked down at this daughter.

"You got your wish, Dad." Victoria smirked. "Just follow us out there. You can leave if you want after we get it all inside."

"I won't." Wes climbed into his truck. "See you in a minute."

The drive only took half an hour, and they rode with the windows down, letting the warm breeze in. Tourists walked the boardwalks, going in and out of stores, eating ice cream and laughing. Their voices floated into the truck on the breeze, and Victoria smiled. Contentment used to be so elusive to her, but now it settled over her like a warm day on the beach.

Rachel was already inside when they pulled up to the beach house. Victoria joined her while the men started to unload everything.

"Good morning." Rachel wore nylon shirts and t-shirt, like Victoria. Neither had bothered with make-up and both had their hair up. Next to Rachel stood a girl a little younger than Addie. She was a pretty brunette with expressive green eyes and a sweet face. "Victoria, meet Ella."

"Hi." Ella waved.

"It's great to meet you, Ella." Victoria shook her hand. "Rachel tells me you're looking for a job."

"There aren't a lot of openings in town for massage therapists right now. I could go to the city, but I'd rather be near my family." Ella's smile was slow in coming, but it brightened her entire face.

"If you want to apply for an assistant position with me, you'd most likely get it. The pay isn't great, though, since I'm only just now starting in the office. I'm hoping to be able to handle more clients from there."

"Any job is better than not having one. I've got to start paying off student loans soon, so whatever I get is fine with me. I worked for a doctor's office in high school. I know it's not the same, but I've got some receptionist skills."

"Works for me. We can set it all up Monday." Victoria told her. Nick and her dad began to bring pieces of furniture into the house. The girls started in the small living room since that's where Victoria felt everything should spring from. The part of the house where memories were made, where families came to spend time together. It was the heart of the home, and she wanted it to be perfect, even if it was just to make the house sell.

Nick and Wes placed a white wicker couch and two bright blue chairs in there, followed by a wooden coffee table and end tables. Victoria, Rachel and Ella, situated the furniture around the room.

On top of the coffee table, Victoria placed a bowl, filled with seashells and sand and put a single white candle on top. Ella grabbed the pictures off of the couch and sighed. "These are breathtaking."

Victoria nodded. "I know. When I saw them, I had to have them." She watched Ella hold up the three pictures in turn to show Rachel. The first depicted a sunrise over the beach, the second the sun high in the sky at noon over the same beach, and the third-the sunset.

Ella then went into the kitchen while Victoria worked on the master bath. Rachel worked on the hall bath, until they all met in the master bedroom. The guys were busy at work on the deck, getting the patio furniture ready.

"It's amazing how much better this place looks. Perfect for the beach, and yet still homey enough for a family." Ella hung some white, gauzy curtains on the window.

"Thank you." Victoria surveyed the room. "I love doing this." She made the king size bed with coral sheets and a white duvet. Rachel placed small coral pillows at the head.

"This didn't take as long as I thought it would." Victoria glanced outside, saw the sun setting over the ocean. Brilliant orange and pink light painted its way across the sky. "I can't believe none of us have eaten yet."

"I'm starving." Ella looked at her watch. "It's after five we've got to get something to eat."

"I'll take you to your favorite place for helping us out." Rachel put an arm around her niece's shoulders.

"Good. Victoria, call me Monday when you're ready." Ella put her number in Victoria's phone. "I can't wait to start working with you."

Victoria joined her dad and Nick on the deck after Rachel and Ella left. "Thanks for you help today, guys. It went by a lot faster."

"Of course." Wes watched the sun set. "Nick needed someone to help him haul in the furniture.

Plus he would've been surrounded by women. He needed some testosterone."

"Thanks." Nick chuckled. "I would've been lost."

"You're mother is cooking dinner. She wants you, Nick, and your sisters to come eat." Wes told them. "She called a little while ago."

"Sure, if that's okay with you." Nick looked to Victoria.

"It's fine with me." Victoria smiled at them.

§§

So it had come to this. Even though he'd technically met her family previously, this seemed a little more formal. More one on one. Tonight he'd be in a more intimate setting than the barbeque and Nick was pretty sure her dad knew exactly what was going on between them. His nervousness made him feel like a teenager, going on a date and meeting the dad for the first time.

The cheery atmosphere of the house enveloped him, taking the nerves down a notch. Cecelia smiled when they entered the kitchen and wrapped him in a hug. She hugged him like his own mother would, and his nerves settled a little more. Addie waved at him, her mouth full of chips.

"Hey. Heard you helped out a lot today." Halle handed him a beer. "I think you deserve to sit down and relax."

"I did work, too." Victoria said.

"But you didn't carry all the furniture." Cecelia patted Nick's cheek. "Have a seat at the bar."

He sat next to Addie. "What did you do to get out of helping?"

"I'm the baby. I get out of a lot of things." Her sapphire blue eyes twinkled.

"It's completely unfair, but Mom and Dad won't believe us." Halle told him.

He took a sip of the chilled beer. The rest of his nerves dissipated.

"We're having some kind of chicken dish Mom's never cooked before, so fair warning."

"I heard that." Cecelia called from the stove.

Victoria laughed. "Quit, Halle. Even if it is a new dish," she told Nick, "it'll most likely be delicious."

"Stop trying to earn brownie points." Addie took a sip of his beer. "You still have to help."

"Bitch." Victoria whispered to her.

"I heard that, too." Cecelia said over her shoulder.

The girls burst out laughing. Nick watched their back and forth, loved seeing the closeness between them. There was something different about their closeness, from his and Luke's, and he realized what it was. It was born from a steady home and having no doubt of how loved they were.

Wes came in, hair wet from his shower, and he immediately crossed to Cecelia and wrapped his arms around her from behind. She tilted her head back on his shoulder and murmured softly to him.

A sharp ache went through Nick's chest for his mother. He hated that she didn't have someone to hold her like that, to help her when she was down, to be her rock when she needed it the most. She always said that she didn't need anyone other than her sons, but how badly he wished that she had that kind of love in her life. Not for the first time, he wanted to hunt his father down and beat him within an inch of his life.

"What's up?" Victoria placed a hand over his. "You look upset."

He forced himself to forget the past when he looked at her. To focus on her and tonight. "No, not at all." He turned his hand over and grasped hers. "Everything is perfect."

"Get a room." Addie elbowed him and laughed.

Victoria rolled her eyes at her sister. "Don't be jealous."

"I'm not. I don't ever want to be tied down." Addie said.

"That's what I thought, too." Nick grinned up at Victoria.

For dinner they all sat around the dining room table, which was formal for him, but the conversation and atmosphere wasn't. Victoria and her family discussed everything under the sun, making sure to include him. Not once did he feel left out because he wasn't a member of the family.

They treated him like he was, though, and he could tell it didn't bother them that he was with their daughter. It seemed Victoria was right, and his fears about them rejecting him had been groundless. He glanced over at her. Even without her make-up, disheveled from their work, she took his breath away. All her walls were down and she glowed with love for her family.

He wanted her to feel that way about him. He wanted to make her glow. It hit him like a bolt of lightning, but it didn't surprise him as much as it should've. It had been sneaking up on him since the day he saw her standing in the office. Like it was kismet, or fate, or whatever people called it. She laughed and his abdomen tensed. He may not have been surprised by the thought of being in love with her, but he needed some time to process it before he told her.

After dinner, the girls cleaned up while Wes took Nick out to his shop to look at some tools. The night was cloudy, proving that summer storms approached.

"I see the way you look at my daughter."

Nick's hand froze over a rustic hammer. "What?" Very eloquent, he thought. That's the way to win him over.

Wes grinned at the stunned look on Nick's face. "I'm not going to shoot you. I just saw how you were looking at her during dinner. It's the same way I look at her mother."

Damn. He hadn't been able to hide that burst of clarity. "Is it a problem?" Nick couldn't deny it and he wasn't going to try.

Wes appraised him. "Are you planning on breaking her heart?"

"No." Nick forgot the hammer, leaned against the counter to look Wes in the eye. "I plan to make her very happy. For the rest of her life."

Wes nodded, the tension thickening for Nick. "I'm a great judge of character, son." Wes looked Nick over and Nick's shame surfaced. Would Wes judge him by his character, or by his upbringing? Wes's face relaxed, and he grinned. "I happen to think you're perfect for my daughter.

It shocked him. He couldn't lie to himself, he'd really thought Wes would reject him for his daughter, even though they'd tried to set them up in the first place. "But what about my childhood? My father? You don't think I'll treat her the same way?"

"Let me tell you something about your dad." Wes placed a hand on Nick's shoulder. "He was an alcoholic bastard who didn't care anything for his wife and sons. But when I look at you, I see your mother. The one who loves her sons and did everything she could to keep them fed, give them a roof and a happy childhood. That's what I see. I don't think your father has anything to do with this situation. You're giving the damn man too much credit."

That rocked through Nick's system. Two significant revelations in one night? His heart might stop. Was he giving his father too much credit? Giving him too much power over his life when he wasn't even around? "Maybe you're right."

"Damn right I'm right." Wes clapped his shoulder. "You and your brother are good men. Don't ever doubt that."

Chapter Twenty-Six

Later that week, Nick stood in his shop, working on some cabinets he was building for another client. The night was cool, so he'd put on a flannel shirt over his tee. He'd even buttoned it to keep the wind off, he'd left the shop doors open. Beyond that he could hear the sounds of traffic out on the road. Ever since he'd had dinner over at Victoria's parents, the weight about his past had lifted. He realized he was more than his father would ever be, and didn't have to live under the cloud of the man's mistakes.

"Nick?"

The smoky voice that drifted into the shop made him cringe. The woman that walked through the door made him want to take a hammer and smash himself in the face. "Stella, what the fuck are you doing here?"

"Oh, I missed you, that's all." She stepped into the shop, wearing nothing but a gauzy blue dress that was practically see through and fuck-me heels. There was a time when she would've woken a storm of lust in him. Not now.

"Stella, I don't want you here. I don't want you at all."

She pouted. Her eyes were outlined in smoky colors, but to him she looked like a raccoon. A rabid one. "Don't say that, Nicky. I know that little puritan doesn't satisfy you." She walked slowly around the table, stopping a few feet from him. She ran a hand down her chest, trying to draw his gaze to her practically naked breasts.

"Stella, I'm not asking you to leave. I'm telling you. I want nothing to do with you."

"You're hurting my feelings." She came closer, ran her fingernails down his flannel shirt. When she went for his buttons, he pushed her hands away.

"Good." His patience was razor thin when he pointed to the door. "Leave."

She broke eye contact to walk around his shop, pretending to inspect everything. He knew she could care less about the work he did here. "You really should give this up and go back to fighting. You were amazing, tough, sexy. You're still sexy, but do you really want to spend the rest of your life in this small town, dating a dowdy mother? I know how you feel about kids. You can't tell me that you've changed your mind."

"I've changed my mind." Nick really needed to get his work done, but he wasn't going to stay here with her. "Have a look around. I'm leaving, since you won't." He grabbed his keys and walked out, leaving her standing in his shop.

Anger rode him hard. He hated that he'd had to leave. *His* fucking shop, just to get away from her. Leaving her there, with all his stuff, probably wasn't the best idea, but he didn't want her jeopardizing what he had with Victoria. He wanted to head straight to her, kiss her, get the sight of Stella out of his mind but he knew she was busy. He headed to the gym instead.

Once inside he went to his locker and changed. He needed to get some of this anger out. Luke glanced up as Nick passed his office and followed him into the locker room.

"What's up?" Luke leaned against the doorframe while Nick changed. "Did you do something to Victoria?"

"Why do you automatically go to that?" Nick slammed the locker door shut. Why was he even so angry about all of this?

Luke held up his hands. "Bro, take it down a notch. If it wasn't that, what was it?"

"Stella showed up at my fucking shop. She wouldn't leave, so I did." Nick brushed past Luke and headed to the weights. Maybe if he worked hard enough he would stop wishing he could run straight to Victoria.

"She showed up at your shop? Here?" Luke followed him out. "What the hell?"

"Yes, here. Do I have a shop anywhere else?"

"Relax. I'm just trying to process this. Didn't you and Victoria give her this huge set down, and Nicola kick her out of the wedding?" Luke stood by while Nick picked up the kettlebells and started his reps.

"Yeah. Obviously it didn't sink in that I didn't want anything to do with the bitch." Nick shook his head. "Why the fuck did you let me go home with her that night?"

Luke grinned. "There was no stopping you. You'd just won the championship, you'd had a lot to drink, and you were high on life. I wasn't getting in your way."

"I thought brothers were supposed to stop each other from sleeping with leeches. Isn't that in the bro code?"

"Probably." Luke shrugged. "How do we get rid of her?"

"No clue." Nick slugged some water, started back on the reps. "She just won't get it. I don't fucking want her. I never really did. And the last thing I want is for Stella to ruin what's going on between me and Victoria." When his brother's lips twitched, Nick flipped him off. "Shut up."

"No, I'm loving this. You always gave me hell for pining over Halle, and here you go falling for her sister."

Nick said nothing.

"Oh, shit. You didn't deny it." Luke scanned his brother's face. "You always freak out if I even casually mention you falling for someone. Like it was the plague or something. You didn't deny it."

"No. I didn't."

"Fucking shit." Luke laughed. "I don't believe it."

"It's not like I'm marrying her or anything." Nick set the kettlebells down and went for the machines.

"Yet." Luke looked around at the other gym rats. "My brother's in love!"

At Luke's shout, Nick sighed. "Can you shut up? I'm still getting used to the idea."

Over the cat calls and whistles, Nick heard his heartbeat pounding in his ears. It wasn't fair for his brother to tease him when he was only beginning to get used to the idea of being in love, and with a woman with teenage daughters.

"Nick, keep an eye on the gym for me." Luke twirled his keys around his finger. "I'm going to take care of your leech problem, okay?"

"You think you can get rid of her, when I couldn't?"

"Oh yeah." Luke shot him a grin. "I'm not worried about her ruining a relationship. I can be as mean as I want, since I never slept with her."

"You're nuts." Nick told him. "But I'm not going to stop you."

He watched his brother leave, wondering if Luke could actually get her to leave. Nick wished she'd leave for good, go find some other poor unsuspecting fool and sink her claws into him. Not for the first time he wished he'd never even laid eyes on her.

§ §

Victoria's office would officially be finished next week. It was Friday, the beginning of summer, and even Helena brimmed with excitement, ready for all the fun the next few months had to offer. Victoria let them sleep, deciding that she could work from home today, let them enjoy it for now. She still had no idea what to do with them after she started working out of the office.

So while she let them sleep, she started to pack up her home office in her room to take over as soon as Nick let her know everything was done. Boxes were sitting all over the floor, some open and some already full and closed. Her dad had the furniture in his shop, and would help Nick put it in. Ella would start work next week and Victoria was sure she'd prove to be a hard worker.

She stood in a pair of boxers and a long sleeve tee and looked over the room, recognizing how far she'd come after Roger left. She couldn't even be bitter anymore. He'd left to find himself and in turn forced her to realize who she was. Now that he didn't control everything going on, she could spread her wings and grow. It just took meeting Nick to realize how far she'd come.

A giant weight lifted since then, and she knew that. She could fully let go of the past and move on, and maybe sine she was able to, she could help Lucia and Helena do the same. All she wanted was to be happy, for her daughters to be happy. It amazed her how she could wake up in the morning now, and instead of the burden of animosity, she woke up in love.

Shit. She paused, her hand above a box. Her skin tingled and her lips parted. She'd fallen for Nick. Fallen hard.

A wide smile cracked her cheeks, and she fanned herself from the sudden flush of heat. Then her smile faded as realized she'd done exactly what she didn't want to do. How was she going to hide it from him? She'd always been an open book. If she wasn't careful, he'd think she was trying to trap him in a relationship and he'd run.

Shaking her head, she took a deep breath. She had to focus on the job at hand. Stuff was laying about everywhere. Papers, files, fabric swatches and concept books. She needed to organize everything. That's why she'd taken the rest of the week off.

She set the concept binder for Mae on the bed so she wouldn't accidentally pack it up, then she rolled up her sleeves and dove into the rest of the packing.

"Mom."

Victoria blinked and looked up. Helena stood in the doorway in her pajamas and smiled hesitantly when Victoria saw her. "What is it, baby?"

"We were wondering if maybe you'd take us for lunch? We're starving."

"It's lunch time already?" Victoria looked around and saw how much she'd gotten done.

"Mom, it's after two." Helena pulled her up. "You probably missed lunch, too, didn't you?"

"I got carried away packing." Victoria gestured around the room. "Go change and we'll go out to eat."

"Okay."

Victoria waited until Helena left to release the breath she held. She'd been waiting for some of Helena's attitude to resurface and was surprised when they'd had a short conversation without either of them losing their temper. She changed into a pair of jeans and a t-shirt and went to find out what the girls wanted to eat.

Chapter Twenty-Seven

The girls wanted IHOP, so Victoria now looked down at the menu, trying to figure out if she wanted blueberry pancakes or chocolate chip. Her train of thought took her straight to Nick and the morning he'd made her pancakes. A flush spread over her face.

"You okay, Mom?" Lucia asked. "You're face is turning red."

Victoria fanned herself with the menu. "I'm fine."

"She's going through 'the change'." Helena made air quotes and Lucia burst into laughter.

"Nice." Victoria had to laugh. "I'm still a little young for that, no matter what the two of you think." God, how she'd missed Helena's hilarious wit and sarcasm. The waitress came around and the ordered.

"What do you girls want to do when my office opens?" Victoria stared across the booth to where her daughters sat together. Side by side, dressed in comfy clothes, they looked so much alike. The same lopsided smile on their faces, the same sparkle in their eyes. Seeing that smile on Helena again almost made her cry, but she held herself back. They'd really think something was wrong if she burst into tears for no reason.

"I don't want to sit at your office all day." Lucia looked to Helena and her sister nodded.

"You're not staying home alone." Victoria nixed that idea quickly. The girls frowned. "Maybe Grammy will let you come hang out with her, and some days you can spend with Addie or Halle."

"We can do that. We don't want to be bored or follow you to all of your houses while you fix them up." Helena took a sip of her chocolate milk. "At Grammy's we can get on the computer, or watch TV."

"It won't be long before you go to your camps." Victoria pushed down the small bit of panic at the thought of them spending time away from her in that type of setting. Sure, they'd spent the weekend with Roger, or with her family, but this was different.

"Has Julie's mom said if she could go or not?" Helena asked.

"No, her father is overseas, and Julie's mom only hears from him once a week. She's waiting to see what he says."

"I wonder what it would be like if our dad was in the army." Lucia glanced at Helena. "At least we can see Dad whenever we want."

"I guess." Helena shrugged, eyes falling to her lap.

"Anyway, I can't wait to go to cheer camp." Lucia switched topics effortlessly. "All my friends are going and it's going to be so much fun."

"I know you will, sweetie." Victoria smiled at both of them. "I saw some interesting stuff in the math and science brochure."

"There was." Helena reluctantly looked up. "They have a giant telescope to look at the stars. That's going to be my favorite part. I love learning about the solar system."

"You always have. I remember when you were younger you used to beg to sit outside at night and count the stars." Victoria told her as the waitress brought their food to the table. "There's a website where you can create an account and they'll email you when there are meteor showers or eclipses, neat things like that. When we get home, you should sign up for it."

"That'd be cool." Lucia nudged her. "Even I'd like to see some shooting stars."

Helena nudged her sister back, smiling. "Okay, I'll do it."

§ §

"Will you invite Victoria and her girls over for dinner tonight?" His mother's voice asked through the phone.

Nick tucked his pencil behind his ear, pulled his glasses off, and wondered if he was ready to take that step. Like when he ate at her family's house, he'd be introducing her as his date to his mother. As more than just a date, and this time the twins would be with them. "Sure. I'll give her a call."

"Good. Call me right back."

Nick hung up, then stared at the phone. His mom had sounded so upbeat, he didn't want to disappoint her. His heart raced and he knew he was too nervous to talk to her on the phone. He told himself he was texting her because she might be busy and he didn't want to interrupt whatever she might be doing.

-Mom wants to know if you and the girls would like to come eat dinner with us tonight.

He set the phone down and slipped his glasses back on. His nerves couldn't handle waiting around to see if she texted him back. Besides, it was only three o'clock, she was most likely still packing for her office move. He focused on the cabinets, sanding them down to just the right texture. When his text alert went off, he was glad no one was around to see him throw his dignity out the window by practically diving for his phone.

Victoria: Sure, what time? Do I need to bring anything?

-No, she wants to treat you and the girls. Do you want me to

pick you up or do you want to meet me there?

Victoria: I don't think we'll fit in your truck.

-True. I'll text you the address. Be there around six.

Before he thought about, he sent another text.

-I miss you.

Yeah, he was definitely a goner. He'd never once thought about missing a girl, much less telling her. Damn it, Colin was right. Once you fell, you fell fast. He felt like he'd been KO'd in the ring.

Victoria: Good, I thought I was alone in that.

He'd never cared if the girl missed him either, in fact he preferred that they didn't. Reading her text twisted his stomach in knots, and not in a bad way. It wasn't just about the mind-blowing sex. It was about how she made him feel.

Now he needed to write a fucking Lifetime movie. Thank God his brother and his friends couldn't read his mind. they'd never let him back in the gym because he'd probably woman the place up. Hug instead of throw punches. Jesus.

He called his mom back and let her know to expect Victoria and her girls, then went back to his work with desperate determination. He had to get this job finished, and couldn't do that thinking about Victoria.

§ §

Victoria tried to hide her nervousness from the girls as she knocked on Charlotte's door. She had a bouquet of daisies in her hand, sweet friendly flowers that she hoped Charlotte liked. The door opened to show Luke standing there.

"Hey, Victoria. Hey, girls." Luke walked them through the house.

It was small but very beautifully decorated. It had a modern art deco design that was very pleasing to the idea. Victoria loved the dark purple and cream colors.

"Nick's on his way, got caught up at work and wanted to take a shower before he came."

"It's okay." Victoria lied. She'd really counted on him being here to calm her nerves. Now she'd have to calm herself down.

"Have a seat in here." Luke pointed them toward the open living room. "Mom wants you to relax and not worry about helping. It's not everyday--well, ever--that either of us bring a girl over for dinner."

"Way to put the pressure on me, Luke." Victoria said.

Luke's lips twitched. "Yeah, well, sorry about that. I'm going to see if she needs any help from me, let her know you're here. Relax."

Victoria blew out a breath, glanced at Lucia and Helena. Their faces were priceless.

"Why are you so nervous?" Lucia sat down next to her mom. Helena came and sat on her mom's other side.

Victoria couldn't tell if Helena was happy or not to be here. She kept her thoughts to herself, no anger or attitude, but neither was she smiling. "I don't know."

"Ms. Charlotte already knows you. She likes you, I can tell." Lucia told her. "She's very sweet."

"You're right." Whatever she had to do, Victoria couldn't keep letting her daughters see how nervous she was. She wasn't setting a great example. Besides, they were right, she had no reason to be nervous.

"Hi, sweeties." Charlotte came into the living room with her apron still on over a pale yellow dress. Victoria stood and held out the daisies, smiled. "These are lovely." Charlotte smiled. "They match my dress."

"You're welcome." Lucia piped up while Helena remained quiet.

"Helena, would you mind going to the kitchen and asking Luke for a vase and putting a little water in it? These flowers would be perfect in here." Charlotte smiled extra sweetly at Helena.

Victoria shouldn't have worried about Helena's attitude, because it obviously didn't extend to Charlotte and for that she was grateful. Helena nodded and went to do what Charlotte asked.

"You look amazing." Charlotte grasped Victoria's hand, looking over the navy blue dress that Victoria wore. "I never looked that great after having two boys, and they were different ages."

"That's not true." Victoria's nerves slipped away in the face of Charlotte's loving personality. "You look great."

Charlotte's hand went to her gray pixie-cut. "My hair is taking forever to grow back. But, I'm glad that I can be here to say that. I was extremely lucky to have my sons here to help me."

"They left the MMA circuit to take care of you, didn't they?"

"Yes, and they were my strength during that time. It was hard to accept that I needed to lean on them. Mothers are supposed to be the rock, but my boys...they took over that role and I have trouble now reminding them that I'm okay. I can be their rock again."

"What happened?" Lucia asked.

"Lucia, you can't just ask people that."

"No, it's okay. I don't mind. Children are so curious." Charlotte smiled down at Lucia. "I was diagnosed with breast cancer. My boys took care of me."

Lucia hugged Charlotte. "I'm glad you're okay now."

Charlotte's eyes misted as she looked over at Victoria. "Thank you, sweetie." When Lucia stepped back, Charlotte asked, "Did you like the sign that Nick made you?"

Victoria's mouth fell open and she blinked. "He *made* it? He didn't tell me that."

"Oh." Charlotte's hand went to her chest. "I'm sorry. I thought he did. He's so modest sometimes."

That brought a whole new meaning to the gift for Victoria. He'd not only picked out a thoughtful gift for her, he'd actually taken the time out of his busy schedule to make it. No wonder she'd fallen for that man.

Nick arrived soon after. Victoria drank in the sight of him, still astonished by his mom's revelation. His hair curled against the back of his neck, damp from his shower. He wore jeans and a long sleeve t-shirt that made her want to run her hands up his chest. He grinned at her and when he hugged her close, his cologne made her knees weaken. They hadn't had much alone time lately, and desire rose at the thought of being alone with him again.

Chapter Twenty-Eight

"Hey, girls." Nick grinned at Lucia, then at Helena as she came back in the room with the vase. "School's out for the summer?"

"Yes." Lucia held the daisies while Charlotte cut the stems. "We don't have to get up early for three months."

"That must be nice." Nick reached out and held Victoria's hand. He wanted to take it slow and not freak the girls out, but he couldn't resist touching her, feeling her skin against his in some way. It had been a while since they'd been alone together. It felt like months to him. "My mom never let us sleep in. We were always up at the crack of dawn to do chores."

"You were not." Charlotte laughed at him. "You know that's not true. You'll have these girls believing I was a monster."

Victoria watched when Helena's gaze fell to her and Nick's intertwined hands. Her brows drew together and Victoria braced herself for an outburst. It had to be weird for her daughters to see her with a man other than their father. Luckily, Charlotte distracted them.

"Let's eat. Nick, take them to the dining room. Luke, you help me set the table." Charlotte ordered.

Nick looked down at her, eyes warm, and certainty struck her. This was where she wanted to be. With him. Hopefully Helena would accept that soon.

"Come on." He pulled her down the hall, the girls following.

"You have an amazing home." Victoria told Charlotte after everyone sat down to eat. "The rooms are put together so nicely."

"Thank you. I don't have your eye for design, so I copied it out of a magazine." Charlotte held the bowl of potatoes so that Helena could take some. "It came together like I wanted, though."

"Still, so many people who try to recreate it from magazine and the internet can never pull it off. You made this house look incredible."

Nick watched the two women in his life getting along. Luke grinned at him from across the table. Would Luke start to resent him for dating Victoria when he couldn't get Halle, or would he figure that it would get him closer to her?

"Mom signed me up for a cheer camp and Helena up for math and science camp. It's on different weeks, but we're still excited." Lucia told them. "Mom was a cheerleader in high school."

Nick raised a brow at Victoria. She'd never breathed a word of that. "You were?"

"Yeah, I was. I don't have that kind of flexibility anymore, but I remember a lot of the cheers." Victoria said. "But I won't do any because I'm sure that would only embarrass the girls."

"What do you do in math and science camp, Helena?" Nick looked over at the girl, who had barely engaged with the rest of the group the entire night. Luke had teased a smile out of her a few times, but other than that she kept silent.

"We'll get to look at stars through a telescope. Learn more about space." Helena spoke shyly at first, but the more she talked about the topic she loved, the more she engaged. "Learn about constellations, things like that."

"You haven't said anything about the math." Luke elbowed her in the side.

A small smile lifted her lips. "I'd rather do the science part. I'd be in a science club at school, but they only have a math club."

"There's supposed to be meteor shower tomorrow night." Nick told them. "A friend of mine has a telescope I can borrow."

Helena's face brightened and she actually looked him in the face. "Really? Can we, Mom?"

Victoria smiled. "Sure, baby. Lucia?"

"Yeah, that'd be fun." Lucia agreed.

"Okay, after dinner, I'll call and see if I can pick it up in the morning." Nick tried to ignore his mom's misty eyed smile.

When dinner was over, Victoria thanked his mom with a hug. His mother squeezed her tightly before telling the girls that they needed to come over some during the summer and that she'd take them to the beach. He walked Victoria and the girls to her SUV, and gave her a quick kiss on the cheek. They both wanted to ease the girls into the relationship, so he couldn't kiss her like he really wanted to.

§ §

Victoria watched Helena bounce around the back seat in excitement. Nick sat in the passenger seat, Lucia in the back with Helena, and they headed out to the beach to grab a spot for the meteor shower. In their part of the country it was rare to be able to see shooting stars and luckily enough tonight was bright and clear. Traffic thickened as they headed toward the beach. It seemed they weren't the only ones with the idea to watch it from there.

"Oh my Gosh. I can't believe it!" Helena squealed. "I want to see a million of them!"

Nick looked back at them, grinning. "Maybe you will. The website said that it would be a big shower. The weather couldn't have been better for it, either."

"No clouds, no light pollution on the beach. The mayor put out a newsletter asking for the houses on the beach to turn their outside lights off for a few hours tonight." Victoria told them. She pulled into the public parking lot and searched for a parking space. Many people had beat them there.

This was it. She and Nick were announcing to the rest of the town that they were together and that she'd introduced him to her kids, which was a big step. Lucia and Helena hopped out of the car and Nick went around to the back and grabbed the box for the telescope. He handed the basket he'd packed to Helena and the blanket to Lucia.

"Want me to carry anything?" Victoria asked.

"You want the telescope or the ice chest?" Nick thought for a second. "You can carry the telescope. The ice chest is heavier."

Victoria watched him reach to pull the ice chest out. His t-shirt rose up, showing the muscles in his lower back. Want and need tangled in her body in a sharp rush that took her breath away. She looked away and swallowed. Her daughters didn't need to see her lusting after him.

Nick winked at her, like he knew exactly what she was thinking. "Come on. Let's get a good spot before they're all taken."

They walked to the beach, taking their flip flops off whenever they reached the cool sand. Stars twinkled overhead brightly, and the thumbnail moon hung high in the sky. It took them a minute, but they found a spot near the water, far enough away that the waves wouldn't reach them. Nick and Lucia spread the blanket out.

"Helena, want to help me set up the telescope? I've never done this before." Nick pulled out the instructions and stared at them, flashlight in hand.

"I know how. We learned in class." Helena told him, all signs of animosity gone.

A tenderness hit her for him. He included both her girls in the date. Roger wouldn't even acknowledge them unless it helped him climb the social ladder. Nick was patient and kind with them, and she had no idea how he'd ever doubted that he could handle this. That he'd end up like his father. Charlotte had raised him, and his brother, to be good men.

"Put the tripod out first." Helena told him.

"This is really cool, Mom." Lucia leaned in for a hug. "Helena's having a great time."

"I know, sweetie. It's great for her. And for you." Victoria hugged her close. "You don't mind being out here, do you?"

"Some of the boys from school will be here. And I think it'll be neat to see some falling stars." Lucia glanced over to where Nick and Helena worked on the telescope. "But don't tell her I said that. I'll never get her to stop talking about it."

"It'll be our secret." Victoria cringed inwardly when she thought about Lucia and boys. She'd never be ready for that day.

Once everything was set up, they still had about half an hour before the shower started. When Helena and Lucia saw some of their friends from school they went to talk to them, leaving Nick and Victoria alone on the blanket.

"This is romantic, right? I get points for this?" Nick joked as they sat on the blanket. He kept an eye on the girls while they talked to their group of friends. "You know there are boys over there, don't you?"

Victoria pressed her lips together to hold in her laugh, but failed. "Yes, you get major points for this, Helena is beside herself. I see the boys over there, sir, and I see you keeping an eye on them."

He looked over at her. "Do you mind that? I'm not trying to step in and take over or anything. I just know what I was thinking, even at that age, and your daughters are pretty. Like their mother."

Under his joking manner, she could tell his question was serious. "I don't mind. I see how protective you are of your mother, even your brother, and I think it's sweet."

"Good, because I wasn't sure if I was overstepping boundaries or something." Nick grabbed a Coke out of the ice chest. "I'm so new at this. I don't know what I should or shouldn't do."

She grabbed his hand, squeezed. "You're doing an amazing job so far. If you did something wrong, I'd let you know. I have a feeling you won't, though. You're mom is an amazing and strong women. She raised you right."

"Thank you." Nick rubbed his thumb over the back of her hand. Chills slid up her arm. "Most people don't realize how amazing she is. They just see her as the woman whose husband ran out on her and left her with two rowdy boys."

"They're blind and damn stupid if that's all they see when they look at her." Victoria frowned. "She did an awesome job raising you two, especially without any help."

"I'll tell her you said that." Nick leaned close and brushed his lips softly over hers. "Tonight, after the girls go to bed, I want to show you how much I've missed you."

The chills spread up her neck. She bit her lip and breathed in his scent, mixed with the salty sea air. "Good, because I've missed you too."

His slow grin made her want to forget about the meteor shower and rush home. She knew she couldn't, so she reminded herself that the anticipation only made it better in the end.

Closer to the start time of the shower, the girls wandered back and grabbed something to drink.

"Lucia's crush was over there." Helena told them. Lucia's eyes widened and she slapped her sister on the arm.

"Shut up." Lucia's face reddened.

"Oh? Who is it?" Victoria stifled a grin. "If I look now, will it completely embarrass you?"

"Yes, Mom." Lucia hissed. "Please don't, he's looking over here."

Nick peeked over Victoria's shoulder. "Which one? Is he the one with the Beiber haircut or the one in khaki shorts and blue t-shirt?"

"Oh my God." Lucia hid her face in her hands. "The one in the shorts. Stop looking, Nick. You're going to scare him away."

Nick looked back at Lucia. "Do I need to?"

"No!" Lucia laughed. "He's sweet. This is the first time he's talked to me."

"He can actually tell the two of us apart." Helena popped a green olive in her mouth. "Even when we're not together."

"That's impressive." Victoria admitted. "Not too many people can do that."

"Is it time yet, Mom?" Helena asked, eyes brimming with excitement.

Nick looked at his cell phone. "It's going to start in about a minute. You want to get next to the telescope so you can get the first look?"

"Sure." Helena bounced up. "You don't mind?"

"Nope. You're the science wizard." Nick told her.

"Yes!" Helena stood behind the telescope and waited.

When the shower started five minutes later, only one or two falling stars appeared over ten minutes. Then, they started shooting across the sky. The sight was breathtaking, the ocean dark beneath the sky, with falling stars shooting past. Helena laughed and pointed, then dipped her head back to watch them through the lens.

After fifteen minutes, Helena reluctantly switched with Lucia. Lucia's face glowed as she watched the sky. Nick held Victoria's hand and Victoria smiled to herself. Tonight was perfect, something she hadn't had in a very long time. Even the girls enjoyed themselves.

To see them this happy, over something so small, warmed her heart.

The shower ended around one in the morning and the girls tried to keep their eyes open as they walked back to the car. Nick carried the ice chest and blanket, while Victoria carried the telescope and basket.

The girls fell asleep in the car, so Nick and Victoria stayed silent on the ride home. Once they got inside, the girls sleepily thanked Nick for taking them, then headed upstairs to pass out. Victoria looked at Nick, a sensuous grin on her face.

"Maybe we should wait an hour, make sure they're asleep?"

"We can lock the bedroom door." She leaned into him, whispered in his ear. "I can be quiet. Can you?"

Nick sucked in a breath, his arms coming up to her shoulders. "Lead the way, baby."

She shut the bedroom door behind them, locked it. Nick came up behind her, hands going to her ponytail. He pulled her hair down slowly, nuzzling her neck. She couldn't breathe with how much she wanted him. His hardness pressed against the small of her back.

His fingers tucked under the edge of her shirt and pulled it over her head. He discarded it, then ran his hands back down her body. She shivered. "I love the feel of your skin. Nothing turns me on more."

She wanted to turn around, but he kept her against the door. He unhooked her bra from the back and her breasts spilled out. The shock of the cold against her warm skin sent heat spiraling through her. When he nipped her shoulder with his teeth, her lips parted.

"I've thought of being inside you all week." Nick brought his hands around to the front of her shorts, unbuttoned them. He pulled her shorts and lace panties down at the same time.

There was something insanely erotic about being naked and pressed against the cold door while he was fully clothed. She wanted him inside her now, could feel the wetness between her legs, and tried to tell him that.

"Shh. I want to see if you can really keep quiet." Nick kissed the side of her neck, his tongue lapping out. His hands slid around to her chest and he tweaked her nipples.

A low moan rose in Victoria's throat. Her knees weakened. Nick wrapped his arm around her waist to keep her up. His other hand slowly traveled lower, torturing her with the wait.

"Fuck, you're wet." His voice deepened, grew rough as his fingers pushed inside her.

She whimpered, biting her lip to keep quiet. He didn't stop moving his fingers in and out, and brought her to an orgasm so fast she had to clamp a hand over her mouth to keep from screaming.

Nick spun her around, not giving her time to catch her breath, and kissed her hard, his tongue slipping into her mouth. She loved the taste of him on her tongue, the way his kiss could light a fire in her. Her arms went around his neck, her legs around his waist. He kept the kiss going, stoking that fire, as he walked to the bed and laid her down. He threw his clothes off, then settled his weight over her.

"Nick. Please." Victoria whispered. She wrapped her hand around his hot cock, loving the silken feel over the hardness. She gripped him, twisting her wrist.

"Tori." He choked out. "Damn it, I need to be inside of you." He pinned her hands above her head after he slid a condom on. "Keep your eyes on mine. I want to watch what you look like when I push you over the edge."

His dominance sent a delicious thrill through her. She arched against him, knowing there was no way she could look away. He owned her, his gaze holding her prisoner, like his body, and all she wanted was for him to push inside her, let her feel that fullness. Her body craved it more than anything else.

When he--finally--pushed inside her, still holding her hands above her head, he groaned. The muscles in his neck tightened as he held himself still. "Give me a second. Fuck, you're so tight and wet. I've got to get control."

Victoria moved her hips, slid up his cock.

His pupils dilated. "Tori."

"I don't want you to stay in control. Fuck me, Nick."

His brows raised until she moved again. His eyes slammed shut. "Fine. If that's what you want." He thrust hard, pushing her into the mattress.

"Yes." Victoria tilted her head back. Her legs went around his waist, tightened around him. "Harder. Now." She didn't know when this sex kitten personality was born, but she'd be embarrassed about it later. Right now, she wanted Nick to move.

His thrusts quickened, his breath panted against her neck as he did what she asked. Her body tightened underneath him. Every movement, every sensation, boiled over and she came, harder than she ever had.

Nick's breath caught as she tightened around his cock. He thrusted three more times, hard, before his head leaned back and he came inside her.

Victoria sucked in air, tried to catch her breath. Her lungs gasped for oxygen like she'd just run a marathon. Her legs shook, felt like jelly, so she didn't even try to move. Nick settled on his side, propped up on an elbow, his other arm draped over her hip.

He kissed her shoulder. "That was phenomenal."

She nodded and tried to force her eyes to stay open. "Yes. It was. I really need to get cleaned up so I can put some clothes on."

"Why would you want to do that?" Nick rolled her over on her back. "I'm not finished with you yet."

Chapter Twenty-Nine

Victoria's newly finished, renovated office now glittered with life for the office warming party. Lights hung in the air and added an atmosphere of glam to the room. She and Ella had invited some of her regular clients, like Rachel and Mae, and a few she hoped would be future clients.

Lucia and Helena stood with Victoria's parents, holding flutes of sparkling grape juice. Wes had no problem with spending good money on champagne and finger foods for the party. The dark gray wall and white trim stood out against the dark hardwood floors, and the chandelier hung above the people, twinkling. She loved the elegant feel of the place and was so glad it was what she picked out.

"Congratulations." Rachel tapped her flute of champagne to Victoria's. "The place looks marvelous."

She looked around the room, full of people she cared about, and peace enveloped her. Near her parents and the twins, Nick talked with his brother and Halle. The cut of his charcoal gray suit hugged his muscles and made his blue eyes pop. She couldn't believe she'd fallen for him. "I've had a lot of help.

From you and the others. You gave me a chance, let me stage homes for you." She willed herself not to let the tears fall, not to ruin her make-up.

"And look how well it worked out for me. Those homes sold way faster than the others I had." Rachel waved to Ella, who chatted up a potential client. "And my niece now has a job as your assistant. It came full circle."

"It did." Victoria beamed. "Everything seemed to work out for the best."

Rachel lifted an eyebrow at Nick, then grinned. "Yes, you've got a hottie on the side."

Victoria kept her smile until Rachel walked off to talk to someone else, then let it fall. Some of her peace vanished. Is that what people thought? That she and Nick were just…screwing around? Was that how everyone saw it but her? What if Nick thought that way? She shook her head. Nick had been nothing but honest with her, and she knew he'd kept nothing from her. He believed, like she did, in total honesty.

"Why are you frowning?" Nick asked as he put his hand on her waist. The heat from his hand burned through her dress. "This is a special night."

Victoria forced herself to forget her murky thoughts. This was a special night, and she'd worked hard for it. "No reason. I'm just realizing how lucky I am."

A corner of Nick's mouth curved upward. "You can get lucky later."

Victoria rolled her eyes. "Stop." She couldn't help but laugh. "Someone might hear you."

"And that would be bad?" His mischievous grin lightened her mood.

"Yes. I'm supposed to be a professional, remember?" She spotted Halle and Luke deep in conversation, saw her sister's glow. "Have you noticed the way your brother is with Halle?" It was the same way Nick looked at her.

Nick rubbed the back of his neck. "Not really. He's just friendly."

"You think?" Victoria tried not to frown. Maybe everyone else saw them correctly, and Nick did just think they were messing around. But, she wouldn't focus on this tonight. "He doesn't seem to like Trevor very much. Every time he comes around, Luke walks away. And it looks like he's angry each time."

"I haven't really noticed that."

Nick's voice sounded weird to her. She looked up at him, but his expression gave nothing away. That still didn't alleviate the churning in her stomach. Nick was hiding something. "There's my mom. I need to ask her something." She didn't wait on his response before she walked away.

§ §

Nick watched her walk away, his gut burning. He knew she could tell something was off, but he couldn't go against his brother's wishes. Luke didn't want anyone to know how he felt about Halle while she was still with her cheating husband, and he didn't want Nick to be the one to tell her or her family about Trevor's indiscretions. Luke didn't want that to shadow how Victoria felt about Nick or a future with Halle for himself.

It didn't seem right, though. He wanted to tell Victoria so she could soften the blow for when Halle found out, or warn her in the first place, so there weren't any secrets between them. The way she'd looked at him before she walked away twisted his heart. The ground was shifting underneath his feet and he had no solid ground to stand on. He didn't like it at all.

Charlotte joined him. "What is it?"

"Nothing." Nick shoved his hands in his pockets. "I'm just adjusting."

She kissed his cheek, eyes full of love. "That's life, baby. We were made to adapt to what goes on around us."

"Yeah, I'm beginning to understand that." He watched Victoria mingle with the people there. She moved with a confidence, a self-assuredness that he loved. She'd had such a solid foundation growing up. Could he adapt his ways to fit in with hers? Would she be able to adapt hers to his? Did she understand that this was all new to him, and the he was still learning how to be in a relationship? He'd only ever been in one-night stands.

"What are you thinking about so hard?" Addie came up beside him, handed him a beer. "You're watching my sister kind of closely. Should I file a restraining order?"

He heard the humor in her voice. "No. Just amazed by her."

Addie nodded. "Finally, a man that appreciates how awesome she is. You know, I've never seen her look at Roger the way she looks at you. It's almost nauseating. She sneaks peeks every few minutes like she's afraid you'll disappear."

"She does?" Nick looked down at Addie. Could Victoria feel the same way?

"Hmmhm." Addie grinned at him. "You look at her the same way. So I say this warning with less violence than I normally would. If you break my sister's heart, I will cut your balls off and make them into a necklace."

Nick's eyebrow's rose. "That was less violence?"

She patted his shoulder. "Go hang out with my sister."

When he approached, Victoria smiled up at him. It seemed she'd forgotten whatever had bothered her earlier.

"Hey, Nick." Halle beamed over at him. Flirting with his brother looked good on her.

"Everyone, I'd like to propose a toast." Wes tapped on the side of his flute. The patrons of the party grew quiet. "Come here, Victoria."

Victoria joined her father by the receptionist counter. Nick thought the pink blooming on her cheeks was adorable. Beside her stood her mother and daughters.

"Now, I want to toast to my beautiful daughter, Victoria. She always loved to decorate things, even as a little girl. Even decorated my tool box, which I used every day of my career. Every time I saw it," Wes smiled down at Victoria, "I knew she'd have a successful career doing what she loved."

"Dad..." Victoria's eyes watered. Beside her, her mom's and daughters' did too. In fact, Nick saw that almost every single one of the women's eyes were teary.

"Let me finish, sweetheart." Wes cleared his throat, fighting off his own tears. "You have worked hard to get here, and I want you to know that we are so proud of you." He raised his glass.

The crowd burst into applause. Nick smiled widely as Wes wrapped Victoria in a bear hug. Charlotte put her arm through the crook of his elbow and leaned her head on his shoulder. "You picked a great one."

"I definitely did." Nick agreed.

After the party, Nick and Victoria took the girls home. He was surprised at how easily he'd come to think of her house as *home*. Uneasiness snuck in and he wondered if it was supposed to be that easy? To just slide into love?

The girls went straight to bed. Nick stood in the kitchen watching Victoria place the dishes she'd brought back from the party into the sink. It wasn't too late in the evening, but Nick could tell by the droop of her shoulders that she was exhausted.

"Baby, don't worry about that right now." Nick took the dish from her. "Let's go to bed." He kissed the top of her head. "We'll clean up tomorrow."

Victoria nodded against his chest. "'Kay."

He led her into the bedroom, making sure she didn't fall asleep while they changed. After he crawled in, he held the covers up so she could slide in with him. She laid her head on his chest and snuggled up against him. It was the most perfect thing he'd ever felt. "Is everything okay?"

She didn't say anything at first and he tensed. Then, "Yeah. I just got a little overwhelmed."

His fingertips rubbed her shoulder. "From the party or from me?"

"The party." She sighed, her breath fanning over his chest. "And you, a little." She pushed up so that she could see him. "I just got out of a long relationship with a person that didn't care about me. I'm a little freaked that I might make that mistake again. You dazzle me, and I can't think straight when it comes to you."

Thoughts tumbled around in his mind. Could he promise not to be a mistake for her? "Tori, I'm not sure exactly what I'm feeling because I've never felt it before. But I do know for sure, you will always be a priority to me. Your needs and wants already come before mine." His thumb brushed her lower lip. "I can't get you out of my head. I don't want to."

Her eyes shone and when she blinked, a tear fell. "That's...wow. That's the most amazing thing anyone has ever said to me."

He leaned up and kissed her softly. "I may not be able to serenade you with Shakespeare, but I can be honest about how I feel."

"I like your words better." She rested her head back down and fell asleep within minutes.

Nick rubbed her back in small circles, and thought about what he'd said. He'd never meant something so much in his life. It was like being in the ring. On one hand, he was the winner, feeling the rush of elation overtake him and in the other, he was the one flat on his ass. Which way would this end up?

Chapter Thirty

Victoria smiled over the stargazer lilies Nick had delivered for her first day at the office. It was the beginning of the week and the beginning of the first day of her big girl career. She had her own office. Even had her own assistant. Ella was invaluable already.

"Those are so pretty. I'm literally going to die of jealousy." Ella sighed. She had her brown hair pulled up in a sophisticated bun and wore natural make-up that made her moss green eyes stand out. "None of my boyfriends have ever given me flowers."

"I can't believe that. You're gorgeous." Victoria stood next to the counter and looked at the calendar. "Are you seeing anyone in town?"

Ella fiddled with the edge of the calendar. "No, I broke up with my boyfriend before I came here. He wanted me to move to Los Angeles with him, but I wanted something closer to home. I didn't want to be that far from my family."

"He didn't understand that?" Victoria asked.

"No. I offered a long distance thing, but he was the jealous type so he said it was either I move or we were done." Ella put on a smile. "Anyway, he's long gone. I'm sure there are some hot men here I could try out."

Victoria smiled back, hoping to bring her spirits up. "Just don't tell your aunt that."

"I won't." Ella pointed to the calendar. "Here are the appointments I've made. We're really starting to get some calls. I also wanted to talk to you about making a new website, with your address and number for the office. We could put pictures of your past work up. That will help draw people in. Some testimonials."

"That's a great idea, Ella." Victoria told her.

"Good. I took some classes in marketing when I went through massage courses. Just give me a few hours." Ella checked the date. "You have an appointment with Ms. Mae at one. I have the concept folder that you made for her on your desk."

"Thanks, Ella." Victoria went into her private office and sat behind the white desk. It had taken her so many years to get here. So much hard work, long nights, worry that she wouldn't make it. She wanted to savor the moment. Roger had constantly talked her down, told her she'd never accomplish anything without him. It took everything she had to not call him up and shout to him that she had and she'd flourished without his negativity. The only thing that kept her from doing it was the girls. She didn't want to cause anymore rancor from Helena. The past week had been nice, no tantrums, no hateful spite. Hopefully that wouldn't change when the girls went to Roger's for a few days.

He hadn't said anything to her since the argument at her house. She'd gotten no phone calls from him, no uninvited visits. In fact, he'd asked through Helena if he could get them the next few days. Maybe her words had changed something in him, because before he never would've offered to get them. And even then he would've acted like it was such a hardship to spend time with them.

Some men just weren't worth the time it took to fall in love.

Later that day, after her meeting with Mae, she picked the girls up from Addie's, then headed home. They needed to pack their bags before Roger got there. She and Nick were going to celebrate her first day at work with dinner and she couldn't wait. She'd miss the girls but looked forward to spending some alone time with Nick.

Roger waited on the doorstep with his car parked in the driveway. Victoria wasn't sure if he did it on purpose, but now she had to park on the street to her own house and wait until he left to park in her own driveway.

"You're late."

Seriously? Victoria ignored him and unlocked the front door. She wasn't late, for once in his life he was early. "Girls, get your bags packed."

They rushed upstairs.

"You're seeing that Nick guy." Roger put a hand on her arm. "He's not good enough to be around the girls."

Victoria shook his hand off. So he hadn't gotten over that. "Nick is a great man, and he actually loves spending time with the girls."

"What is that supposed to mean?" Roger's hazel eyes narrowed. "I love being with the girls. Did I not offer to come get them for a few days?"

"Yes." Victoria crossed her arms. "And why is that? I normally have to beg you to spend time with them. Is it because Nick is doing a better job at being a father than you are?"

"He is nothing but a piece of trash. His own father didn't want him."

Victoria's hand connected with Roger's cheek before she even thought about it. Her eyes widened, but the only thing she was sorry for was that she hadn't balled her fist up first. "Get out of my house. You are a miserable piece of shit. Don't *ever* talk about him like that again."

Roger touched his cheek gingerly. "You hit me."

Victoria opened the door. "I slapped you, stop being such a damn baby. You deserved more than that. Wait for the girls in your car."

"Victoria--"

"Now." She hissed. "Do not come back inside this house for any reason." She resisted the urge to slam the door behind him. Who the hell did he think he was, saying stuff like that about Nick? How could he even mention Nick's father when he was hardly one to judge?

"Bye, Mom." Lucia hugged her. Victoria forced down her anger and wrapped her arms around Lucia.

"Bye, baby. Have a good time. Don't hesitate to call me if you need me." Victoria opened her arms and pulled Helena close. "I love you."

"Love you." Helena squeezed, then was out the door without a look back.

Lucia waved, then shut the door behind her.

Victoria stood in the foyer, listening to the silent house. The entire atmosphere felt different with the girls gone. There was something about knowing they weren't going to be here for a few days that made Victoria's heart heavy. She'd missed them so much.

To pass the time until Nick got there, Victoria picked up a novel she'd started almost four months ago and curled up in her chair. Nick walked in a little while later.

"What's going on, Belle? Beast run out on you?" Nick leaned against the side of her chair.

"Ha, ha." Victoria shut the book and set it on the bookshelf behind her. "I needed something to do to take my mind off the girls."

Nick pulled her up. "Well, I can help with that after dinner. You do know it's six o'clock, right?"

What?" Victoria's gaze snapped to the yellow clock on the wall. "No. Let me jump in the shower. I'll hurry."

Nick grinned. "I'm going to watch TV until you're done."

Victoria rushed through her shower, halfway dried her hair before throwing it up in a messy ponytail, and threw on some clothes. Nick looked up when she entered the living room. The look in his eyes sent a thrill through her.

"You look perfect."

"Don't lie." Victoria laughed. "I don't even have make up on."

"You don't need it." Nick kissed her, pulling her close. "What do you want to eat?"

"I don't care."

Nick gave her a look. "You know you do. I can eat anything, so you pick."

"I hate all these decisions." Victoria shrugged. "I could really go for a burger and fries."

"Stop my beating heart." Nick placed a hand over his chest. "You are so romantic."

She slapped his arm. "I'm serious. It's what I want."

"Then that's what you'll get."

Nick picked a small diner that he said served the best burgers. They sat in a checkered booth near the back. Not many people were there, most were probably eating on the boardwalk for tourist season.

Not all of the shops stayed open year round. "Have you ever been here?"

Victoria looked around. "Once, a long time ago."

"They serve the best food. You'll love their burgers." He linked their fingers together on the table as he looked at the menu. The waitress came to take their order. "I want a Southwestern burger, fries, and a Coke."

Victoria glanced over the menu. "I'll have the bacon cheeseburger, fries and a sweet tea."

"Good choices." The buxom waitress winked at Nick as she left.

"Don't give me that look." Nick squeezed her hand. "I've never met her before."

"That's not why I'm giving you that look." She leaned back in the booth. "It's just ridiculous how many women throw themselves at you."

Fire pooled in her abdomen at his intimate look. Like he wanted to devour her. "I only see you."

She could tell he spoke the truth, especially when he looked at her like that. He made her want him in the worst way. She needed to change the subject so she could focus on food. "How is the remodel on the kitchen going?"

"We just started today, so we've only started gutting it. That'll take a day or two, then we'll start making the cabinets she wants. I started on some for another customer, but I'll have to put those on hold for a week or two." Nick thanked the waitress when she brought their drinks. True to his word, he didn't look away from Victoria.

"How's your mom?" Victoria asked. She sipped out of the straw and watched Nick's eyes narrow on her mouth.

"Fine. She's fine." Nick cleared his throat. "If you keep doing that, we're going to miss dinner."

Victoria bit her lip and squeezed her thighs together against the sudden ache. How did he make her think of sex constantly?

"Tori, I'm serious." He whispered across the table. "I'm holding myself back right now, because we both need dinner. We're supposed to be celebrating."

She sent him a sexy smile. "I can think of better ways to celebrate."

He cursed under his breath, his fingers tightening around hers. Electricity seemed to jump between their hands and run up her arm. "You're killing me."

Teasing him like this gave her a surge of power. She loved how she affected him, how she made him crave her. That kind of power was addicting.

The waitress brought their food and they scarfed it down, paid, and ran to the truck. Victoria giggled at the crazy way she acted, but she was high on life. She'd finally opened her office, she had a hot, gentle man, and her girls were finally happy. Nothing could ruin tonight.

His hand stayed on her upper thigh on the drive home. Every few minutes he would gently squeeze and she'd bite her lip. The anticipation was killing her. Finally, they turned into the neighborhood. The truck lights illuminated a car in her driveway.

"That's Halle's car." Victoria's heart sank. "She wouldn't come over unless something was wrong. She knew we were going out tonight."

As soon as Nick parked the truck, she threw the door open. Halle sat on the porch steps, head in her hands. She still wore her scrubs, so she hadn't even been home. When Victoria heard the sobs, she ran to the porch. "Halle?" Victoria knelt down beside her sister. Halle's shoulders shook. When she glanced up at Victoria, mascara ran down her cheeks. "Halle, what happened?"

Halle's eyes were red and puffy, her nose running. "Trevor." Her voice cracked.

"Was he in an accident?" Victoria helped her stand. "Do I need to call Mom and Dad?"

"No!" Halle shook her head. A flash of anger shot through her eyes. "I wish the bastard was dead."

Victoria shot Nick a look as she unlocked her front door. He followed them in, standing awkwardly while Victoria led Halle to the couch. "What happened?"

Halle took a few deep breaths, like she was gearing herself up for the words. "I walked in on him at the office." She sobbed again. "How was I so damn blind? So stupid?"

Victoria looked to Nick and he pointed toward the door. She mouthed "sorry" to him and he shook his head. She figured he understood and that it would be uncomfortable for him to sit while Halle hated on men.

Chapter Thirty-One

Victoria rubbed Halle's back in soothing circles. Halle's sobs shook her body and Victoria wanted to kill Trevor with her. From what she was able to piece together from Halle's words, Halle had walked in on Trevor and one of the nurses from the office. She'd gone home, forgot her cell phone, and gone back to get it. Apparently, Trevor and the nurse, Jenna, were getting freaky in one of the exam rooms.

"What am I supposed to do now? That's my job, the only place I've ever worked." Halle took deep breaths, tried to calm the sobs. "That lying bastard."

"He is a bastard. Halle, I'm so sorry."

Halle wiped the tears from her eyes. Victoria went and got her a warm washcloth to wipe off the mascara that ran down her cheeks. "I can't believe he'd do this to me."

Victoria sat back down, her heart in her stomach. Her sister was hurting, therefore she was too. "Do you want me to call Addie?"

Halle nodded. "I need a bitchfest right now. I want chocolate, wine, and ice cream and I want to punch that fucker in the face."

"Done." Victoria sent the text to Addie. "You can stay here as long as you need. I have plenty of room. You're not planning on going back to him are you?" Please, please don't go back to him.

"Hell no. But that house is mine. I decorated it, I'm the one who spends time in it every night. If he thinks I'm giving it up, he's lost his damn mind."

"That's my girl." Victoria took Halle's hand. "I hate him. I'm sure Addie will punch him in the face for you."

"It wouldn't be nearly as satisfying." Halle's chin wobbled and tears started falling again. "Why can't I stop?"

"Because your husband is a cheating bastard and no matter what anyone says, you did love him and it hurts."

"I knew." Halle shook her head, pissed at herself. "I *knew* deep down, but I ignored it. I thought, that can't happen to me. We're perfect for each other. Like a fairy tale."

"No one wants to think that the person they love would do that to them." Victoria said, sadness in her voice. "It still hurts just as bad. Don't try to stop crying. You need to get it out, get the hurt out until you get mad. Then we can get your house back."

"I feel so humiliated. It was right under my nose! He was having his affair, more than likely many, right there in the office. Was it going on the whole time? Did he have sex with me before or after he left them?" Halle sucked in a breath. "It feels like someone is sitting on my chest. I'm going to throw up."

Victoria's eyes welled up when Halle ran to the bathroom and vomited. Her heart ached for her, she hated seeing her like this. She checked her phone.

Addie- Wtf?! Be there in 5.

Good, Victoria thought. She sent Nick a quick text, apologizing for cutting their night short, even though she knew he understood. Halle sat back down, holding a cold washcloth to her forehead.

"I'm sorry. Just the thought--"

"Don't think about that." Victoria rubbed her arm. "You shouldn't be humiliated. He's the dickhead who couldn't keep it in his pants. None of this is your fault."

Addie didn't knock, just came in the front door carrying several grocery bags. "I've got chocolate, ice cream, and Jack Daniels. Wine was too tame for this. We're going to get this going right now."

Halle sniffed. "Thanks, Addie."

"No problem." She took the bags into the kitchen. "Get your asses in here and we'll begin."

Victoria's eyes rounded as Addie pulled three shot glasses out of one of the bags and set them on the counter. "Oh no."

"Shut it." Addie said. "Our sister needs us. She can't drink alone and if there was ever a time to drink, it's now."

"True." Victoria agreed. She grabbed some bowls and dished out the ice cream. "The girls are with their dad, so it should be fine."

"Damn right." Halle bit her lip when it wobbled. "I refuse to cry again. At least for tonight. I just want to forget it."

"Your wish is my command." Addie filled each shot glass up. "Cheers."

They tapped the glasses together before throwing them back.

Half of the bottle in, the doorbell rang. Victoria set her spoon down. It was after nine, so she wondered who it could be. "I'll get it." She opened the door without checking, something she got on to her daughters all the time for, and blinked when she saw

Trevor standing on the porch. For a moment she just stared, let him squirm. The man was attractive, tall and blond, with bright blue eyes. The fact that he was a doctor only inflated his ego more. He held a bouquet of roses and a box of chocolate. Did he honestly think that was all it took to make up for being a sleazy manwhore?

"Is Halle here?"

"She doesn't want to see you." Victoria glared out at him. "You need to leave."

"I have to talk to her. Tell her I'm sorry." Trevor pulled a puppy dog face.

That wasn't going to work, was he serious? "Maybe you should've thought about that before you cheated on her."

His puppy dog expression vanished, his face turning red. The cruelty in his eyes made her uneasy, but the Jack Daniels made her forget it. "I'm her husband. I demand to speak to her."

Victoria let her bitch laugh out. "I don't think you have that right. Not anymore."

"Is there a problem?" Addie came up beside Victoria. Now they presented a united front, blocking him from getting inside.

"Where is she?" He grit his teeth, hands tightening on the roses.

"I believe Victoria told you to leave. I'm going to give you one minute to do what she asks." Addie said.

"Look, you little bitch--"

Addie swung, connected with his jaw. Trevor crumpled to the ground, crushing the roses. "That's a warning, you stupid bastard. Go. Away!"

Victoria turned to Addie, her mouth hanging open. She didn't know whether to cheer or laugh.

"Holy shit. You hit me." Trevor rubbed his jaw, all semblance of tough guy gone.

"It'll be worse if you don't leave. I'm going to go inside, shut the door, and wait. If you aren't gone by the time I look back out, I'm grabbing my gun and I will shoot your dick off." Addie pointed. "Now go."

Once inside, Victoria let the laugh out. "Oh my God. You punched him in the face!"

"I can't believe that!" Halle ran from the kitchen and jumped on Addie, hugging her. "You are the best sister ever."

"I know." Addie shook her hand. "Can I get some ice? I can't feel it right now because of Jack, but I want to get a handle on the swelling."

"That was amazing!" Victoria grinned. "I didn't think you'd actually do it. And shoot him? Do you even own a gun?"

"No." Addie smirked. "But he doesn't know that."

Later that night, after Halle was tucked away in the guest bedroom, Addie and Victoria sat on the couch with the TV on. Neither paid attention to it, but both wanted the background noise.

"She's going to hurt for a long time over this." Victoria rubbed her forehead. The alcohol was beginning to wear off and the headache was starting. "She didn't deserve this. She needs someone who will love her for real. Respect her, give her everything of themselves."

"We all thought Trevor was a good guy in the beginning. I think the fact that he had an MD behind his name made him feel invincible. I'd like to find the little whore Halle saw him fucking and break her face." Addie sipped her water. "This is why I'm never getting married. Men aren't raised to be gentleman like they used to be, back in Dad's generation."

"No kidding." Victoria agreed, although she hoped Nick was better than the others. "Should we call Mom and Dad or let her tell them?"

"I don't know. She may want some time to wallow before Mom and Dad get involved." Addie said. "We'll ask her in the morning."

"I'm glad she never had kids with him. I know she wants them, but it only makes the process harder. Although Roger never cheated on me. That I know of."

"He doesn't seem like the smartest person. You would've known."

"True." Victoria sipped her own water. She needed to get hydrated for work tomorrow. "I just hope she doesn't decide in the morning that she can forgive him."

"We won't let her. We'll protect her from making that colossal mistake." Addie promised.

Chapter Thirty-Two

Victoria knocked on the open door of Nick's shop. Since Halle was staying at the house the last few nights, they'd hardly had any time for each other. She didn't blame Halle, and neither did Nick, but she missed him. She drank in the sight of him in holey jeans and gray t-shirt. He had on a pair of the most adorable black, thick framed glasses. The way he mumbled to himself as he worked made her heart turn over.

"Nick?"

His head shot up and when he saw her his face lit up in a sweet smile. "Hey, baby."

She stepped inside, curious to see what the area he worked in looked like. "I hope you don't mind. I wanted to see you before I went home."

He dropped the pencil, crossed to her, and pulled her into a hot kiss. "Of course I don't mind. I'm just working on measurements for a lady's cabinets."

"I've missed you." She ran her arms up and down his back. Being in his arms brought her stress level down.

"I've missed you." Nick tilted her chin up and kissed her again. "How's Halle?"

"As good as can be expected, I guess." Victoria said. "She's still hurting pretty badly. The anger hasn't set in yet."

"That guy needs to be shot. Luke told me about Jenna a few months ago." Nick said.

Victoria stilled. Then she pulled away and looked at him with an incredulous stare. "You knew? For a few months?" Her voice rose on the last word.

Nick's face twisted with confusion. "Yeah. The guys at the gym talk about it."

"They *talk* about it? And you didn't say anything to me?" The anger rose in her voice. She stepped back from him, needing some physical space to digest this. He'd kept something from her, something so important.

"I didn't know how to bring it up." Nick shrugged. "I don't understand why you're so mad."

Victoria shook her head in amazement. "How can you not understand? You kept it from me. You heard people talking about my sister, behind her back, a whole freaking gym of men, and you couldn't say anything to me? I thought we didn't have secrets, that we'd always be honest."

He winced and crossed his arms. "I have been honest. I've never lied to you."

"But you *kept* it from me. It's called a *lie* of omission. It's my sister. That's a big thing to keep from me."

"Just calm down, we can work this out."

Her head snapped up and the fire in her eyes told him he said the wrong thing.

"Calm down?" She threw her hands up in the air. "You can't expect me to calm down. You weren't honest." She knew she kept repeating the same thing, but damn it, that lie hurt her. It also hurt her sister. What was Halle going to say when she found out? "You didn't just hurt me, you hurt Halle, too. You let this keep going on, all the while you slept with me, promising not to lie."

Nick leaned back against the table. His jaw flexed, but he didn't say anything in his defense.

Maybe he didn't want to, she thought. Maybe she'd been wishing for more, and he'd only led her on. "I should've know this wasn't going to work."

"What does that mean?" He stood again, posture stiff.

"You've never been in a real relationship. You don't know *how* to respect your partner. Maybe you didn't even want to be in a real relationship." Pain burned in her eyes. "Maybe you only wanted me to be another notch."

Her lack of faith in him snapped his temper and shredded deep in his chest. He could just tell her about Luke making him promise, but did she deserve that? Now that she was telling him what she really thought about him, ripping through his emotions? "Maybe you were." The flash of pure anguish on her face cut him, but he kept going. He needed to hurt her like she hurt him. "Maybe I didn't want to be tied down."

Victoria gasped at his words, the pain tearing through her. "I see." She steadied herself. "I guess you're right."

Instantly he wanted to take it back, to show her that's not what he meant, to tell her everything. But it was too late. She was already walking away from him.

"Don't call me, don't show up at my house. I'm done." She called over her shoulder softly.

He could hear the tears choking her voice. His chest heaved. To survive the pain, he focused on his anger. How the fuck did she think he wasn't being honest with her? She was the only one he'd been honest with. He'd been prepared to change his life to be with her. What a damn idiot he'd been. All women, besides his mother, were crazy bitches. Thank God he'd seen the real her before they'd gotten too serious.

Adrenaline coursed through his body. As he stood there, he realized why he felt so hurt. He thought she believed in him, that she'd at least give him a chance to explain himself. She'd railroaded him and by the time he could've explained, he'd been too hurt and angry to say so. So instead, she'd believed the worst in him from the second he'd opened his mouth.

He was fooling himself if he thought he was getting any work done. He needed the gym, needed to spar. While he was there, he could kick Luke's ass for getting him into this mess. If Luke hadn't been so fixed on having Nick keep the shit a secret, he could've been honest with Victoria.

When he walked into the gym, Luke took one look at his face and tried to duck. Nick's fist slammed into Luke's mouth, blood flying.

"What the hell?" Luke stumbled backward. "What the fuck did I do to you?"

"Damnit. It's your fault Victoria's pissed at me." Nick breathed hard through his nose. He couldn't hit Luke again without starting a real fight and right now, he wasn't sure he could stop if he started.

"Why would Victoria be mad at you because of me? Luke swiped a hand across his mouth. He gestured to the employees that stood nearby, waiting to break up the fight. Gym goers went back to their workouts.

"Because Halle caught her fucking husband with that girl and now Victoria's mad I didn't tell her, because you wanted me to keep it a secret!" Nick forced through clenched teeth. "Which it doesn't fucking matter now. Victoria's too damn snobby to believe anything I say. She doesn't want to see me anymore. That's fine. That's fucking fine with me."

Luke watched Nick's tirade with his hands on his hips, waiting on Nick to blow off steam. When Nick stopped, Luke raised his brows. "Is that what you really want?"

"Yes." Nick swallowed the hurt. "Because she didn't have faith in me. She didn't trust me, even after knowing me."

"You're sure?" Luke asked.

"Yeah. I need to fucking hit something."

"It won't be me a second time. I'll hit back. And I'm not letting you loose on my customers either. I want them to come back." Luke steered him toward the punching bags. "So, do you know if Halle's leaving her husband?"

"Fuck off, Luke, or I'll forget you're not a punching bag."

Luke backed away with his hands in front of him. "I just had to ask."

"Of course you did." Nick snarled. Not caring if he wasn't dressed for it, or wearing gloves, he attacked the bag like it was trying to kill him.

§§

Victoria walked into her house in a fog. Halle sat on the couch, still in her pajamas, her hair a hot mess. She looked up when Victoria plopped down beside her. Even in her own misery, she noticed Victoria's.

"What's the matter?" Halle paused the show.

"Nick knew about Trevor cheating. He kept it from me. He kept it from us." Victoria tried to stop the tears. "I thought he'd be honest with me. Not hide anything. I thought we could make it."

"Oh sweetie." Halle hugged her, reversing their roles from the other night. "Don't be upset with him because of me and Trevor."

Victoria shook her head. "No, after I asked him if I was just a notch on his belt, he said I was. And if he keeps something like that from me, how easy will it be to keep other things secret? He knew how important honesty was, he even said he'd be completely honest with me. How could he say that when he didn't tell me?"

"I don't know. Men are assholes." Halle stood. "I'll get the ice cream."

"He didn't stop me when I left. I told him we were over, I was so mad." Victoria rubbed a hand over her chest to try and assuage the ache. When she and Roger split up, it'd never hurt like this and she'd only known Nick for a couple of months. Thank God she'd never told him how she felt. That would've been a disaster.

"Maybe he was as upset as you are and wasn't thinking. Maybe you should've let him explain. Could he have had a good reason not to tell you? Even though I'm angry he didn't tell you. I could've been prepared for this."

"Would you have believed him?"

Halle stayed silent for a minute. "No." She shook her head. "No, because I wouldn't have believed it. I was so wrapped up in Trevor, it took walking in on it to really believe it. There were so many hints, so many lies that were so transparent. I could've known if I hadn't been so selectively blind."

"We were suspicious, but didn't really know anything." Victoria sighed. "Men really suck."

Victoria was happy when the girls came home, not just because she missed them, but because they'd be a good distraction from her and Halle's thoughts. When they walked in, though, she could tell something bothered them. It seemed to be the night of hurt and pissed off females. Helena pushed by Victoria, sending her a hateful glare, before she stormed upstairs. She didn't even say anything to Halle, who was usually her favorite aunt. Lucia tried to smile but managed poorly. She took her bag into the living room and plopped next to Halle. Victoria turned around to see Roger smiling and looking smug.

"Good-bye, Roger." She shut the door in his face. She wasn't in the mood for his games. Something was wrong with her girls, and she intended to find out what it was.

Since Lucia sat with Halle, Victoria settled on her other side. "What's the matter?"

"Dad talked about you and Nick the whole time, Candace even joined in. He talked so *bad* about Nick, how he was violent and mean, and trash. That he would hurt you, or us." Lucia's eyes watered. "Is it true? Candace said that she dated him and that he hurt her so bad she was in the hospital."

"What?" Victoria looked at Halle, then back at Lucia. "No, Nick has never hurt me. Has he ever seemed mean to you?" Even angry at Nick, Roger's tactics pissed her off. Lucia shook her head. "And Candace is lying. He would've said something that day of the barbeque." But would he? He seemed great at keeping secrets. "Let's not worry about that right now."

"Okay." She turned to Halle. "Why are you here and not at home?"

Halle's eyes flickered with pain, before she smiled bravely at Lucia. "Uncle Trevor and I are getting a divorce."

"I want you to be happy, Aunt Halle. Trevor wasn't nice to you." Lucia kissed Halle on the cheek.

It always seemed so simple in the eyes of children.

Chapter Thirty-Three

A cloud of confusion and hurt hung over Victoria the next week. She tried to fully listen to Elizabeth, a new client who had bought a summer home on the beach, describe the style she wanted to decorate it in. All Victoria could think about was how much she missed Nick. They hadn't spoken since that night and that horrible argument and Victoria began to think that maybe she'd overreacted. Halle hadn't seemed that upset to find out Nick knew. Victoria didn't know if she could trust him though.

"I want the kitchen colors to be bold, with light hardwood floors. I don't want tile anywhere but the bathrooms." Elizabeth touched her blonde hair to make sure none of the strands were out of the French twist. "I want the furniture to be antique looking, if not actual antiques. I'm thinking of teal and brown in the living room."

Victoria nodded, numbly taking notes with a pencil. She gave up on using a pen a long time ago because clients more often that not changed their minds. "What about for the master bedroom?"

Elizabeth sat back. "I'm not sure about that yet. I don't know if I'm going to bring any of my furniture from Los Angeles."

"Are you planning on living here full time?" Victoria couldn't help but be curious. Maybe if she focused on someone else's life, she wouldn't have to worry about hers.

"Until I find something in New York. I want to open my own modeling agency, I'm honestly over the go-all-the-time of the modeling world. I need a break from the hustle, take time for myself. When I'm ready to go back, I'll keep this as a summer home."

"You'll definitely get a break out here. Tourist season is busier, but I'm sure it's nowhere near what you're used to."

"It's what I'm looking for. Jetting all over the world, the parties, the shoots...I never slept enough. I wasn't taking care of myself like I should and I finally decided I needed to get away from it." Elizabeth's blue eyes looked into the past. She focused on Victoria after a minute. "It may not seem hard, but it was. The constant pressure alone was enough to kill you."

"I believe you." Victoria thought about never having time to spend with her family, the constant pressure to always look amazing. "I think you made the right choice. Not many people can."

"Thank you." Elizabeth's smile was radiant. "No one thought that way. I may have an idea for the master bedroom, if I don't bring mine. I want something elegant. I loved the hotels in Paris. I kind of want something like that. White, chandeliers, some Versailles type furniture."

"I can look some stuff up, give me a few days to get the concepts together, and we can go take a look at the house." Victoria stood and shook her hand.

"Thank you. And if you wouldn't mind, could you not mention I'm in town?" Elizabeth grabbed her massive purse, put it on the crook of her elbow.

"Of course." Victoria led her out of the office. "Make a follow up appointment with Ella, so I can make sure I'm here." After Ella opened the calendar, Victoria shut the door to her office and sank back into her chair. She rubbed her temples, trying to stave off an oncoming headache. Ever since the argument, her nights had been restless. She could feel herself folding, wanting to pick up her phone and call Nick, but she clenched her jaw and made herself leave the phone alone. He didn't seem to be missing her any, he was the one that told her that she didn't mean anything to him. That familiar ache in her chest pierced at the thought. How could she have been so blind, so stupid to think that he felt the same thing she did?

§§

"Damn it." Nick threw the ruler across his shop and ran a hand through his hair.

"Hey! That almost hit me." Luke came into the shop holding the ruler up. "This thing has a sharp edge, you know."

Nick tried to reign in his temper by breathing deep a few times. "Sorry."

Luke set the ruler down and handed his brother a beer. "Look, dude, I don't mean to get all in your love life, but it's beginning to become a problem." He ignored Nick's death glare. "No, it is. You have been in a fucking awful mood and it's only got worse. You look like shit, no joke. You've missed dinner at Mom's and she's worried about you."

Nick's stomach twisted at the thought of making his mom worry. "Didn't you explain what happened?"

Luke nodded. "She called us both idiots and that she raised us better than that." He tipped his beer up and swallowed. "She said you should've told Victoria from the beginning and she understands why Victoria's upset."

Nick groaned. "Women. How the hell are we supposed to understand them?"

Luke shrugged. "No clue. Though I'm hoping to learn soon. Halle hasn't gone home. Oh, I heard from Grant that Addie punched Trevor that night he came to Victoria's."

"He went to Victoria's?" Nick tried to tamp down the protectiveness but it was useless. "Why did Addie punch him? Did he hurt Victoria?"

"And you say you're over her." Luke sighed. "No. From what I hear, Trevor wouldn't leave, called Addie a bitch, so she dropped him."

Nick smiled reluctantly. "Victoria said that Addie was the feisty one."

"Are you really done with her?" Luke asked.

"I want to be." Nick stared down at the beer in his hand. He missed her so much it was a physical ache. "I don't know. I don't know what to do, or if she even wants me back. I told her she didn't mean anything to me, that she was just another notch."

Luke whistled. "I wouldn't want to get back with you."

"Fuck off." Nick growled at his brother.

"Hey, I'm just telling you the truth. That was too harsh. You want her back? You're going to have to beg for mercy."

Nick knew he was right. He'd really, really fucked up this time. So bad that he didn't know if he could fix it. "Since you're here you can help me finish this blueprint, then we'll head to Mom's. It's about time I went and saw her anyway."

His thoughts turned back to Victoria. Could he forgive her for not believing in him? Could she forgive him for being an ass and not telling her? Was he being a hypocrite, trying to get her to see his side but not trying to see hers? He couldn't lie to himself, he hadn't been the same since that night. He needed her back.

§§

"Mom, I can't find my brush!" Lucia hollered down the stairs.

Victoria sighed. Lucia was supposed to have packed everything last night. Four thirty in the morning was not the time to search for things. "Look in your room!" She hollered back up. Three weeks without Nick, with that pain, had her nerves on thin ice.

Helena sat on the couch in a pair of sweats and a hoodie. She had the hood pulled up and her iPod on, effectively cutting her off from Victoria. Even though Nick wasn't around anymore, her attitude hadn't changed. Victoria knew Roger was behind this but she didn't know how to fix it. Helena ignored her when she talked, had refused to go to the math and science camp next week, saying that it was for dweebs and that her dad thought she should do something more social.

Victoria wished she'd punched him when she had the chance. The slap wasn't nearly satisfying enough.

"Found it! I'm ready!" Lucia ran down the stairs, her bag in one hand, her carry on in the other.

"Are you sure you have everything?" Victoria asked. When Lucia nodded, Victoria nudged Helena's shoulder.

"What?" Helena snapped.

Victoria clenched her teeth before she started an argument and made Lucia late. "We're leaving." She grit out.

They loaded the bags in the car. Once in, she headed toward the mall where the greyhound bus would meet them. "Now, remember that the cell phone I gave you is prepaid. You are only to use it to call home or in case of emergencies. There are only so many minutes on it so don't use it to call your friends."

Lucia rolled her eyes. "All of my friends are going to be there with me."

"You get what I'm saying." Victoria was almost happy that it was so early in the morning. All the tourists were still asleep, so the drive was quick and easy. The mall parking lot was eerily empty besides the bus and few cars in the corner near the road. She tried to hold her nervousness in as she parked so Lucia didn't see it. "And have fun. Don't get into trouble."

"Mom, I'm going to be fine. And I'll call every night. Don't worry." Lucia told her. She smiled at Victoria, her excitement plain on her face.

"Wait here, Helena. I'll be right back." Victoria didn't move until Helena jerked her head in a nod. Then she climbed out and grabbed Lucia's bag. Students lined up, waiting to put their bags in the cargo area. A few of the chaperones and teachers walked up and down, checking people in. Victoria and Lucia joined the end of the line. Lucia hugged the girl in front of them, both of them squealing.

"Mom, this is Natalie." Lucia beamed up at Victoria. "And this is her mom."

Victoria smiled over at the petite girl and her tall mother. "It's nice to meet you."

"You, too. I'm Kathy." The woman looked around. "It's too early for all this."

"Victoria. And I agree." Victoria wrapped her arms around Lucia's shoulders. "It's her first trip away."

"Mom." Lucia blushed.

"Natalie's gone to cheer camp since she was in fourth grade, so she can help Lucia adjust." Kathy told her. "She loves it, I'm sure Lucia will. And the worrying gets a little easier, but it never goes away."

"Great." Victoria laughed. "That's what I'm afraid of."

"They take good care of them." Kathy assured her. "Natalie usually has so much fun, she doesn't want to come home."

The cheer coach came by with a clipboard and asked the girls their names. Soon after, they called for the kids to load the bus.

"I love you, Lucia." Victoria hugged her close as the driver took the girls' bags to put them in the cargo area. "Call me when you get there."

"Mom, I'll be fine. I love you, too." Lucia pulled back. "I've got to get on."

Victoria reluctantly let her go. "When you get there. Remember!" She called as Lucia climbed on the bus. She sighed.

"I promise it gets easier." Kathy said. They walked back toward their cars. "If you have any concerns, feel free to call me."

"Thanks." Victoria took her number, just in case.

Helena had her hood up still, her head lying against the window. Victoria couldn't see her face, but she imagined the same bland look was there.

"I'm going to miss Lucia." Victoria started the car and made her way home. Helena didn't move, stayed silent. "Helena?"

Nothing.

Victoria stopped trying to engage her in conversation. There was only so much she could do and there was no reason she should have to make her daughter talk to her. It hurt, though, adding on top of everything else.

When they got home, Helena slammed the car door and went straight upstairs. Victoria trudged in the house, her body weary. She needed a good rest, even if she only slept for a few hours. Luckily it was Saturday, so she didn't have to go in to work today. She could try to sleep in.

With Lucia gone, it would be lonely in the house. Helena wasn't talking to her, she and Nick were over, and Trevor had given the house to Halle. She'd filed for divorce, paying for the best lawyer with her savings. Victoria knew she was looking for a job at the hospital, and hoped the interview Monday would go well.

Victoria changed back into shorts and a cami and slid underneath the covers. One hand ran over the empty spot next to her. Nick had only ever stayed a few nights at a time, hardly enough for her to get used to his warmth being next to her, but she missed him with an ache that never went away. It wasn't just her body that missed him. She wanted to see his smile, to share her day and hear about his. She wanted him to make her laugh, to take care of her. How could she have been so wrong about that? His actions had clearly said he cared for her, or was that just her imagination?

Chapter Thirty-Four

"I got the job!" Halle burst into their parents' house, jumping up and down.

Victoria refrained from jumping but hugged her sister close.

"That's great, Halle!" Addie high-fived her. Even Helena smiled at her aunt.

"When do you start?" Cecelia asked as she placed food on the table. "You only had the interview a few hours ago. They must've loved you."

"They were right to love you." Wes kissed Halle's cheek.

Halle grinned. "In three days. I have to get all my paperwork together, make sure I have a current copy of my nursing license. I'm going to be working on the Labor and Delivery floor, which I've always wanted to do." Her usual haunted look was replaced with her happiness at finding a job.

Victoria knew that Halle doubted herself those few weeks after she found out about Trevor, but they'd all talked her confidence up.

They sat at the table, Helena sitting between Wes and Halle. The past two days were hell at Victoria's.

Every time she tried to engage Helena, ask her to come eat or watch something with her, it had ended up in a shouting match. Victoria was over it but she wasn't sure how to get Helena to stop.

"What will your hours be?" Addie scooped some mashed potatoes on her plate before passing the bowl.

"I'll be working three days a week, with every other weekend off. I'll go in at seven and get out at seven at night. I'll work overtime if they need me to."

"Are you nervous? You haven't worked in a hospital since school, right?" Cecilia asked.

"Yes, a little. But you guys have faith in me. So I know the skills will come back to me." Halle bit into her food.

"Well, I'm just glad you're eating again." Cecelia told her.

"Mom." Helena sighed. "Anyway, I know some of the nurses on the floor, I went to school with them. I'll know some people there."

"Great, honey." Wes patted Cecelia's hand to reassure her. "We're so proud of you." He turned to Helena. "Now, do you still have the stubborn idea not to go to your camp next week?"

Helena shrunk down in her chair and mumbled, "I don't want to go."

Victoria watched Wes and Cecelia exchange a look.

"Why is that? You were so excited a few weeks ago." Cecelia kept her voice soft.

"I just don't want to." Helena snapped.

Victoria's lips parted. Her baby girl had just back talked her grandparents. When had it gotten that far?

"Now, Helena, you know that we have nothing but love for you." Wes set his fork and knife down. "But if you keep up this attitude here or with your mother, no one is going to want to be around you."

Victoria and her sisters looked at each other. They remembered when he'd given them those lectures, spoke in that deceptively calm voice. It meant they were in big trouble.

"Fine. Whatever." Helena glared at each of them. "You're all on her side anyway."

Addie shook her head. "There aren't any sides. We just don't understand why you're so mad at your mom."

Helena screeched in frustration and startled Victoria. "Because she's a liar. She's the reason Dad left. She's the *reason* he doesn't want me and Lucia around. She made him leave, then she started talking to Nick, who's nothing but a piece of trash."

By the end of her tirade, everyone's mouths hung open.

"I'm done eating. I'm going to sit in the car." Helena stood up and stormed off. No one moved until the front door slammed.

"Oh my God." Halle looked over at Victoria. "I had no idea it was that bad."

Victoria frowned. "I don't know what Roger's filling her head with when she goes over there."

"I think I need to go have a talk with her." Wes stood and set his napkin down. "Her attitude is unacceptable. She doesn't need to talk that way about anyone, especially her own mother. Victoria, give me your keys. If I'm driving, she'll have no choice but to listen."

"I'm going to get some wine." Cecelia said as Victoria fished her keys out of her purse and handed them to her father.

"Can I go punch Roger in the face? I think it'll make me feel better." Addie growled. "What the hell is wrong with these men?"

"Who knows?" Halle came and sat beside Victoria. "Are you okay?"

"I don't know." Victoria rubbed her eyes with the palm of her hands. " I just can't believe he would turn her against me like that, or that she would believe it so easily." At that thought, she realized how Nick must have felt when she'd believed he wasn't serious about them so easily. Great, now the guilt could pile on the confusion and hurt.

"He poisoned her mind. She's a daddy's girl and he's using that to his advantage. He could care less about her, he just wants to hurt you."

"I don't understand that. He's the one that left, that decided we weren't right for each other. Never mind the fact that he was obviously correct. But why does he have to do this?"

Cecelia walked back in with the wine bottle and glasses and poured them each one. "Hopefully Wes can talk some sense into her. If she's going to listen to anyone, it'd be him. And even if it doesn't work right away, your father has a way of talking to someone that sits in their brain for a few days. She'll come around."

"I know that when they hit a certain age kids challenge their parents, but this is a little extreme."

Addie sipped her wine. "And I remember rebelling a little later than this."

"You girls were never this bad. But you also didn't have one parent trying to turn you against the other." Cecelia ran a comforting hand down Victoria's hair.

Victoria let the comforting caress sink in. This reminded her that she didn't have to face any of this alone. "Thanks."

"We wouldn't let you deal with this by yourself." Cecelia kissed the side of her head.

§§

Helena's attitude didn't change over the next few days. By Friday, Victoria was so stressed that when Helena asked to go to Julie's house before Julie left for Math and Science camp, Victoria didn't even hesitate. Julie's dad was home on R&R and they were planning to go mini-golfing. Now Victoria was in the silent house, sitting on her bed, wondering what the hell to do with herself. Her cell phone sat in front of her and she stared at it. A constant debate raged in her mind over whether or not to text Nick and try to work out what the argument had ruined. There wasn't a day that went by that she didn't wish they could have handled it differently.

The phone beckoned her. It pulled her in, lured her to text him, just once, to see if he'd even answer. Just when she reached for it, the phone rang. Victoria stared down at the screen, not recognizing the number.

"Hello?" She answered. In the brief silence, her heart raced.

"Hello, this is St. Michael's hospital. Are you Victoria Copeland?"

Victoria couldn't breathe, but whispered, "Yes. I am." Did something happen to her dad, or her mom? Or one of her sisters?

"I'm sorry to inform you that Helena has been in a car accident with her friend."

Victoria shot off the bed. "I'll be there in five minutes." She hung up the phone without thinking about asking which room or about particulars. She refused to contemplate a worse reality. She threw on flip flops and her hands shook as she dialed her parents' number.

"Mom, Helena's been in an accident." Victoria's voice cracked. Hot tears poured down her face, but she blindly wiped them away.

"Don't move. We'll be right there. You don't need to drive." Cecelia told her.

"Hurry." Victoria hung up, arms hanging limply at her sides. The room spun around her and she shut her eyes. A sudden coldness took over her body and she blinked rapidly to try and get control. Helena had to be okay. Her baby had to be okay.

Her parents pulled into the driveway in under five minutes. She was out the door and in the car before they could get out.

"It's okay, Victoria." Cecelia reached back and took Victoria's cold hands. "I called your sisters. They're going to meet us there."

Victoria jerked her head in a nod. She couldn't speak over the lump in her throat. She had to see her baby.

Her father sped through town with his hazard lights on. Cars moved out of the way for them and for that Victoria was thankful. He pulled the car up to the emergency room doors. Victoria jumped out, forgetting to shut the door, and ran straight to the receptionist desk.

"Helena Copeland. What room?" Victoria gulped in air, but it didn't feel like enough.

The woman looked in her computer. "ICU, ninth floor."

Victoria's knees gave out. "The ICU?"

Wes caught her and held her up.

Thank God for her parents. They kept her strong right now and without them she would've been lost.

Wes led her to the elevator. The harsh lights of the hospital burned into her eyes and sharpened her headache. "What if she's not okay?"

"Shh. She's going to be fine." Cecelia pushed the button for the ninth floor, then wrapped her arms around her. Victoria laid her head on her mom's shoulder, but couldn't feel any comfort through her numbness.

The rise to the ninth floor seemed to take forever, but finally the doors opened. Victoria's legs didn't want to move. She was so afraid of what she'd see if she walked in there. Wes took her hand and gently pulled her out.

The first person she spotted was Julia's mom, Erin. Erin's tan skin was mottled with bruises and jagged cuts. She sat in one of the waiting room chairs, hands clenched in her lap. When she saw Victoria, she rushed over and threw her arms around Victoria.

"I am so sorry. A drunk driver ran a red light and we didn't see him. We didn't see him, and he hit Mark and Helena's side." Erin's tears wet Victoria's neck and she shook against her.

"How are they?" Wes asked.

"Mark and Helena are in the back. They haven't let us see them yet. Julia is down in the ER with my mother getting stitches in her forehead. I...I don't know how it happened. I'm so sorry." Erin repeated.

Victoria managed to find her voice. "It wasn't your fault, Erin. The drunk driver shouldn't have been driving."

Erin nodded, blinking a few times. "The doctor said they were taking them both down for CT scans to check for internal bleeding and that they'd be right back. That was thirty minutes ago." She ran her hands down her blood-stained jeans.

"Let's go sit down. Dad, can you grab some coffee?" Victoria asked. Erin was in worse shape than she was, and needed someone to lean on.

Wes nodded. "Sure. You wait to hear what the doctor says."

Victoria led them all to a row of chairs and they sat. She fought off her own hysteria. She had to hold it together for everyone, had to get it together for when she saw Helena.

Chapter Thirty-Five

Her sisters arrived a few minutes later and her dad returned with the coffee. Victoria tried to ignore the smell of disinfectant and old pee and focused on the aroma of coffee and the warmth of the hugs her sisters gave her. Maybe both would get rid of her shock. Worry for Helena burned in her chest and she knew if her family wasn't here, she'd succumb to it.

"I need to call Roger." Victoria reached for her phone, but Wes grabbed it.

"I'll call him. You don't need to deal with him right now." He kissed the top of her head. "I'll be back in a minute. They won't let me use the phone up here."

"We're all right here." Halle sat next to her. Dark half moons hung under her eyes. "Have you heard anything?"

"They took her and Julie's dad down for a CT. Erin said they should be back in a minute." Victoria's legs bounced. She couldn't keep still, felt like she should be doing *something* for Helena besides waiting. All of her and Helena's fights over the past few weeks kept running through her mind. If anything happened to her...Victoria shook the thoughts away. If she kept thinking like that, she'd shatter.

Victoria's glance bounced from the waiting room to the counter, to the doors that led to the ICU. She watched a woman try to keep her three young boys in line. She snapped at them, sighing and rolling her eyes in frustration. Victoria wanted to stand up and yell at the mom to not take her children for granted. That she'd made the same mistake. She bit her lip and instead focused on her hands, which she clutched together in her lap.

The atmosphere in the hospital darkened the longer Victoria waited to hear from the doctor. Her family stayed next to her, talking quietly, and their whispers drifted over her in a fog.

"Family of Helena Copeland?"

Victoria's head snapped toward the direction of the voice. A gray haired man in a white coat and scrubs stood next to the elevator. She stood and crossed to him, her family following. "I'm her mother."

The doctor nodded. "I'm Dr. Black. Helena's CT scan came back okay, no signs of internal bleeding. She has a fractured left radius, some abrasions, and a concussion. I want to keep her overnight for observation."

Tears burned the backs of Victoria's eyelids. Her trembling hands covered her mouth, and her knees threatened to buckle, but she held herself together. "Can I see her?"

"She's getting a room on the fifth floor." Dr. Black checked her chart. "They're moving her to room 533. I'm going to speak to Mr. Smith's family and then I'll come down to Helena's room and speak more with you."

Victoria nodded. "Mom, do you want to find Dad and let him know where we'll be?"

"Of course." Cecelia smiled at her daughter, relief on her face. "We'll meet you in Helena's room."

The sisters rode the elevator in silence, holding hands. The doors opened to the fifth floor and they searched for Helena's room.

"I'm going to text Mom and tell her where it is." Addie said before they went in. "I'll be in when I'm finished."

Victoria slowly pushed the door open. A nurse stood next to Helena's bed, checking her vitals. Helena looked so small in the hospital bed. Her black hair stood out against the white of the sheets and pale color of her skin. The bruises and scrapes on her skin looked even darker. Victoria was glad Helena was asleep and couldn't see the look on her face.

"I'm Lydia. I'll be her nurse until seven in the morning." The nurse told Halle and Victoria. "I hear that she's going to be just fine. I'm going to have a cast tech in here in a few minutes to go ahead and put a splint on her wrist. We won't be able to cast it until some of the swelling goes down. You'll probably be home then, and can go to an orthopedic doctor for that."

Halle thanked her. Victoria already stood next to Helena, focused only on her. She took Helena's right hand in hers and softly kissed her forehead.

"She has an IV with morphine, so she'll probably be asleep for a while." Lydia gestured to the door. "I'll be right outside if you need me."

Victoria nodded, not taking her eyes off her daughter. After the nurse left, she grabbed a chair and slid it to the bed. In the dimmed light, Helena's skin looked yellow now. "Baby, I'm so sorry."

"It's not your fault." Halle crossed to the opposite side of the bed and stared down at her niece. "It's not Mark or Erin's fault."

"I know that." Victoria sighed and looked up. "I just hate that this happened and I wasn't there for her."

"You are now. The only reason she's staying overnight is to keep an eye on the concussion." Halle said. "They're all very lucky."

Addie stepped into the room, stopped when she saw Helena. "Oh, she looks so bad."

"Did you talk to Mom?" Halle asked.

"They said they'd be up in a second." Addie stood next to Victoria and placed a hand on her shoulder.

A few minutes later the cast tech came in. He quickly made the splint and wrapped her arm in an ace bandage while Helena slept. He repeated the part about her taking Helena to the orthopedic doctor, then left. Her parents came in right after. Wes's red face and scowl warned the girls that his conversation with Roger didn't go well.

"What is it?" Addie squeezed Victoria's shoulder.

"I swear, I try to be nice and give him the benefit of the doubt, but Roger is such a bastard." Wes grit his teeth.

Victoria knew her dad was pissed because he didn't normally curse in front of the girls. "What did he say?"

"He asked if she was okay and when I said we hadn't heard yet, and I even told him how bad the wreck was, he merely told me to call him when we heard. That he was at a prestigious dinner party in New York and couldn't leave. That Candace was counting on him to be at her side."

"I'm going to break his face." Addie threw her hands up. "I don't understand him."

Victoria couldn't worry about Roger right now. She was just glad that Helena hadn't been awake to hear what a shit for a father he really was. All of the family that mattered stood in this room, besides Lucia.

"If you give me your house keys, I'll go grab you and Helena some clothes." Cecelia's gaze roamed over Helena. Victoria could tell she tried to hide her concern, to be brave for her daughter and Helena. "She'll probably want something comfortable to wear when you head home tomorrow."

Tomorrow. Victoria fought off the overwhelming urge to break down. "Lucia comes home tomorrow. Can you pick her up from the mall? It'll be around noon."

"Of course. Don't worry about anything, darling." Cecelia took the proffered keys. "Wes, are you riding with me?"

"Sure." Wes hugged each of his daughters, kissed Helena's forehead. "She's going to be just fine. I'll grab some food and we'll be back in a minute."

"I'm going to turn the TV on, it's too quiet in here." Addie grabbed the remote and switched it on. "Maybe the noise will make her feel more at home."

Victoria didn't say anything. Some of the shock was wearing off, and now that the burst of adrenaline fizzled, exhaustion was setting in. She wouldn't sleep until she'd had a chance to make sure Helena woke up, heard her sweet voice.

Someone knocked at the door to the room. Halle motioned Victoria to sit. "I'll get it."

Victoria didn't pay attention to who was at the door until she heard Nick's voice. Despite the fact that they weren't talking, her pulse still jumped. She wanted to throw herself into his arms, to feel safe. She managed to make herself stay in the chair. At first she was confused as to how Nick heard about the accident, but then she remembered Addie had his number. She shot a questioning glance at her sister, but Addie was talking to Halle and Nick.

His brows furrowed, but when his gaze landed on Victoria the tension left his body. Not a second later, he was beside her. "How is she?"

The concern in his voice almost undid her. "Okay." Her lips quivered. "She has a broken wrist and a concussion.

He knelt next to her chair and tucked a strand of hair behind her ear. "Mom and Luke are in the gift shop downstairs getting her something."

"That's very sweet of them. And for you to come by." Victoria wasn't sure how to take it that he was here. That he came to check on Helena when her own father neglected to. Holding it together was becoming hard, she knew she was going to break soon if she wasn't careful.

Nick stared at her for a moment, his look tender, before he replied, "You and the girls are important to me. When I heard," he ran a hand through his hair, "all

I could think about was getting here. I was at Mom's having dinner, and they insisted on coming with me."

"I'm glad you're here." She hoped he could see it in her face, in her eyes.

His lips lifted slightly. "Do you need me to get anything from your house?"

"Mom and Dad just left to go get some stuff. She only needs to stay overnight because of her concussion." It didn't get any easier saying the words so Victoria had to force them out.

"It's good to hear it's not worse. How are the rest of the people that were with her?"

His words steadied her. "Julia is in a room in the ER and her dad is having a CT too. I haven't heard how he is. Erin had a few nasty bruises and cuts from the glass."

Luke and Charlotte came in, carrying a giant pink teddy bear and some red and white balloons. Charlotte's kind look bolstered Victoria a little. She'd been a little afraid when Nick mentioned they were here that Charlotte would be upset with her. Luke stood next to Halle, a hand on her elbow, whispering softly. Halle leaned into him, her eyes wide and shimmering with tears. Addie set the teddy bear and the balloons on the table next to Helena's bed.

"Is there anything we can get you?" Charlotte laid a hand on Victoria's where she held Helena's.

"No, thank you. I'm just waiting on her to wake up. The drugs they gave her made her drowsy."

"Well, dear, if you need anything, don't hesitate to call. Lucia's coming home tomorrow. Do you need me to pick her up?"

Victoria burst into tears as the wall she built crumbled. These people truly cared about her daughter and it touched her. "I'm s-sorry." She hid her face in her hands.

Nick pulled her to him, whispered to her, ran a hand down her hair. "It's okay, baby. Don't apologize. We're here for you."

She nodded against his chest, letting his strength melt into her.

Dr. Black entered the room, checked Helena's vitals and her chart. "Everything looks great. Did the nurse explain to you about the cast?"

"Yes, she did." Victoria glanced down at the splint on Helena's arm. "We'll go to an orthopedic doctor for the cast in a few days, after the swelling goes down."

"Good." Dr. Black smiled kindly. "I'm going to have the nurse come in every two hours, waking her up, making sure she's lucid and there's no lasting effects from the concussion. We'll keep her on the morphine for the night to help with the pain."

"Thank you." Victoria looked around the room at her friends and family. "How long are we allowed to have visitors?"

"Only for a few more minutes actually. After that, only one other person can stay until morning." Dr. Black told them. "Sorry, it makes it hard for the nurses to do their jobs if the room is overcrowded."

"I understand." Victoria rubbed Helena's hand. "Should we wake her up now, or wait?"

"She was awake for the CT, so I'd let her sleep for now." Dr. Black suggested.

After he left, Charlotte and Luke hugged Victoria and Addie and Halle made her promise to call if she needed anything.

Chapter Thirty-Six

Victoria realized that she and Nick were essentially alone now. The tension stretched across the room, brushing along her skin.

He cleared his throat. "I know now probably isn't the best time, but I wanted to apologize for not telling you about Trevor."

Victoria exhaled. He looked so right, so good sitting there, and she wasn't sure how to tell him how much she missed him. "I may have overreacted a little. I value honesty so much and I believed you'd be honest with me."

"I know." Nick's face was somber. "I didn't mean what I said about you just being a notch. You're more than that to me. And Luke made me promise not to say anything. He's had a crush on Halle ever since high school and was afraid if I told you, it would kind of ruin his chances with her."

"He has a crush on her?" Victoria couldn't help but smile. "I could kind of see it at the barbeque when he talked with her. But I don't understand how you telling me would ruin his chances with her."

"I don't either, honestly." Nick said. "But I couldn't promise that, which was before you and I got involved, and then go back on it."

"I guess." Victoria glanced down at her daughter, so pale and bruised. "You're right, though. Now isn't the time to discuss this. We can talk about it later."

"Will we?" He stared at her, his eyes searching her face.

Her heart raced. Was he as anxious as she was? She nodded.

He blinked, smiling a little. "Do you want me to stay, keep you company?"

She wanted it more than anything, but didn't think it would be good for Helena to see him as soon as she woke. She'd already been through enough stress. "No, thanks. I think I need to focus on her tonight."

"I understand." He stood. "If you need anything, give me a call." He leaned down and pressed a kiss to the top of her forehead.

Victoria let the sensation of his lips on her again wash over her as he left. She almost called him back to the room, but refrained. She had to stick by her decision, for Helena.

§§

Later, after her parents dropped off the bag and left, Lydia came in to check on Helena. Victoria had fallen asleep with her head next to Helena's legs, holding her hand still, and sat up when Lydia placed a hand on her shoulder.

"How are you doing?" Lydia smiled down at her.

"I'm okay." Victoria blinked the drowsiness away. "Is it time to wake her up?"

"Yes." Lydia walked around to the other side of the bed. "I want you to try and wake her up. I'll check her pupils, her vitals, then let you talk with her for about fifteen minutes. If she's okay, then we can allow her to go back to sleep."

Victoria brushed a strand of hair softly back from Helena's forehead. "Baby, it's time to wake up."

Helena's eyelids fluttered but didn't open. Victoria clamped down on her panic and tried again. "Helena, I need you to open your eyes."

After a few seconds, Helena did. Her eyes opened, the hazel color a little dim. It took a minute for her to focus on Victoria, but when she did, her eyes watered. "Mom."

"Hey." Victoria whispered. "How are you feeling?"

Helena swallowed, looked around and saw Lydia. "My head hurts. My body hurts."

"I know. Can you let Lydia check you out for a minute?" Victoria asked.

Helena nodded slowly.

Lydia took out the penlight and checked her pupils, then asked her several questions from her chart, like her birthday, name and the city she lived in. When she was satisfied that Helena was okay, she charted it and left.

"Mom. I'm sorry." Helena grasped Victoria's hand. Tears leaked out of the corner of her eyes.

"It's okay, baby. You don't worry about anything right now." Victoria brushed a hand across Helena's forehead, wishing she could ease her daughter's pain. When she realized how close she came to losing her, the only thing that assuaged that ache was to touch Helena, to realize that she was here and alive.

"No, please listen." Helena squeezed her eyes shut. "I heard what Grandpa said about Dad. Is it true?"

"About your Dad?" Victoria's eyes blurred as tears rose. She forced herself to blink them back, to be strong for Helena. As much as she hated her daughter's attitude, she didn't want her finding out about her dad this way. "Baby, please don't worry about him. You need to rest and feel better."

"Did he really say he wasn't coming to the hospital because of a dinner with Candace?" Helena turned her head on the pillow to look Victoria in the eyes. "Tell me the truth. Please."

Victoria let out a long, slow sigh. "Yes. He said that to Grandpa." She wouldn't have chosen today to be the day that Helena realized the truth about her father, but apparently she believed Wes when he spoke of it.

"Does he really not care?" Helena let a sob loose, then held her hands to her head where pain blossomed.

"Baby," Victoria rubbed her arm and kissed her cheek, anything to get her to calm down. "I need you to forget about this right now. I know it's hard because you love him, but you're only making your head hurt more."

Lydia came back in and administered more drugs into Helena's IV. Whatever they gave her helped out, because after a few minutes of silence Helena drifted off to sleep.

It amazed Victoria that Roger hadn't even been the slightest bit worried about their daughter. That he couldn't care less that she'd been in a car accident and landed in the ICU for a little while. That violence rose in her again, and she bit her lip to keep it in.

Throughout the night, Lydia came in and woke Helena up with Victoria, talked to her for a few minutes, then let her drift back off to sleep. By the next morning, Dr. Black was okay with Helena going home. Helena sat silently in a wheelchair next to the counter as Victoria signed the discharge papers. She stayed silent on the drive home.

Once they got inside the house, Helena laid down on the couch.

"I'm going to grab you a pillow and a blanket." Victoria laid their bags on the floor. "Do you want to watch TV or a movie or anything?"

"I love you, Mom."

Victoria turned from the movie case to look at her daughter. Helena smiled through her tears when Victoria beamed. "I love you too, sweetie."

"Can you call the aunts and ask them to come over?" Helena asked. "I want to see them."

"Sure." Victoria texted both of them. "Now, a movie?"

"How about Beauty and the Beast? We haven't watched that in a long time."

Victoria pulled the DVD out of the case and popped it in the player. "That is an excellent choice." She grabbed a blanket and pillow from the hall closet and covered Helena up, made sure she was comfortable. "I'll get you some water and your pain medicine. Be right back." She set her phone down on the couch and returned within a few minutes to see Helena's secret smile.

Halle and Addie arrived within ten minutes and both snuggled up on the couch with Helena and Victoria. Halfway into the movie, Helena nodded off on Halle's shoulder.

The sisters snuck into the kitchen so they wouldn't wake Helena.

"I went and stayed with Mom and Dad last night, figured they could use a distraction. They were worried about Helena and pissed about Roger." Halle snapped her mouth shut at Victoria's sudden look. "What?"

"Last night Helena heard Dad after he got back from his call with Roger. We thought she was asleep. She asked me about it the first time the nurse woke her up. It tore her up inside." Victoria sank onto a stool.

"What did you say?" Addie started the Keurig.

"The only thing I could. To not worry about it right now." Victoria shook her head. "He is such a bastard."

"I can punch him too, the offer still stands." Addie half-joked.

"I'd love that, except I'd miss out on hurting him." Victoria laughed at her sister's surprised faces. "I can't help it. He makes me violent."

"I see that." Halle cocked her head to the side. "So, Nick came to see Helena, and you, last night. How did that go?"

"He apologized. Told me that there was a reason, a promise that kept him from saying anything." Victoria avoided Halle's gaze. She didn't want to give Luke's crush away. "I can understand why he did what he did, I just don't know if right now is the best time for a relationship."

"You should've thought about that before you fell in love with him." Addie pointed out.

Victoria knocked her coffee over when she jumped. "What?"

Halle shared a look with Addie as she grabbed a towel. "We're your sisters. We can tell these things."

"That's not fair!" Victoria placed her palms to her heated cheeks. "I only realized this with certainty after our fight. This is really not fair."

"I say you go for it." Addie told her. "I know I'm not one for commitment or anything of the sort, but Nick seems like a great guy, unlike Trevor or Roger, and he truly cares about you and the girls. He wouldn't have shown up at the hospital if he didn't."

"He wanted to stay last night, to keep me company." Victoria said. "Do you think he could still want a relationship after I basically told him I didn't believe in him?"

Halle nudged Victoria's shoulder with her own. "I could tell by the way he looked at you in the hospital that he still wants one. He misses you."

Her sisters were right. She needed to go to him. "Will you sit with Helena while she's asleep? I'm going to text him and see if he's home. Go talk to him."

"I don't think that will be necessary." Addie said with a mischievous grin. "Helena texted him from your phone before we arrived. You've got about five minutes before he gets here."

Victoria's hands flew to her hair. "I haven't showered. Wait--Helena texted him?"

"Yep. Apparently she thinks you two should work it out."

Victoria digested that, then, "Why didn't you tell me earlier he was coming?"

"I wanted to see the panic in your eyes." Addie laughed at her.

"Bitches." Victoria reluctantly smiled. "I'm going to at least change."

Chapter Thirty-Seven

Nick stood on Victoria's porch, knots in his stomach. He kept licking his lips. They felt dry. His throat felt dry. If his heart pounded any harder, he might just have a heart attack on her porch. He'd already planned on coming over, but when Helena sent him the text he jumped to go. He had to make Victoria realize that she was it for him. That she was his total knock out.

His hands shook when he knocked on the door. He mentally called himself a coward, but damn. He'd never done anything like this before. Never wanted to call a girl his own. Especially one that might turn him down because he lied to her. At least he had an unlikely ally.

"I'll get it." He heard Addie call from inside.

Great, was she going to punch him like she did Trevor? As the door opened, he straightened, trying to appear confident. Addie's eyes narrowed on him, assessing. "You look like crap."

He frowned. "What? I showered and changed. I had to work earlier. I can't help that."

She laughed. "I'm just kidding. Your face was hilarious, though." She stepped back, allowed him to come inside. "She's in her room, getting dressed. Your best bet is to ambush her there."

Nick nodded and tried to hide his shaking hands. He really didn't like being this nervous. He passed Halle and Helena on his way to Victoria's room. Halle shot him a wink, and Helena's eyes were closed. He reached Victoria's door and paused. The door signified a line. Did he want to cross it? Once he did, there was no going back. No single nights, no one night stands.

Hell yes he wanted to cross that line. He pushed the door open and stepped inside, shutting it softly behind him.

Victoria spun around, wearing a cami and short boxers, her hair sticking up everywhere. "Damn. I thought I had more time."

He couldn't help the grin that spread across his face. "You look beautiful. You are beautiful, just like this."

"Oh." Victoria licked her lips. "So Helena texted you."

"Yeah." Nick didn't move. She seemed skittish, just as nervous as he was, and he didn't want to push his side, have her completely shut him down. "Is that okay?"

Victoria smiled shyly. "I was going to call you in a little while. When I'd had a shower and changed."

The corner of his lips rose. "I like your look now. Like when I used to wake up next to you. I miss that."

Victoria's breath hitched at the solemn look in his eyes. "You do?" She wanted to be articulate but the way he stood there, watching her intensely, made her feel naked, like he could see past all her barriers.

"Oh, yes." Nick stepped forward, stopping only an inch away from her.

She could feel his body heat and her own body reacted, but she reminded herself that they had to talk first. "I don't know if I can do this."

He let his fingertips trail down her arm, watched the goose bumps pop up. "Do what?"

She swallowed. She couldn't concentrate when he touched her like that. "To let you back in." His hand fell away and she barely stopped herself from leaning into him.

"Tori, I'm sorry that I kept what was going on with Trevor from you. It was wrong, I know that. I knew it then, but Luke was adamant." Nick hoped she saw the regret on his face, the desperation in his eyes. "I won't do it again. I've learned my lesson. Watching how much it hurt you, it tore me up inside. I've barely survived these past weeks."

Victoria let his words wash over her. She wrapped her arms around his waist and laid her head on his chest.

"Before I met you, I was going through the motions. I just didn't realize it. I went through life doing what I needed to do, having meaningless one night stands, and my soul became numb to anything that felt good. That was good for me." Nick tilted her chin up so that he could look into her eyes. "You woke me up. You breathed life back into me and I don't want to go back to that. I want to wake up next to you every morning. I want to be your partner, forever, one you can put your trust in. A rock in the storm. I want to help you raise your daughters, not that you need help. I want to be yours, and yours alone."

The breath left Victoria in a rush. No one had ever spoken to her this way, with this sort of raw truth. Nick was baring himself to her, becoming vulnerable in a way he never had. "I want that too. I want to be your partner, the one you can talk to, the one that can wake you up everyday of our lives. But if you lie to me again, I will kick you out of my life, out of the girls' lives."

He nodded. "Good, because I respect that. And I won't. Luke will just have to trust that you'll keep his secrets too."

Victoria rose up on her tiptoes and kissed him. The pressure of his lips on hers was so right, so normal, that she wrapped her arms more tightly around him. He pulled her closer, drawing the kiss out. She pulled back, breathless, and said, "We can figure out all the details later. We can take this slow, that way both of us can adjust to being in a real relationship, because what I had with Roger was nowhere close."

"I love you, Tori." Nick kissed her forehead, her cheeks, the corner of her mouth. "More than anything." He pressed a quick kiss to her lips.

"I love you, too." Victoria's smile broke through. "Now, let's get out there. Lucia will be home soon, and I know my sisters are dying to hear what I said to you."

Nick took her hand, led her out of the room. "I'm going to have to get used to sisters."

"You won't. I'm not even used to them, and I've lived with them all my life." Victoria laughed. She smiled because things had a way of turning out for the best. Maybe she'd had her relationship with Roger so that she could appreciate Nick better. Now, her sisters needed their happily-ever-afters.

About the Author:

I'm a multitasking mom of four. When not writing/doing laundry/changing diapers, I like to catch up on episodes of Supernatural and Castle. If you can't find me in front of the computer, I'm most likely watching my DVR.

I've been writing since the first grade, where I wrote a one page story titled "If I was an Indian". My warrior husband was going to be the best hunter, I was going to live in the best teepee and apparently, I was having an affair with the Chief. Racy, I know.

Of the things I'm addicted to sweet tea, movies, and books top the list. My favorite authors include Nora Roberts, Lauren Kate, Kresley Cole, and Gena Showalter. Few of many I love.

Thanks so much for reading!

Sam :)

www.facebook.com/SamanthaLongAuthor

www.samanthamlong.com

www.pinterest.com/smbyrd18

https://www.goodreads.com/author/show/7142522.Samantha_Long

Author's Other Works:

YA Paranormal Series
Awakening (Guardians, #1)

Sacred (Guardians, #2)

Coming in Summer 2014

Addie and Finn's story

Taking the Heat